PLAY BY
Heart

A HARMONY OF HEARTS NOVEL

ARIELLA ZOELLE

D1295910

Cover Design by Cate of Cate Ashwood Designs

Editing by Pam of Undivided Editing

Proofreading by Sandra of One Love Editing

Layout by Ariella of Sarayashi Publishing

ISBN: 978-1-954202-08-5

Dedication

This is for Iason who has patiently stayed by my side for the past seventeen years while waiting for me to become a good enough author to tell his story properly. It's also for Daimon, who taught me about the ecstasy an amazing singer's voice can offer.

Welcome to Sunnyside

Immerse yourself in the world of interconnected series set in Sunnyside!

Full of cute sweetness and sexy fun, every story ends with a satisfying HEA and no cliffhangers. Since all of the following series are set in the same town, you can expect to see cameos of some of your favorite characters! The books are funny, steamy, and can be read in any order.

To access the Sunnyside universe reading order guide, please visit www.ariellazoelle.com/sunnyside

Chapter One

ORION

I CLOSED my eyes as I immersed myself in Iason Leyland's beautiful music. His dulcet tone was like a comforting hug from a good friend, making all of my problems feel a million miles away. Although it was only an open mic night in the Hurly-burly Bar and Grille, his angelic voice filled the space as he kept his audience enraptured. It was a rare treat since he normally performed in front of tens of thousands at sold-out theatres and arenas. Tonight was a fan club–exclusive event I had brought my sister to, who was staring up at him from the front row of tables with adoration.

When I opened my eyes, I discovered Iason looking straight at me—and not for the first time. An electric thrill sparked through me as our gazes met again. Even across the crowded bar, his piercing blue eyes seemed to see right through me. It made me feel as light-headed and dramatic as my teenage sister. I couldn't look away as it felt like he was singing only to me. It was an absurd thought to have, especially as a straight man, but it didn't change the giddiness I experienced from having someone as famous as him notice me.

It was almost disorienting when Iason's mic cut out and silenced him, breaking the moment. Like the pro he was, he continued playing the rest of the song without missing a beat. Without the sound system boosting his volume, I could still hear the fullness of his huge voice that had no problem reaching me.

A hulking man with the biggest biceps I had ever seen in real life weaved through the crowd to the stage. He announced the event would temporarily halt while they worked on fixing the audio issues. Both he and Iason disappeared into the back, leaving an audience of chattering fans behind.

"You seem to be enjoying the show," Nyla teased from her place beside me. She was my ex-girlfriend, who I was close friends with despite our breakup. Although we weren't together anymore, I still appreciated her beauty as one would appreciate fine art. She had long, raven-black hair and strands of rainbow streaks peeking through. Her colorful ink-stained overbust corset from her favorite designer, West Easton, drew the attention of every straight man around us.

I flushed with embarrassment, despite the lack of

judgment in her tone. "I'm not as fanatical as my sister, but I appreciate how wonderful his voice and lyrics are."

"And he's certainly easy on the eyes." She gave a dreamy sigh. "It's not fair that he's prettier than me."

"In fairness, he's prettier than pretty much everyone," I said. The man was undeniably attractive. Even remembering the way our gazes had met made my heart skip a beat as I experienced the same jolt of excitement. That it had happened more than once during the performance was surprising, but I had the same reaction every time.

"Do you think Iason is his real name or his stage one?" Nyla asked.

"It's too strange to not be fake. He pronounces it 'Yay-son,' but his real name is probably just Jason and he's trying to be a mysterious musician."

"Yeah, you're probably right." She tossed her long hair, exposing her bare shoulder. "I swear he's been looking at me this entire concert. Have you noticed?"

It made more sense that he'd be glancing our way because of Nyla and not me. What reason would he ever pay attention to me? Clearly, I was letting my appreciation of him as a fan cloud my senses. "It seems like it, doesn't it?"

My younger sister came over with a pleading look in her big doe eyes. Lyra wore a T-shirt with the logo for his current world tour and a pair of ratty jeans and high-top sneakers. At fifteen, there was no one more obsessed with Iason than her. "Rion, could you pretty please help me?"

Despite the fifteen-year age gap between us, we were still a tight-knit family. "What do you need?"

"Would you mind getting the spare CDs from the basement? We're almost out at the merch table." She helped run it as part of her duties as a member of Iason's street team.

I frowned at the request. "Isn't there someone on staff who should do that? I can't imagine they'd be thrilled with me going down to their basement. And who put the CDs there, anyway?"

"Iason's best friend, Duke, owns the bar and keeps stock down there for us." She took hold of my hand and tugged at me, leaving me with no choice but to follow. As we walked into the staff-only section of the restaurant, my paranoia about getting in trouble spiked. She pointed to an open door that led into darkness. "I have to get back to the table, but they're down there in a big box up front. Thanks!"

Not only was I afraid of being punished for trespassing, but it was also the kind of place you went to get murdered. Everything in me told me not to go down, but when I didn't budge, she gave me a not-so-subtle nudge. I consoled myself that the sooner I went down, the quicker I could return to the safety of light. Steeling my nerves and turning on the lights, I headed down the rickety wooden stairs into the dim area.

When I reached the bottom, I swore when I saw a

ton of boxes strewn about with seemingly no order to them. How the hell was I supposed to tell which one contained his CDs? The last thing I wanted to do was snoop. I started with the closest box since it was the most obvious choice. But it was sealed and had the label of a local microbrewery on it. I checked all the nearby boxes, but none of them were what my sister had asked me to bring.

As my frustration mounted, I froze when I heard someone ask from behind me, "Who are you?"

I spun around in shock, only to stare into the gorgeous face of the man I had come to see. Even in the yellow glow of the scattered incandescent light bulbs in the shadowy basement, Iason's blue eyes captivated me. They were more beautiful than any sky in the heavens.

He wore a cobalt shirt under his leather jacket, which further enhanced the color of his eyes. His tight white jeans left nothing to the imagination. The dark hair falling in front of his face gave me the strangest urge to reach out and run my fingers through to push it back. His tone had been curious rather than accusatory, but my heart still raced from the unexpected encounter with one of the most famous musicians in the world.

My words came out in a nervous rush over being caught and because being so close to Iason was doing strange things to me. "Sorry, my sister, Lyra, is on your street team, and she asked me to come down

That *definitely* shouldn't have been my reaction as a straight man.

My cheeks were red-hot as I tried to collect myself. "I'm over here, Lyra."

"Oh my god, you can't see shit down here." She stumbled into a box with another swear. "What a stupid place to keep the spares! I understand leaving the posters down here because not everyone can have him on their ceiling or wall, but we always run out of CDs. Who could hear his voice and not want to buy one?"

"I assume most people already have it or stream it."

"Sorry, Duke moved the CDs when they received their shipments in today. They're over here," Iason said as he stepped into the light where she could see him.

My sister yelped in surprise before she breathed his name, staring at him with hearts in her eyes. Was that how I was looking at him when he embraced me?

He gave her a charming smile. "You must be Lyra." It impressed me he had picked up her name from my earlier rambling. No wonder his fans adored him for caring about them.

"You know who I am?" She covered her mouth to hold in her excited squeal of delight.

If her obsession was bad before, it'd be even worse now that he knew she existed. She'd probably construct another shrine for him.

"Of course. You're a valuable member of my street team. You'll have to forgive me for the delay. I came to help Orion, and we got sidetracked by talking."

Funny, there seemed to be way more touching than talking. But I couldn't say anything because I was too shaken up by what had happened and the things his touch had stirred within me. Why did I feel like Lyra's sudden arrival had cheated me out of something amazing? *You're straight, remember?*

She made a noise of protest. "You aren't supposed to help! That's why we're here."

I picked up the box Iason indicated was his CDs. While I was a huge fan of his music, I wasn't as fond of carrying it up the stairs as my sister yammered nonsense at him. I appreciated his lyrics as pure poetry, given life by his sensuous tenor voice. Lyra, on the other hand, loved him because he was "absolutely fucking gorgeous," as she so eloquently put it. She wasn't wrong. He was a god amongst men with his striking blue eyes, soft features, and stunning body, which had felt so good pressed against mine. Wait —*what?* The strange thought almost caused me to drop the box when I tripped up a stair in shock.

When I emerged from the basement, someone took the CDs away from me as Lyra continued to gawk at her idol. I leaned back against a wall as I watched them.

"You'll really sign stuff for the team? I can tell

them?" Lyra's brown eyes were wide as she stared at Iason with unadulterated joy.

"You girls help me out so much, it's the least I can do." He gave her a benevolent smile. "I'd be more than happy to do it after my set is over."

Lyra turned to me with a pleading gaze. "You don't mind staying a little later for me, do you, Rion? Please?"

It went without asking. "Sure, I'd be happy to."

"You're the best brother ever!" She gave me a hug before she hurried off with an excited squeal.

With her gone, Iason shifted his attention to me. Pinned under his intense gaze, I forgot how to breathe again. It took an effort to remember how to act normal. "I appreciate you being so nice to my sister. She's a huge fan. It's always been a dream of hers to meet you."

"It's the least I could do for you." His sonorous voice sent shivers through me while his words confused me.

That didn't make sense. "For me?"

Before he could answer, someone called out a warning to him. "Ias! Five minutes!"

Ignoring it, he answered me. "In order to see you again." He walked away with an enigmatic smile, humming a song I had never heard before.

What the fuck did *that* mean?

Chapter Three

ORION

I COULDN'T GET Iason's lyrics out of my mind that echoed what he had said to me in the basement. What did being "made out of wishes on stars" even mean? Surely, it couldn't be that he had been praying to meet *me*. Why would someone as famous as him think a nobody like me was his long-lost soul mate? We didn't even know each other! It was downright absurd. But how else could I describe the magnetic pull I felt to him? Why was it every time our gazes met across the room, it felt like my heart might leap out of my chest? And why did I want one more chance to be near him to figure out what the hell was going on?

Despite my confusion, I still lost myself in Iason's voice as his show continued. It calmed my nerves and brought me a comfort no other musician had ever inspired within me. I couldn't help but mourn when he ended the concert after an encore.

How could anyone deny that beautiful, begging blue? I certainly couldn't. "Sure."

My sister gave me a running hug before Tisha escorted them away. Just when I thought it was safe to breathe, Iason looked over his shoulder and winked at me before they rounded the corner.

I blinked several times as I tried to understand what had happened. Why would he want to talk to me alone in his dressing room? And more importantly, why did a bar have one?

A man in his early twenties with auburn hair approached me with an amiable smile. Red was a bartender I had become friendly with over the years since I was a regular. He wore his uniform of jeans and a white shirt with a black vest. "Hey, Orion! Did you enjoy the concert?"

"I did. What about you?"

"Yeah, it was amazing, as always. Plus, Iason's fans are generous tippers, so my night has been awesome so far." He grinned with happiness. "Speaking of which, he wanted me to show you to his dressing room."

I followed Red as he walked in the direction Iason had headed earlier. "Why does a bar have one of those?"

"It's normally our break room, but it's where he gets ready, so we call it his dressing room as a joke." Red opened the door to let me inside. He winked at me with a suggestive tone as he said, "Don't worry, it locks. You two have fun."

My cheeks burned at the implication. I mumbled my thanks to him before Red left to go back to work. The area was minimal, with a small kitchen, a table and chairs for taking lunch breaks, and a black leather couch for stretching out on to rest.

Iason must have stopped in to freshen up before meeting with his street team because it smelled like his spiced cologne. What was it about the scent that teased my senses and stirred things within me I had never experienced before because of a man? It made me heady as I struggled with my reaction to Iason.

Sure, I was a fan of his, but I wasn't anywhere near Lyra's level of fangirl fanaticism. His fame making me nervous was logical, but it didn't explain why I got all tongue-tied around him as my stomach did cartwheels because his body pressed against mine like he was about to kiss me. I was straight, so why had I reacted that way? Shouldn't I have pushed him away?

But I was flattered, confused, and curious if I was being truly honest with myself. I had to remind myself that Iason probably had his pick of groupies hanging around, so I certainly wasn't anyone special. Someone like him would never be interested in me. It was ridiculous to pretend I stood a chance. Besides, it wasn't like I wanted that chance. I was straight and had never been attracted to a man before. Thirty was a bit late to have a sexual awakening.

A knock on the door startled me out of my thoughts. I opened it with a shaky hand, trying to brace myself for whatever Iason wanted to talk to me about. Maybe he was only interested in a casual tour of the museum. But instead of him, it was Lyra on the other side.

"I feel bad asking after making you wait for me, but is it okay if I get a ride home with Tisha and her mom? Mom and Dad said I could spend the night at her house since we have off tomorrow for teacher conferences."

"They probably didn't want to be kept up all night with your fangirl ravings," I teased. Every time after a concert was the same, only it would be worse since she had actually met Iason in person. I could only imagine the screeching phone call she had made to our parents.

"Please?" She clasped her hands together in prayer.

"Yeah, that's fine." As an afterthought, I added, "I'm glad you had a good time tonight."

She hugged me tightly. "And it's all because of you. Thank you so much! You're the best!" She ran down the hall, and I watched long enough to see her jump on Tisha with an excited whoop.

I closed the door behind me, surrounded by silence once more. Since Lyra had left, that meant I no longer had a reason to stay. I could leave and never find out what Iason wanted from me. It was the coward's way out, but that was fine since I wasn't feeling brave.

Decision made, I squared my shoulders and opened the door. To my surprise, I revealed Iason standing before me. He brushed past me into the room, which now felt far too small for two people. He thanked me for being kind enough to open the door for him. With defeat, I shut the door, knowing there was no escape now. Whatever was about to happen was up to him.

"Your sister's sweet." He tossed a marker on the table he had used for signing swag.

"She has her moments." I laughed, almost at ease. If we could keep it at that level, maybe it would be okay.

He held his hand out, gesturing for me to come closer with a seductive smile. I noticed there was black ink on his hands, probably from signing autographs. Somehow, it lent him an authenticity as an artist. "Why are you still by the door? Please, make yourself comfortable."

Without thought, my body obeyed him by taking a few steps closer. I was careful to stay just beyond his range of touch, so he couldn't confuse me again. "No, I probably shouldn't. Your crew will want to get out of here soon, since the show ended."

"Then come to my hotel with me."

His bluntness amazed me. A disconcerting part of my brain that was almost curious enough to accept. "I really shouldn't."

"Scared of the paparazzi?"

"Then here is fine, I guess." It seemed safer to have the security of people nearby, rather than alone in a hotel where there would be no one but him. I avoided looking at his smile, afraid of confusing myself further. Everything about Iason's presence overwhelmed me.

"So, what did you think of your song?"

It didn't make sense to me why he called it that. "It's impossible for you to have written that in five minutes." I couldn't stand the thought of something that beautiful being for me when I didn't deserve it.

"Is it?" He didn't seem the least bit convinced.

"Yes."

He closed the space between us, forcing me to meet his gaze. It suddenly felt like there wasn't enough air in the room to breathe. "I had the idea for the song that I've been working on for almost two months, but it finally found its meaning in you."

"How?"

"Because you're everything I've been dreaming about. You're even named after a constellation." When I tried to argue that he didn't know me, he cut off my words by caressing my cheek. Once again, the simple touch flooded me with heat and filled my stomach with churning lava. "That means you're made of all the wishes I've made on every star. I want you so much, Orion."

There was genuine desire in his blue eyes that seemed to see straight through to my soul. It overwhelmed me when combined with the romantic sentiment and the scent of him that filled me with urges I didn't understand. Unable to bear his intensity, I looked to the floor to collect my bearings. My head was swimming from the rush of confusing feelings. Why couldn't I quit noticing how incredible he smelled?

He lifted my chin up with a crooked finger, holding my gaze. "I mean it."

At that moment, I wanted to trust in the sincerity in his beautiful eyes. He gazed at me with such conviction that it swayed me despite my heterosexuality. God help me, he looked at me like he wanted to kiss me, and I almost wanted it. I was powerless to pull back as he leaned in closer.

A sharp knock on the door caused us both to startle. From the other side, a woman's voice called out, "Ias! We need to be out of here soon. Hurry up in there!"

He didn't let me move away. Instead, he pressed his body against mine with a seductive sway of his hips. It made it impossible to think about anything other than how good—how *right*—it felt to be embraced by him. Wasn't I supposed to be protesting what was happening? Wasn't it wrong when I was straight? Then why did I want to be brave enough to take what he was tempting me with despite all of that?

The confidence in Iason's blue eyes was stunning, momentarily sweeping me away with fiery passion. It was only when he leaned in to kiss me and broke our gaze that I jerked back. My heart pounded as I trembled from confused desire. What frightened me more than him kissing me was how much I hadn't wanted to pull back from him. When Iason took another step closer, I lost the battle of wills. I fled the dressing room like the coward I was, too scared to stay and find out things about myself I wasn't ready to accept.

Chapter Four

IASON

IT HAD BEEN DISAPPOINTING when Orion ran away, but I wasn't about to let him escape from me without a fight. I was a man who knew what he wanted, and I would do whatever it took to get him into my life.

Showing up at the museum he worked at seemed a little desperate, but I *was* desperate for another opportunity to be near him. I had blown it yesterday by coming on too strong because I had gotten carried away by the cosmic coincidences that brought him into my path. Given my level of fame, it was no wonder he had been scared off. But I intended to take things slower with my second chance.

I waited until about fifteen minutes before the museum closed to go there. A bored young woman sat at the admission counter, whose brown eyes flew wide when she saw me.

"Oh my god, you're Iason Leyland," she breathed, resting her hand over her heart in shock.

"I am." I stopped in front of her with a charming smile. "How are you today?"

"Feeling like I've died and gone to heaven." She flushed when I chuckled at her cute answer.

"Would you be willing to help me out with something?"

"I'll do anything you want." The blush on her cheeks turned brighter at her accidental innuendo.

I leaned in closer to act secretive. "How about helping me surprise my friend?"

She nodded before turning shy. "Could I ask for your autograph first? And maybe a selfie?"

"I'd be happy to." It was a small price to pay to see Orion again.

She dug through her large tote bag on the floor, pulling out one of my CDs. She looked a little embarrassed as she handed it and a pen over to me. "I was at your concert yesterday and bought this to give to my friend at dinner tonight, but I can give her a different one. My name is Laura, by the way."

I accepted them from her, then pulled out the insert to write, *Laura, Here's to fun surprises*. I signed with a flourish, giving the ink a moment to dry before sliding the insert back into the case.

Laura quickly took a selfie with me, squealing in excitement when she checked it on her phone. "Seriously, thank you *so* much! I've been a fan for a long time, so it means a lot. I never thought I'd get to meet you in person!"

"I appreciate your support, and your help with surprising Orion."

Her jaw dropped at his name. "You're friends with *Orion?*"

"I am."

"He never told me." She still sounded shocked.

Based on his bashfulness yesterday, I made a guess about his personality. "You know he's not one to brag."

"That's true." She smiled at me. "Let me call him for you."

I waited as she called to inform him he had a friend who wanted to see him. My excitement built as I waited for him to arrive.

When he entered the lobby, he took my breath away. He wore another well-tailored suit that flattered his body. It was paired with a black shirt and a pink jacquard-print tie. The longing in me intensified, especially when he stopped in his tracks with a dumb-founded expression.

"Iason?" He stared as if he didn't believe I was actually standing there in front of him.

Unable to resist the temptation, I walked over and embraced him. It pleased me when he reflexively returned the hug. I couldn't resist murmuring in his ear, "It's so good to see you again."

The sound of my voice caused him to shiver

against me, sparking my desire. It seemed he had sensitive ears, and damned if that didn't make me want to exploit his weakness with some fun teasing.

He pulled back from me, clearly shaken by the greeting and my sudden appearance. "Why are you here?"

I had to swallow down my first response of telling him it was because I wanted him. That was the exact opposite of playing it cool. "I wished to see you. Could we maybe talk in your office for a few minutes?"

Orion looked almost shell-shocked. For a moment, I thought he would refuse me. I held my breath until he relented. "Um, sure, I guess?"

Before walking away, I remembered to thank the person who had made seeing him possible. "Thanks for your help, Laura."

"You're welcome!" she called after me as I followed him through the museum to the administrative area in the rear that was off-limits to the public. I glanced around at the art on display as he led me to his office. It was crammed to the gills with art history books on the shelves dominating the space. I was unsurprised to find that his desk was neat and well organized, with everything in its rightful place.

After I entered behind him, I shut the door. It amused me when he startled at the sound of it closing. Instead of going over and pinning him against the desk and kissing him until we were both breathless, I sat down in the chair across from him. "Thanks for seeing me."

He sat in his desk chair, still looking overwhelmed by my sudden appearance. "How did you know where I work?"

"You told me last night, remember?"

"Oh, I guess I did." He smoothed his tie with a trembling hand. "But why are you here? The museum is about to close, so it's too late for a tour."

"I wanted to ask if you would join me for dinner tonight?"

That apparently wasn't what he had been expecting to hear. "*What?*"

His stunned reaction amused me. "Dinner."

He pointed at himself. "You mean dinner with *me?*"

I gave him my most winsome smile. "Yes, you and me, enjoying dinner together tonight. There's a great Japanese restaurant near here that I'd love to take you to."

"*You* want to have dinner with *me* tonight?" His shock was adorable.

"I do. I want to get to know you better, and I'm hungry. Dinner with you solves both problems."

"Why?"

I remained patient with him. "Because I like you."

"But I—what? I don't understand." It was cute

how he struggled with his words in disbelief. "You don't even know me."

"Which is why I want to have dinner together. We can get to know each other better. Will you join me tonight?"

His expression turned wary. "Just for dinner?"

I couldn't blame him for being suspicious of my intentions after how strongly I had come on to him last night. Although I wanted so much more, I assured him, "Just for dinner."

He remained silent for so long that I worried he was going to refuse. "I *do* like Japanese food."

"Then you'll love this place. It's about a ten-minute drive from here."

Orion checked the time on his watch. "I have a few emails I need to send before we can go."

My face lit up with a smile when I realized I would get what I wanted. "I'll wait for you as long as it takes." I meant it far more than he knew. I'd wait a lifetime if that was what it took for him to be mine.

"Thanks." He turned to his computer to finish what he needed to do.

I silently waited, figuring the less of a distraction I was, the sooner we could leave and continue with the rest of our night. His fingers flying over the keyboard filled me with a longing to feel his touch all over my body. God, he looked so good in that suit. It made me hunger for so much more than only dinner.

Baby steps, I reminded myself. Something told me remembering that would prove to be a real challenge, considering how eager I was to see his suit decorating my floor while I pleasured him in bed. I shifted uncomfortably in the chair as I struggled against getting aroused.

To distract myself from being a total creeper watching him work, I turned my attention to his bookshelves. I grinned when I realized they were all in alphabetical order by author. It almost made me feel bad for being such a chaotic complication in his pristinely organized life. I wasn't sure why, but I had unwavering certainty that we needed each other. Trusting my instincts had gotten me everything I wanted so far. I wasn't about to doubt myself now.

While I wasn't overly familiar with art, I knew enough of the big names to recognize his books covered a wide time period. As I let my gaze travel over the spines of the books, one jumped out at me.

"What's so funny?" Orion asked, making me realize I chuckled out loud.

"I wasn't expecting to see such interesting book titles. I must say, *Exposing Nudes* sounds like it would be a rather fascinating read."

"It actually is!" He was so precious in his excitement that I wanted to hug him. "It's about the evolution of nudity, looking at how art styles and social mores changed the meaning and presentation of nudes over the centuries. They start with the earliest—"

When he abruptly cut himself off, I looked at him questioningly. "They start with the earliest what?"

"Sorry, you don't want to hear me ramble about art." He waved it away. "I know it bores most people."

"I'm not most people."

He grinned at my words, which felt like sunshine warming my soul. "No, you're really not."

"I promise, you could talk to me about nudity for hours and I'd never get bored." It was impossible to resist the urge to throw in a wink for good measure. "Especially if you're showing me some examples."

His laughter was a beautiful sound. It made me want him even more. He rubbed the back of his head with a sheepish shrug. "I'm used to people's eyes glazing over whenever I talk about art."

"It must be awful being so erudite around a bunch of cretins." I loved that my smart-ass comment earned me another laugh.

"No, it's nothing like that. It has more to do with the fact that both of my parents are scientists, so they're more interested in the analytical than in art. My sister thinks stuff created by dead people isn't worth talking about."

It was a surprising piece of information. "Then how did you get interested in the field?"

"I took an Art History AP class in high school,

and I fell in love with the stories behind the art. Hearing the tales about how the work was created, or about the lives of the subjects featured, or even the artist themselves, made ancient things feel alive. Knowing the truth behind a painting makes it so much more interesting than a static portrait with no context."

"That's beautiful." I loved that that was something he valued.

He looked so adorable that it was hard to resist the urge to hug him. "Thanks."

"I wish more people were passionate about things. Life is so much better when you really love something." I held his gaze, the dual meaning lingering in the air.

"That's so true." His lips turned up in a small smile. "I'm finished with my work, so we can go now."

"Did you drive here?"

"Yeah, I parked my car over in the garage." He packed his messenger bag before slinging it on his shoulder. "I can drive us."

"Great." I followed him out of his office, eager to get on with the rest of our evening together.

"WHY ARE you so familiar with this area?" Orion asked as he drove to the restaurant.

"I grew up around here and went to Sunnyside University before moving out to Manhattan."

He glanced over at me in surprise. "Really?"

"I'm sure you can imagine how *thrilled* my parents are that I'm wasting my college education on a music career."

"But you're one of the most famous musicians alive! How could they be anything but proud?"

"That's not really their style." I didn't want to ruin the evening talking about my awful parents. "I studied business and hated every minute."

He gave me a sympathetic look. "I'm sorry. That sucks you couldn't study what you loved."

"After I graduated, I felt obligated to do what my parents had envisioned for me, so I got a job at a fabric distribution company."

"How did you end up doing that?" Orion asked. "I didn't know that was a thing."

"Neither did I until I worked there. It was one of those 'a friend of a friend knows a guy' arrangements. I tried for five years to be satisfied with it. But I eventually realized that I'd rather live with my parents' disappointment for the rest of my life than be miserable every day at a job I hated. I did what was best for me, although they thought I had lost my damn mind."

His sympathetic expression comforted me. "What happened?"

"I was sent out to LA to handle an issue with one of our fabric suppliers. My boss was so cheap that I ended up staying with a friend from college who lived out there. Levi was an accountant who also was a musician. After I returned from work, he invited me to go to the open mic night at a bar with his friends. He had a spare guitar, so I figured what the hell, why not?"

"Wait, isn't that how you got discovered? I remember Lyra talking about it."

I nodded. "She's right. The person who became my agent was there and offered me a meeting at the record label the next morning. I blew off work to meet with them instead. After I signed with them, I quit my job and moved out to New York. My parents were so livid they didn't speak to me for over a year."

"Holy shit, really? That's terrible."

"I don't live my life waiting for their approval." He seemed to be the sensitive type, so I didn't mention that their prolonged silence had actually been a gift.

He looked over at me with a sympathetic expression. It made me want to lean over and kiss him. I refrained since I didn't want to wreck the night with a car crash. He said in a sad voice, "That must be so hard not having their support. I can't imagine not talking to my family for that long."

"As my mother always said, I march to the beat of my own drum," I replied with a wry grin. "I don't let it bother me."

"Well, that's good, I guess."

"Oh, you want to turn right up here at the next light." I pointed at the area ahead. "It's in the middle of that strip mall."

He followed my instructions, then parked the car. "I can't believe I've lived here almost all of my life, but I've never been here before. I drive past it every day to and from work."

"I'm glad I get to be your first." I loved the blush that graced his cheeks from my teasing.

Before entering the restaurant, I put on a pair of black glasses I used as a disguise out in public when I didn't want to be recognized. It didn't always work, but I wanted to minimize the chances of us getting interrupted by a fan.

After we were seated and looking at the menu, I suggested some recommendations. I liked the intimate vibe of the small restaurant. It had low lighting, with dark red walls that were covered in bamboo umbrellas with painted flowers on them. They usually weren't busy, so it was easier to stay as long as you wanted without being an inconvenience.

After we placed our orders, we returned to making small talk. It pleased me to see Orion relaxing as he got more comfortable during dinner. I was at my most charming, even as I became increasingly captivated by him. As we chatted over our meals, it was a true joy watching him open up like the most beautiful flower blossoming.

The longer I spent with him, the more convinced

I was that I had to be with him. I knew the logistics of it didn't make a lot of sense. We lived on two different sides of the country, I was always traveling on tour, and long-distance relationships rarely worked. But none of that changed how much I desired him or my certainty that he should be mine.

For the past several months, I had been considering moving back to Sunnyside. I had been looking for a reason to return other than my selfishness, and he was the best incentive I had so far to make the move. It was absurd to consider relocating for someone I had only known for a few hours. But if all the stars had aligned to bring him into my life, why shouldn't I take advantage of fate's generosity?

"My sister would never forgive me for going out with you," he said as we finished eating.

"I think I could endure her wrath for the pleasure of dating you."

His cheeks flushed beautifully. "I meant for dinner. Going out with you for dinner. Without her. That's what I meant."

He was so damn cute. I couldn't resist the urge to tease him a little more. "Oh, but she would be fine with us dating?"

"No, she would straight up murder me." The utter certainty in his voice caused me to laugh.

"I'd protect you."

I had to hold back my smirk when it sent a visible tremor through him. Clearly flummoxed, he protested, "No, you don't understand. She's practically in love with you. Trust me, she would take it as a personal affront and betrayal of the worst kind."

"Really?" I asked, although it wasn't all that surprising after being around Lyra backstage yesterday. She was incapable of hiding her extreme fangirl reactions, which entertained me. Dedicated fans like her were responsible for my career being such a meteoric rise.

"She loves you and your music."

"What about you?"

"I love you, too." He turned bright red when he realized what he had said. "I mean—I like you, too. And love your music. But I didn't mean—I'm not— it's not like I'm in love with you or anything weird like that."

His panicked rambling made me want to kiss him into silence. "Yet."

"Yet?" His voice came out as a startled squeak.

"The night is still young."

"I couldn't—I'm *not* going to fall in love with you. Not that you're unlovable because you're *amazing*. I'm not—" He gave up protesting and hid his face in his hands with a groan. "Forget it. I'm digging myself deeper into this hole and making everything worse."

Orion's embarrassed bumbling was precious. His flustered reaction gave me hope I was making more progress with him than I thought. "But you're so cute when you're doing it."

"Cute?"

"Very." I couldn't stop my broad smile at his reactions. "I won't say no to hearing you explain why you love me, too."

His adorable pout drew my attention to his full lips. "I didn't mean it like that!"

"Then how did you mean it?"

He drank water to avoid immediately having to answer. "I appreciate your music."

"Is that all?" I asked in mock disappointment.

"Your lyrics are wonderful." His expression showed his concern that he had somehow insulted me. "And your voice is so beautiful."

There was a sense of awe in his tone that I loved. "And my face isn't half-bad, either."

I finally made him laugh again. "You don't need me to tell you that you're attractive," he said in amusement, losing some of his self-consciousness from earlier.

"No, but my ego loves hearing it."

His laughter left me eager to leave and move on with the rest of our night—provided I could get him to agree to keep it going.

As if summoned by my thoughts, our server appeared to deliver the check. I picked it up before he had the chance.

He reached for his wallet. "How much do I owe?"

That he intended to pay rather than accept a free dinner from me said so much about him. I pretended to look over the bill. "It says here you owe me a confession about what your favorite song of mine is."

"It does not!" His laughter delighted me. "Seriously, how much do I owe?"

Once again, I acted as if I was closely studying the bill. "I double-checked the math. It clearly says that's your part of the bill." I put my credit card in the holder before handing it over to the server. "But I could be persuaded into accepting a kiss instead, though."

He failed to smother his soft squeak of surprise at my offer. God, he was driving me wild without even trying. He remained silent until he chuckled when I was signing the receipt. I gave him a questioning look, then noticed that ever-present blush started creeping up on him again.

"Sorry, I realized that you're essentially giving them an autograph. I imagined a server being a fan and stealing your receipt to take it home as a souvenir."

I grinned at the thought. "As long as it doesn't lead to credit card fraud, they're free to do that."

He hesitated a moment as he fidgeted. "To answer your original question, it's 'Midnight Magic,' if you must know."

Now *that* was a surprise. "Midnight Magic" was one of my most sensual songs, an ode to making love all night long. I never would have imagined someone as tightly wound as him would pick that song out of everything I had ever done. It seemed there might be hope for me to get my way after all.

Even though I warned myself to back off, it was too tempting of a segue. I pinned him under a heated gaze. "I'd be happy to share my inspiration with you later tonight."

"That's…" Orion trailed off when words failed him. He abruptly stood up so we could leave. "Where's your hotel?"

"Planning on spending the night with me there?"

His cheeks were as red as the walls. "Sorry, I didn't mean like that! I need to know where to take you next, that's all."

I guided him out by the small of his back, feigning being hurt. "Are you that eager to get rid of me?"

He stopped in the parking lot and turned to face me. "Of course not! This has been fun when I'm not making an idiot out of myself."

I used my height to my advantage to get into his personal space. "Then let's keep the fun going at your place."

"My apartment?" His lips were parted as he looked up at me with wide eyes.

Everything in me wanted to cover his mouth with mine, but I held back. It wouldn't pay to push him too far too fast. Not when going home with him filled me with hope that I might get the chance to make him mine. I lowered my voice to a dark rumble. "Would you deny me?"

I could see the war inside of Orion as he struggled between doing what he thought he should and what he wanted to do. He took a shuddering breath before nodding. "Okay."

And suddenly, my good night got even better.

Chapter Five

ORION

IASON WAS SHOCKINGLY easy to talk to when he wasn't confusing the hell out of me and getting me all mixed up inside. He was so charming that I got swept away by his beautiful smile and teasing without realizing it. In true me fashion, I had made an ass out of myself at the restaurant, but he had the good grace to not make me feel bad about it. That was why I had agreed to bring him to my apartment without considering the ramifications.

My nerves ramped up into high gear the closer we got to my place. What would I do if he made a move on me? But surely, he wouldn't be interested in someone like *me*. There was no way he'd try anything with me, right?

The only thing that distracted me from my chaotic thoughts was hearing him softly singing along to Jeff Buckley's "Last Goodbye." I couldn't help but watch him in awe as we waited at a stoplight. The street lighting illuminated his face, making him look like an otherworldly deity. I had never seen anything so bewitching in my life.

A horn blaring behind us made me jump. It took me a moment to realize the light was now green. He laughed as I hurried to drive.

"Sorry, was I distracting you?" He wasn't the least bit remorseful.

"A little," I sheepishly admitted.

"And here I was trying to be on my best behavior."

I took the next turn, bringing us that much closer to our destination. "Hearing you singing one of my favorite songs, I…"

"You should hear me do his 'Grace' sometime. I love tearing into that one."

The thought of Iason's beautiful voice opening up on such a huge song raised chills on my skin. I had never imagined him performing it before, but now I was desperate to hear it. Without meaning to, the words "Oh, *god*" slipped from my lips, my tone indicating *exactly* how much I'd enjoy that.

Out of the corner of my eye, I could see his eyes dancing brightly with amusement in the darkness. "Like that, do you?"

I nodded, not trusting myself to do anything more than that without humiliating myself.

"If you ask nicely, I'll sing it at the next concert you come to."

Since I didn't know what to say, I stayed silent. When we pulled into my apartment development, I paid attention to parking. The last thing I wanted was to humiliate myself by hitting something in my distraction. But in my defense, how was I supposed to focus on anything else with Iason crooning along to my favorite songs?

I was a little unsteady when I got out of the car. Taking a deep breath, I reminded myself that it was too late to bail now. I squared my shoulders as I led the way to my apartment, overly aware of how close he was.

Once we were inside, I turned on the lights and shrugged off my suit jacket. I tossed it on the back of my kitchen table chair. The track lighting in my living room was still dimmed from last night, giving the area an intimate atmosphere.

My heart hammered when he sat down next to me on the couch. My hand shook as I straightened my pants. I prayed he didn't notice how nervous I was. "Do you want anything to drink?"

"No, I'm good. Thanks."

My one-bedroom apartment felt claustrophobic with Iason's overwhelming presence. I loosened my tie, needing air. Taking a deep breath didn't help when I got a whiff of his cologne. It stirred things inside me I didn't understand. Since when had I ever paid attention to how a man smelled before? When had the scent of *anyone* made me feel like I needed to lick them for a taste? Apparently since Iason. I didn't know what to make of that.

"Am I making you nervous?" He once again sounded entertained by my reactions.

Instead of answering, I was honest. "I don't understand what you want from me."

"I told you that I want you. What's not to get?"

"Why?" I questioned, sounding more distressed than I meant to. "Why me?"

"For so many reasons." The affection in his eyes as he studied me sent my heart racing. "Throughout the entire concert last night, I kept getting distracted by how moved you were by my music."

The truth escaped from me against my will. "Hearing you singing live was intense, especially in such a small venue." His voice had filled the space and all the empty places inside me.

"In that moment, I knew I wanted you." He shifted closer to me. "The cosmic universe brought you into my life for a reason."

My couch creaked as I shifted my weight, subtly trying to get away from him and his earnest gaze. "What do you mean?"

"Shall I show you?" His voice was a sensual rumble that sent a shiver through me. He offered me untold possibilities that part of me couldn't stamp out my interest in, despite being straight. I couldn't resist that magnetic attraction I had toward him.

I didn't know how to answer. Instead, my mind catalogued everything about the moment, as if I would want to remember it later in great detail. His high cheekbones, his delicate features, and the dark hair that fell in front of his face that gave him an air of mystery. And then there were his azure eyes that were as heavenly as the sky, and his beautifully long eyelashes.

Everything got clouded when he pressed closer, leaning in for a kiss. The world was suddenly in slo-mo while my mind still raced. What the hell were we doing? I was straight, yet my body was responding to him. How did I ignore the fact that there was a part of me that was desperately praying that he kissed me? I couldn't listen to it, though.

"I can't do this," I told him in a shaky voice before I lost the will to put a stop to things.

Iason exuded a sensuality I couldn't handle. He cupped my face in his hand as he caressed my cheekbones with his thumbs. "I promise you can. You're in good hands."

"I'm straight," I blurted out, although he had made me question if that was true anymore.

His voice was a dark rumble, sparking desire deep within me when he leaned in to murmur next to my ear. "Don't let that stop you."

I kept waiting to open my eyes and find out this

was some bizarre dream. But then I felt his warm breath before he made my heart stop by sucking on my earlobe. That was one of my erogenous zones, so him tugging on it with his teeth wrenched a moan out of me. It pushed me dangerously close to the point of no return. My body betrayed how turned on I was by the sound of his voice and his teasing. As he nibbled at my ear, it became increasingly difficult to remember why I wasn't supposed to want him.

I got so lost in the exquisite feeling that I didn't realize he had somehow laid me back on the couch. He straddled over me as he toyed with my ear in a way that made my dick stir. While I may have had my protests, my body had no such hang-ups. I arched against him as my hands wrapped around Iason's neck to pull him closer as he continued teasing me. And it felt *so fucking good*.

Lust blazed within me as he trailed kisses down my neck until he reached my collar. I offered no resistance as he undid the knot of my tie, pulling it free with several slow tugs. The act was stunningly sensual. I couldn't find it in me to resist as he unbuttoned my vest and dress shirt next. My breathing grew shakier with every button that came undone.

When he finished, he studied me with an appreciative look in his eyes, which were dark blue from desire. He shocked me by stripping off his sweater, tossing it aside. Good god, the man was *beautiful*. His muscles were chiseled perfection, but I didn't have the chance to appreciate the view because he pressed himself against me. It took my breath away with the shock of his bare skin touching mine.

It had been months since Nyla and I had broken up. I hadn't been with anyone, so the intimate contact made any thought of stopping him flee. All I could think about was how Iason's body was utterly *perfect*.

When he leaned forward, I discovered I wasn't the only one aroused. Could he seriously be turned on by being with *me*? How was that possible? And why the fuck wasn't I freaked-out?

My thoughts came to a screeching halt when he resumed trailing kisses down my neck, allowing me to feel his smile. He kissed down my body, adding in little nips that made my hard-on twitch in the confines of my pants.

"So beautiful." He spoke in an awed voice before he traced the ridge of one of my hip bones with his tongue. I was overwhelmed with ecstasy as he sucked and nibbled on it.

Overcome by desire, it didn't matter that Iason was a man. Why should I care when it felt so good? Was it so wrong to want to be physically close to someone after months of being alone? I whimpered his name as I lost the battle against my body. "Iason, *please*." I wasn't sure what I was pleading for, but I needed whatever it was. *Desperately*.

"Please what?" He had a mischievous look in his

eyes. "Do this again?" He teased my other hip bone, earning him an aroused keen from me.

When I didn't answer, he continued. "Or maybe this?" Before I could ask what he meant, his hand snaked down to cup my arousal. My hips bucked into his touch, aching for more as he undid the button of my pants.

I bit my lower lip to prevent from crying out again. Despite being a surreal situation, my body hungered for his touch. I saw myself reflected in his ocean-colored eyes, and in them, I looked beautiful. Was that how he saw me?

"Or would you rather have me kiss you before going that far?"

I couldn't say the words out loud. It was impossible for me to string any sounds together when I was distracted by his hardness pressing against me. Why did that make me yearn for the rest of our clothes to come off?

Iason ran his thumb over my lower lip with a tender expression. "I've been wanting to kiss you since I first laid eyes on you."

As he moved closer, I tilted my head up in offering, even as my heart frantically beat in anticipation and confused desire. Nothing mattered more to me than tasting him.

Right before our lips met, Nyla's voice interrupted us. "Well, *this* explains a fuckload of things."

It was like getting doused with freezing water.

Although we weren't dating anymore, panic set in as I tried to explain to her why I was caught in such a compromising position with another man. "This isn't what it looks like, Nyla!"

She crossed her arms over her chest with a skeptical eyebrow arched high. "Really? Because it sure looks like the two of you are engaging in some sexy foreplay from where I'm standing." She sounded amused, but it didn't stop my panic.

"I can explain!" They were big words, considering I had no idea what the fuck was going on. My mind was in a chaotic free fall, unable to process the fact that I was more upset about being interrupted by Nyla than being caught with Iason.

Before I could protest, he got off me to stand. His warm playfulness had disappeared, leaving an aloof coldness that pained my heart. "That's my cue to go." My body cried out in agony at the loss. He pulled on his sweater, covering all his perfection. The realization that he was leaving sent cold dread through me.

It wasn't until he reached the door that I found my voice. "No, wait! Iason!"

But in the blink of an eye, he disappeared. Only the lingering hint of his cologne and my half-undressed state served as proof he had ever been there at all. It devastated me he left before I could explain that she was my *ex*-girlfriend. The realization that he thought I was a cheater made me sick to my stomach. I wanted to chase after him and tell him he misunderstood, but it was probably too late. He'd never trust that I was telling the truth when he had no reason to believe me. Denying she wasn't my girl-friend was the exact thing a cheater would say.

It left me on the verge of tears as I looked up at Nyla with all my chaos and the anguish of losing my only chance to figure out what I felt for Iason.

While I couldn't put my messy feelings into words, she seemed to understand. She came over to sit beside me on the couch. "Okay, tell me what's going on."

I hid my face in my hands with a sob that broke free. How did I answer her question? There was an even more pressing one, though. "Why didn't he give me a chance to explain?" Thinking about how upset he was at the perceived betrayal gutted me to my core. Had someone cheated on him before and that was why he was devastated enough to leave? The last thing I wanted to do was add to his trauma. "What do I do now?" I had no way of contacting him, so how could I undo the harm I had unintentionally done?

She reached over and rubbed the back of my neck in comfort. "I'm sorry I accidentally fucked every-thing up. I thought you were at your parents' house for family dinner night, so it didn't occur to me to knock first. I just came to get my coat I left here last weekend. Seeing you with Iason was such a what-the-fuck moment, I didn't know how to react."

There wasn't enough space within me to be mad at her. I had let her keep her key after we broke up since she was a friend, so it was my fault. And now Iason probably hated me. I would never know how his lips tasted or feel such incredible pleasure again. I was going to be sick. What a shitty way to discover I liked him more than my heterosexuality.

"I really like him," I whispered. Saying it out loud made it even more real that he had left. "How do I fix this?"

"You talk to your sister."

The suggestion was strange enough to get me to look up at Nyla. "Why would I talk to her about *any* of this? She'd fucking kill me if she found out I went out with Iason alone and lived out her fantasy of being with him. Well, *almost* being with him."

"She's your only chance at finding out who can put you in touch with Iason. Since she's part of the street team, she might know his manager and can put in a good word for you."

"But then I'd have to explain *why* I need to talk to him. I can't do that. She'd never forgive me."

"I'm sorry, sweetie. That's the only idea I have. You could try reaching out on social media, but it's probably run by his people and not him, so I doubt you'll get very far with that."

I sighed as I fell back on the couch. "How did this get so fucked-up so fast?"

She looked over at me with curiosity. "How did it even happen at all?"

"I met him backstage after his show yesterday. He

came to the museum today, and we went out to dinner together. For some inexplicable reason, he's attracted to me. And I feel the strangest attraction to him I can't ignore. It's so *weird*." In a calmer moment, I realized something. "Wait, what did you mean seeing us explained a fuckload of things?"

She laughed at my question. "For starters, I realized he wasn't looking at *me* during the concert. He couldn't take his eyes off *you*. And you blushing through the second half of the show after you came back from getting CDs for your sister meant you probably met him while they were fixing the audio issues, didn't you?"

"Yeah." The memory of my first encounter with Iason filled me with complex emotions. "He told me the song about someone being made out of wishes on stars was about me."

Nyla made an impressed noise. "Damn, that's smooth. I wonder how many times he's used that line before?"

She was probably right that he did that to anyone that struck his fancy while he was on tour. But something in me couldn't believe that. Not when he had been so earnest and genuine with me. Everything about him had been open and sincere, which was why I wanted to believe him. Was I being foolish?

Did he make everyone feel like they were his entire world when he went out with them? Or was I being stupid and caught up in the glamour of his fame? My common sense immediately told me I was being ridiculous for thinking the time we had spent at dinner had been anything other than him trying to get into my pants. But something in my heart steadfastly refused to believe that about him. I was an excellent judge of character, and nothing about him set off any of the warning alarms about being a player out for only his own satisfaction.

"What if it was just me, though? What if he was serious about that?"

"Then you'd be the luckiest man in the world." She wrapped her arms around me in a comforting hug. "For your sake, I hope that's the case."

It tore me up inside thinking I'd never see Iason to explain what happened. But if he genuinely believed I was made out of his wishes on stars and all his hopes and dreams, hopefully he'd give me a second chance. And if I was *really* lucky, maybe I'd *finally* get to kiss him without being interrupted.

Chapter Six

IASON

I WAS the world's biggest dumbass. Instead of being a mature adult, I had fled Orion's apartment like a coward when Nyla interrupted. His panicked denial that it wasn't what it looked like was the same thing I had heard other men explain to their girlfriends when caught in a compromising situation. There was never any point in sticking around after that. The guy always fucked his girlfriend to reaffirm his heterosexuality, and that was the end.

I *hated* being involved with a man who was dating somebody else. My father cheated on my mother throughout their entire marriage, so nothing disgusted me as much as that. I'd *never* be a pathetic excuse for a human like him. The thought that I had been caught in that kind of situation again had made me flee the scene.

But once I returned to my hotel room after calling

a ride share, I realized my mistake. The woman interrupting us hadn't sounded pissed off. She had almost been amused, which didn't make any sense. Normally, there was rage, fury, and sometimes throwing things. But there wasn't any trace of hurt in her tone. Why not?

As I analyzed the situation from every angle, I recognized the importance of what Orion had said. He had told me he was straight, not that he had a girlfriend. What if that woman was just a roommate and I had misunderstood their relationship? What if his protests that he could explain were because they had an agreement about not bringing people to their apartment and not about him betraying her as a boyfriend?

The worst feeling was hearing the echoes of his desperate plea for me to wait. He had tried to stop me, but I had let my emotions get the best of me and left him behind without a single glance back. Why had he wanted me to stay? What if it was because he had been prepared to choose me over his sexuality?

It was madness to believe that was true. I knew better than to mess with straight guys. They inevitably got scared off by their new feelings, leaving me nursing a broken heart and a bad case of blue balls. I had learned that lesson the hard way in college and swore I would never let myself fall for one again.

What kind of sick cosmic joke was it to have Orion appear in the guise of my perfect soul mate, only to make him straight? Or worse, have a girlfriend?

But in my defense, how the hell was I supposed to tell that he wasn't gay? All of his blushes whenever I looked at him, the way he shivered when I caressed him with my voice, and his moans when I teased his ears: those were not the reactions of someone who was straight. He may have claimed to be heterosexual, but his hard-on said otherwise.

But the thing that gnawed away at me the most was I should have known better. He wasn't a callous asshole who didn't care about who he hurt in his pursuit of pleasure. He was a shy sweetheart who blushed and loved someone with all of his heart. Although I had only known him a short time, he obviously wasn't a cheater who didn't care about his partner's feelings.

I wanted to go back to his apartment and apologize, but I couldn't bear the thought of being wrong. What if he was reaffirming his sexuality by having sex with Nyla? That would be an even worse rejection.

It would have been so much easier if I could call him directly and talk to him. However, in my excitement, I had neglected to get his number during dinner. In fairness, if everything had gone according to plan, I would have done it in the morning when I was leaving after an incredible night of learning every inch of his body as I made him come over and over again. So much for that. Jerking off to fantasies about how our first time should have gone was hardly a good consolation prize.

It infuriated me that my sense of certainty that he was supposed to be mine hadn't left me, despite the mounting evidence that it was an increasing long shot. The rational part of my mind warned I should give up before I got hurt further. But my heart wanted Orion, regardless of how difficult it would be. There had to be a way to make him understand we were meant to be together.

Waiting to visit him at the museum on Monday was too creepy, especially since I suspected I might not receive the warmest welcome. However, if going to his apartment or work wasn't an option, that left me with only one choice: trying to use Orion's sister to reach him. The trick was doing that without tipping her off as to why I wanted to see him. It was a desperate grab at straws, but it was my only chance.

That was when I came up with a brilliant plan. I texted my manager, Dylan, and asked her to set up a last-minute brunch with my Sunnyside street team. If I invited everyone, it wouldn't look as suspicious as singling out Lyra.

It wasn't a surprise when she was the first to arrive. She lit up like a kid at Christmas when she spotted me, hurrying over to say hi.

"Thank you *so* much for this, Iason!" She was practically vibrating with excited energy. "I can't believe this is happening!"

"It's the least I could do after the inconvenience the technical difficulties caused you girls the other night at the concert." It was my best excuse to cover up my less than savory intentions. I tried to sound casual. "Is Orion parking the car? He's welcome to join us."

She frowned, sending my hopes crashing to the ground. "No, he wouldn't bring me today."

The rejection hurt more than I'd care to admit. He was probably desperate to do anything to keep as much space between us now. I guess he must have chosen her over me after all. The thought physically pained me. I couldn't keep the concern out of my voice when I asked, "Is everything okay?"

"It didn't sound like it." She furrowed her eyebrows. "But he wouldn't tell me why he was so upset. It's not like him to ice me out."

Did that mean he was devastated that his girl-friend had broken up with him because she caught us together? Or was it because I had abandoned him without giving him a chance to explain what was going on? Both options made guilt eat away at me. Unsure of what else to say, I could only apologize. "I'm sorry. I hope he's okay."

Before we could continue talking, Lyra's friend Tisha appeared with Dylan right behind her. As the two teens became immersed in their conversation, I realized I had lost my chance to find out more about Orion. After all, I couldn't ask Lyra, "Hey, I'm worried I freaked out your brother by making a move on him. Would you mind giving me his phone number so I can check on him to see if he's okay?"

My best hope was waiting until the end of the brunch to try again. If that failed, I wasn't sure what I would do. All I knew was that I had to meet Orion again, no matter what.

AFTER BRUNCH FINISHED, Lyra and Tisha were the only two members of the street team left. They were waiting on Lyra's mom to pick them up, so I stayed with them to pass the time. I wanted to ask her about Orion again, but I couldn't do it without sounding suspicious.

Lyra waved at a woman who entered the restaurant. She was petite, with a pretty face and a warm smile. Her dark hair was twisted up into a rhinestone star clip, which matched her dangling diamond star earrings. I loved her ostentatious, neon pink coat covered with silver glitter stars that sparkled as the light hit them.

"Sorry, I'm late," the woman apologized in a thick Southern drawl when she reached our table.

Now that she was closer, I could see the resemblance in her smile to Orion's. It made me miss him all over again. "Please, come join us." I gestured to one of the empty chairs. "It's no trouble."

"Oh, aren't you a peach?" She shook my hand before sitting down. "I'm Estelle, Lyra's mom."

"A pleasure. Can I get you anything?"

"No, I'm good, thanks." She studied me with curiosity. "So, you're the famous Iason?"

Lyra looked mortified, as only dramatic teenagers could. She indignantly hissed, "Mom!"

"You can't be upset with me before I've had a chance to properly embarrass you yet." Estelle's playful chiding made me laugh. Lyra looked like she wanted to crawl under the table when her mother turned her attention to me. "I have to say, you're even prettier in person than on the posters she has hanging up in her room."

Lyra hid her face in her hands with a pained groan. Her friend sympathetically rubbed her back. It struck me how similar Lyra's reaction was to Orion's.

Estelle's outgoing personality amused me. Lyra definitely took after her mother in that department, whereas Orion was more reserved. I wondered if that meant he was more like his father. "You're too kind."

"I'd pay you a nicer compliment, but I'm not entirely certain that my daughter won't spontaneously combust from humiliation." Estelle's blue eyes were bright with mischievous amusement.

The chance was too tempting to resist. "Your son seems to suffer from the same affliction."

She lit up at the mention of her son. "Oh, you've met Cherry?"

"Cherry?"

"That's what Mom calls Rion," Lyra explained.

If nothing else, I had to see him for that alone. "His nickname is *Cherry*? He neglected to mention that."

"He's such a darling boy, but you're right, it doesn't take much to turn him into a blushing cherry tomato." The sound of Estelle's delighted laughter warmed me. She was the polar opposite of my own frigid mother, who only laughed when bad things happened. "It's so fun making him maraschino cherry red. You can obviously tell how the nickname came to be."

I took my last shot at a reunion. "Now, I *really* have to meet him again."

"Do you have any plans for tonight?"

I wasn't above playing the pity card. "Just sitting in my lonely hotel room."

"Oh, don't be ridiculous! Why don't you come to dinner tonight? We can have Cherry over and make an evening out of it."

Estelle was officially my new favorite person. "That sounds delightful if it's not too much trouble. Can I bring anything?"

"Just your sweet self and that lovely smile of yours." She reached across the table to pat my hand. The casual show of affection was so different from what I was used to with my own family.

Lyra looked torn between being over the moon

and worried. "Mom, I don't know if Rion will come. He's really upset about something. Do you think he got into a fight with Nyla?"

"I can't imagine that. What would they have to argue about?"

"What if she rejected Rion after he asked to get back together?"

Estelle shook her head. "Trust me, honey. They're never getting back together. Cherry has made his peace with that."

Her words overjoyed me. So Nyla was an *ex*-girlfriend. That tidbit shed light on why she hadn't seemed mad about catching me with Orion. But why was Estelle so certain that they'd never get back together? There was a story there I was clearly missing.

Lyra frowned as she tried to figure something out. "I don't understand why they broke up, but they're still good friends. It doesn't make sense."

"It will when you're a little older." Estelle pulled her cell phone out to call her son. When he answered, her voice was as sweet as sugar as she greeted him. "Hi, Cherry, it's Mom. You're coming home for dinner tonight, okay?"

Although it was phrased as a question, there was no room for argument in her tone. A frown crossed her face as she listened to his answer. "Nope, no excuses. You're coming over tonight, and that's final. I'll pick you up myself if I have to." There was a brief pause before she snorted in amusement. "You think I won't come get you? I'm sorry, have you met me?"

Lyra mouthed the word "Sorry" at me, causing me to grin. Her mother's antics were entertaining. She was so lively and full of warmth, unlike my icy mother, who could only make time for me when she needed to inform me how disappointed she was in me and my life choices.

"We're having a guest over for dinner, so you have to be there." Estelle laughed at something he said. "No, I promise it's not your Aunt Sharron. I met Iason when I went to pick your sister up from their brunch. Since I can't bear the thought of him sitting all alone in his hotel eating room service when he could have a home-cooked meal, I invited him over."

Whatever he said made her grin with amusement. "Yes, *that* Iason. I expect you home by 6:00, understood? No, I'm not joking. Do you want to talk to him yourself? He's sitting right here."

I held my breath, my heart pounding in anticipation as I begged every cosmic force in the universe to make him agree. My prayers were answered when she passed her phone over to me.

Very aware of the three ladies watching me, I played it casual. "Are you checking if I really exist?"

Orion's voice sounded so small and miserable that it hurt. "I'm so sorry, Iason."

"You better not be saying that because you aren't

coming tonight," I said in a teasing tone, even though the thought of him doing that gutted me.

"No, I meant about yesterday. You won't believe me, but Nyla is my ex-girlfriend I'm still friends with. I swear I'd never cheat on anyone. I'm sorry I couldn't get the words to come out right last night. I thought you'd probably never want to see me again, but—"

I couldn't say what I wanted to, so I hoped he could read between the lines. "No, I really want you to join us for dinner tonight."

"I want to see you, but I don't know what'll happen."

"We'll have a great time." I would make sure of it. "You know I'm not getting off this phone until you agree to come over, right?"

His laughter warmed my soul like bright sunshine after a stormy day. Amusement colored his tone as he asked, "I suppose you want me to pick you up to bring you over?"

That was an even more generous offer than I expected. Could he be that eager to see me? "I'd like that. I'm in room 609 at the Luxurian Suites Hotel on the West Side."

"What time?"

"As soon as you're ready." I hoped he would arrive early so we could talk before we had to go to his parents' house for dinner.

"So, in like, twenty minutes?"

"Works for me." My voice betrayed how eager I was. "I'll see you then, thanks."

I passed the phone back over to Estelle. "That settles it, then. We'll see you both at 6:00. Love you, Cherry." She hung up, looking as triumphant as I felt. "Thank you for convincing my stubborn son to join us."

"It's my pleasure." Talk about understatements.

"Well, we should get going. I need to go to the grocery store for tonight. Iason, do you have any dietary restrictions or allergies?"

Her consideration touched me. "As long as there aren't any pine nuts, I'm not picky."

"Fantastic! Then we'll see you soon."

"Thanks again for brunch," Lyra said, looking at me with hearts in her eyes. "I can't believe you're coming over to *our house* for dinner!"

I smiled with all the joy I felt that I'd be having my reunion with Orion. "It's my pleasure. We'll have fun."

After a few more parting words, I left the café to wait at my hotel for him. Hopefully, my good day would get even better very soon.

Chapter Seven

ORION

I ARRIVED at Iason's hotel in record time. As I stood in front of his door, I took a deep breath. My life would change forever as soon as I went into his room. It should have been terrifying, but it was exciting. For once, I wanted to be brave enough to act on my instincts instead of questioning myself into paralysis. For better or for worse, I was as ready as I would ever be.

Taking a deep breath to steady my nerves, I knocked on Iason's door. My heart stuttered in my chest at the sight of him when he opened it. He wore tight black pants and a light blue V-neck sweater, which made his eyes even more stunning. His pleased smile evaporated any lingering doubts I may have had.

He gathered me into a hug when I stepped inside. All was right in my world at last. I returned the embrace, hiding my face against his neck. The scent of him comforted me while also sending desire rocketing through me at the same time. I wasn't sure how long we remained like that, but I never wanted that perfect moment to end.

"I'm sorry I overreacted yesterday." His apology surprised me. "I should have let you explain everything."

"I hated knowing you probably thought I was the worst kind of cheater." To convey my sincerity, I pulled back to make eye contact with him. "I would *never* do that. If I'm with a partner, I'm *only* with them. That's why Nyla and I aren't together anymore."

His expression reflected his shock. "You're still friends with someone who cheated on you?"

I shook my head. "She didn't. But she wanted to open our relationship and explore her polyamorous desires she was coming to terms with. I couldn't do it, though. I can't be one of many. I don't resent her for being true to who she is, but it's not for me. That's why we're only friends now."

"I'm not a cheater or liar. My father is both, and I can't stand it. I'll *never* be like him." He swore it with a conviction I believed. "I would never betray you. You would be my one and only, Orion."

His words went a long way toward reassuring me about my unspoken fear. It gave me the strength to press my lips against his, claiming the kiss that had been denied to me so many times. He made a surprised noise before his arms wrapped around my waist, pulling me closer in encouragement. It was heavenly when he kissed me back with a tenderness that swept me away. He let me go at my own pace as I lost myself in the taste of him. It was better than I had dared to dream, as it stirred my desires.

We were both breathless when we parted. Never in my life had a single kiss made me feel so much before. If just kissing was so amazing, what would it be like if we kept going?

"I've gotta say, I'm liking this bold side of you, Cherry," Iason teased.

I groaned at the nickname. "You can't call me that!"

He chuckled. "But it's so cute. Not to mention appropriate, given how much you blush."

"It's my mom's stupid nickname for me. I—"

My next words disappeared when he ran his tongue along the shell of my ear. I moaned when he tugged on it. Shit, and I had thought it felt great before. Now that I wasn't trying to resist the pleasure, it was even better.

"I'm dying for a taste of you, Cherry."

The nickname may have been annoying when my mom called me that, but hearing him murmur it next to my ear was sexy as fuck. A whimper escaped me when he continued teasing my sensitive spot. I could only hold on to him, trembling with my building arousal.

"I have been since I first laid eyes on you." His fingers snuck under my shirt to stroke my skin, making me pull back with a gasp. Rather than being displeased, my reaction seemed to delight him. "I love how responsive you are to the slightest touch."

Before I could reply, he removed my black long-sleeve shirt. He leaned forward and placed a trail of warm kisses against my collarbone, sending a shiver through me. "It makes me want to touch every inch of you and see what happens."

The word "please" slipped from my lips in a pained groan. My desires might have scared me, but that didn't change the fact that I wanted what he was tempting me with. I kicked off my boots and toed off my socks in anticipation of what was about to happen.

His hands slid down my torso, moving across my stomach, pausing long enough to stroke the prominent ridges of my hip bones. When he reached the waistband of my jeans, he looked at me with a sultry expression. "Will you let me pleasure you, Orion?"

There wasn't a person alive who could turn down that kind of offer from Iason. I didn't have to think about my answer. "*Yes*."

He stripped me of my pants and briefs before he lowered to his knees. "With a cock like this, you should have a bigger ego." He ran his fingers along the rigid length of my erection. "It's as magnificent as the rest of you. I'm *so* going to enjoy this."

I wasn't oblivious to the fact that I was well-endowed, but it was still a confidence boost to hear the awe in his voice. Unsure of how to respond, I could only awkwardly shift on my feet. "You're the only one who has ever felt that way about me."

He leaned forward and ran his tongue along the length of it, savoring his first taste before my words registered. "Wait, what do you mean? Your ex-girl-friends weren't grateful for being blessed to suck this beautiful cock?"

"Nyla couldn't because her gag reflex was too bad. My girlfriend before her refused to do it because she said blow jobs are demeaning."

"Demeaning?" Iason repeated in outrage. "What the fuck?"

"Indra had a lot of weird hang-ups." That was an understatement, but it wasn't worth getting into details. "She didn't see why she should have to when men use 'suck my dick' and 'cocksucker' as insults. She also hated having to do all the work for me to get off while she got nothing out of it."

He shook his head with a disgusted look. "No offense, but she's a selfish idiot."

I shrugged. "It didn't matter to me enough to push the issue when we were having actual sex."

"Does that mean it's been a while since you've gotten good head?"

Although there wasn't any judgment in his tone, I

was still embarrassed to admit the truth. "Um, I've actually never come from a blow job before."

Instead of making fun of my inexperience, his eyes lit up with excitement. "I'm going to be your first?"

"There will be a lot of firsts today."

He surprised me when he stood up and took hold of my hand, leading me over to his king-size bed. "Lie on your back."

I felt horribly exposed when I stretched out, my heart hammering in nervousness. When he spread my legs wider to kneel between them, I reminded myself to take calming breaths. It confused me why he was still wearing his clothes, but the thought evaporated when he moved up to kiss me.

The distraction helped lessen my nerves as I lost myself in his kisses and caresses that made me harder than I had ever been in my life. Being the center of his attention overwhelmed me but in the best of ways.

Lulled into a sense of complacency, I startled when his tongue teased my heavy sac. When he took one into his mouth, I inhaled with a sharp gasp from the unexpected sensation. He repeated the action on the other, drawing a whimper from me.

I propped myself up on my elbows, transfixed by the sight of him taking my cock into his mouth. The wet warmth was unbelievable. I had never seen anything so erotic as watching myself disappear between his lips, as his cheeks hollowed to heighten my pleasure. I gave in to my urge to slide my hand through the silken strands of his hair that fell in front of his face. It earned a pleased moan that almost caused me to shoot my load when I intimately experienced the vibration.

Iason looked like he was in ecstasy from being able to suck me off. How could such a simple thing feel so incredibly good? I gasped and moaned fragments of his name as I raced toward my climax. As much as I wanted to hold out and not humiliate myself by coming too soon, the onslaught of pleasure was too intense to handle.

He paused for a moment, making me bite back a groan of frustration. "You can come in my mouth. In fact, I want you to." The roughness of his voice excited me in a way I didn't understand. My heart rocketed into the stratosphere when he ran his fingers over my entrance. "Can I touch you here?"

I would have agreed to damn near anything to get him to keep going. "Sure."

The moment his mouth returned to my hardness, my ability to form a complete sentence disappeared. The overwhelming pleasure of his skill made me come undone, especially as I looked deep into his blue eyes that radiated joy at seeing me losing my mind.

When I was almost pushed to the very edge of my limits, he eased a lubed finger into my ass. It wasn't unpleasant, but it was an unexpected sensation. Where the hell had he gotten lube? However, his oral attentions made it too hard to focus, so I relaxed into the touch as he worked me open.

I didn't resist when he added a second finger, but the weirdness of it drew me from the blissful haze of his incredible blow job. Without warning, his fingers ghosted over something inside of me that almost caused me to shout from the intense sensation as he swallowed at the same time.

While he had said it was okay, I tried to warn him I was close to finishing. The feelings built up inside me, stoked to new heights by his fingers teasing that spot within me that had me seeing stars. It was too much to withstand when he started humming one of his songs. "Ias!"

I watched in awe as he swallowed my release and put on a show of licking my cock clean of every drop of cum. It was unbelievable that a mouth could bring so much pleasure, but he had sent me to the heights of heaven.

"Feeling good?" He sounded smug, but after his performance, I couldn't blame him.

Words were beyond me. "Mm-hmm."

"This isn't hurting you?" He moved his two fingers inside of me.

I realized I needed to answer with more than monosyllabic grunts. "No, but it's odd."

"I promise it'll be worth it." He added a third finger, giving me time to adjust to it before moving again. "My cock will feel even better."

"I don't know how anything can feel better than what you just did." I hadn't expected such an intense orgasm from oral sex, which had never done much for me in the past.

"Trust me, the fun is only getting started."

I acutely felt the loss when he withdrew his fingers from inside me. However, the sight of him rising on his knees and stripping off his sweater caused all my thoughts to come to a screeching halt. I swallowed hard as he undid his belt and stood up to take off his pants, kicking them aside with his briefs.

His naked body stole my breath away. All of his beautifully defined muscles filled me with the strongest urge to touch. I felt inadequate in the face of his perfection, especially when I allowed my gaze to drift down to the large, thick cock. It proudly stood out from a neatly trimmed nest of dark hair.

I swore when he reached down and stroked himself. Instead of turning me off, it lit a fire within me. "See what you do to me? This is because of you, Cherry."

It was almost more than I could wrap my mind around. "Sucking me off is that enjoyable for you?"

"Getting to take you inside of me and taste your pleasure makes me want you even more." He rolled on a condom, making me swallow hard. "I could come right now just thinking about being inside you."

I had no idea what to say to that, but fuck if it didn't sound sexy as hell. While I was turned on, my nerves took over the afterglow of my incredible release. Iason's cock was massive, and I found it difficult to believe that it would fit without hurting.

"Don't worry, I'll make you feel so good, you'll forget to be nervous."

"If you can fuck the anxiety out of me, I'm going to marry you." It would be a miracle, given what a challenge it was for me to let go of my apprehensiveness normally.

He repositioned himself, pressing the head of his cock against my entrance. "Then I'll make you come hard enough to hear wedding bells." It was such an outlandish claim that I laughed while he pushed into me. "Remember to breathe and stay relaxed."

"Isn't this supposed to feel good?" I asked as he entered me. The stretching didn't hurt, but it wasn't pleasant, either.

His hands caressing me kept me focused on him and not the weird sensation of being penetrated for the first time. "Don't worry, I promise it'll get better soon."

While I logically knew there had to be some kind of pleasure to be had from anal sex, I wasn't impressed so far. It mostly felt awkward and a little uncomfortable. I shifted my hips, reminding myself to breathe and stay patient. It took forever before he was fully inside me. He stayed still to give me time to adjust to the unfamiliar fullness. It wasn't great, but at least it didn't hurt.

"I'm going to move now, okay?" He started with small movements, which didn't do much for me.

I wondered if something was wrong with me until he canted my hips for a more aggressive push. It gave me the first glimmer of a pleasant sensation. I grabbed his toned bicep to steady myself. Something about the feeling of his hard muscle excited me. I slid my hand up his arm and onto his shoulder. Another well-aimed thrust caused me to grip him harder. "*Oh!*"

"That's it," he encouraged me. "Let go and feel good."

It wasn't until he lifted my hips and hit something deep inside of me that I cried out in intense pleasure. I clapped my hand over my mouth to hold in the moans that wanted to escape me.

He moved my hand away. "I want to hear you, Cherry."

"Your neighbors don't."

Despite my protests, the next pump of his hips made me gasp his name. It came as a surprise since I had never been noisy during sex. The responsible part of my brain reminded me to stay quiet and not disturb the people in the adjoining room. However, I lost the fight against my normally reserved self. I moaned and called out Iason's name as my body undulated under his masterful manipulation of my desires.

As it grew more intense, I looped my arms over his neck while my legs wrapped around his hips. It allowed him to hit even deeper inside of me than before. I couldn't hold back my cry at how incredible it felt to have him moving within me.

I achieved a new level of sexual satisfaction when he reached between us to stroke my reawakened hardness. A gasp got caught in my throat as he made me feel things I never imagined possible. Sex had never been so intense and incredible before. I couldn't think of anything other than *good, so fucking good*.

"You're beautiful." He gazed at me like I was the most gorgeous thing he had ever seen. "So damn beautiful, Orion."

At that moment, I believed him. I truly felt beautiful as he looked down at me with such warm emotions in his enthralling blue eyes.

It was too intense for me to last. My orgasm hit so hard that I forgot how to breathe, how to exist, how to do anything other than feel the extraordinary pleasure crashing over me. I lost myself in sexual ecstasy, which was further heightened when he came while moaning my name. I had never experienced anything so glorious in my life.

Although it was over, I couldn't make myself let go of him yet. He leaned forward and gently kissed me, eliciting a soft whimper from me when it caused him to shift inside me. My heart skipped a beat when he caressed my cheek. It was stupid to think there was anything more between us than lust. But as he looked at me with such fondness, I felt like I actually mattered to him.

He broke the moment with a joke. "When's our wedding, Cherry?"

It took a second for me to remember what he was referring to before I laughed at the absurdity of the idea. "Yeah, right. As if somebody like you would ever marry someone like me."

"What kind of person am I supposed to marry?" He pulled out of me, making me feel weirdly empty.

"A famous, gorgeous, talented person." I shifted to look at him when he lay down on his side beside me.

He brushed my hair from my face. "Do you think my ego would want to compete with another famous person?"

"When you're walking the red carpet to win your next Grammy, you'll want a stunning model or actor on your arm, not me being awkward as fuck."

"I love how you say when and not if." He leaned closer for a teasing kiss. "Why would I ever choose a vacuous model when I could have you?"

The response surprised me. "But I don't matter."

Iason moved to hold my gaze, all traces of playfulness replaced with a serious expression. He sounded genuine as he adamantly told me, "You absolutely matter to me, Orion. This isn't a meaningless fling."

"Isn't it, though?" I tried not to let my hurt show. "I'll fade into a distant memory once you're off to the next stop of your tour."

"That's not true at all." It surprised me how sincere he looked. "I still want to see you after I leave."

"Really?"

The warmth in his voice filled me with heat. "Really."

"But what does that mean?"

"I want to spend every night with you here before I leave, Cherry." He caressed my cheek as he looked deep into my eyes. "It means I want to text you on Thursday after we go our separate ways. I want you to come to my San Francisco shows next Friday and Saturday so we can meet up there. I want to call you while I'm on the road and see you again when I'm back in town."

It was impossible to wrap my head around what he was saying. "Why?"

"Because I really like you." He said it as if it was as simple as that. "When I told you I want you, I meant for more than one meaningless night."

"You don't know me, though."

His smile melted my resistance. "Not yet, but I want to. Will you let me?"

Before I could talk myself out of it, I agreed. "Okay."

Iason's face lit up in excitement, a look so beautiful that it took my breath away. "You don't know how happy you just made me, Cherry,"

"You're right, I have absolutely no idea," I replied with a laugh. "I'm just a nobody."

"No, you're somebody to me."

Although I warned my idiot heart not to misunderstand what he was saying, his words moved me.

He grinned when I didn't respond. "You don't look convinced."

"That's because I can't comprehend how it's possible. You're a world-famous singer who looks like a god descended from heaven, and I'm a scrawny assistant curator at a small museum. We don't live in the same worlds at all."

"We're together now. That's all that matters."

He interrupted my next protest with a demanding kiss. It stirred my desires despite being satiated. Heat flared through me, which was why it confused me when he got up to leave. "Where are you going?"

"I'll be right back." He disappeared into the bathroom and emerged with a warm washcloth.

A deep blush spread across my cheeks when he gently tended to me. In some ways, it almost was more intimate than sex as he washed me. While it embarrassed me, I had to admit that I felt better. "Thank you."

He kissed me with a sweetness that caused my heart to race. "I'm happy to take advantage of any excuse to touch you." He tossed the washcloth onto the nightstand and set an alarm on his phone. Then he lay down on his back once more, gesturing for me to come closer.

I moved to lay my head on his shoulder as I nestled against his side. He wrapped an arm around me to hold me close. I relaxed into the position, surprised to discover I enjoyed being held that way. The steady thrumming of his heart calmed me.

"Get some rest." He pressed a tender kiss on my forehead. "I set my alarm to give us plenty of time to go to your parents' house."

After barely sleeping the night before, I drifted off. I had never felt better in my entire life.

Chapter Eight

IASON

ORION GREW anxious the closer we got to his parents' house. I worried he was having regrets about what we had done. While we waited at a stoplight, I reached over to rub the back of his neck. He dropped his head forward, closing his eyes for a moment as he melted into my touch.

"What's wrong?" I asked.

"Sorry." He sounded miserable.

I did my best to reassure him. "You don't have to be sorry. Tell me what's wrong, Cherry."

"They'll know."

"Know what?"

There was a faint blush on his cheeks. "What we did this afternoon."

I couldn't stop myself from grinning. "It's not like I left a hickey that would give it away. They won't know unless you tell them."

"No, you don't understand. Mom will figure it out," he said with complete conviction. "She's got a ridiculous sixth sense about this kind of stuff."

"Is it a problem if she does?"

He growled in frustration as he made another turn. "If she figures it out, then Lyra will, and all hell will break loose."

"You're this worried about a teenage tantrum?"

He glanced over at me with a troubled expression. "I *really* don't think you understand how much she worships you."

I tried to reason with his fears. "If she worships me, nothing would make her happier than me being happy, right?"

He shrugged. "I guess."

Since we were at a stop sign and there was no one behind us, I turned his head to meet my gaze. "Nothing makes me happier than you, Cherry."

His gray eyes flew wide at my declaration. "Really?"

"Really." I leaned over to kiss him. "If she gets mad, she'll get over it."

He remembered to drive again after checking both ways twice. His grip on the steering wheel was so tight that his knuckles turned white.

"She has to understand that as a thirty-five-year-old gay man, I won't be interested in dating a fifteen-year-old girl."

"I don't think she knows you're gay." He frowned

as he sighed. "In all her fantasies, you're straight and one backstage meeting from sweeping her off her feet."

"Even if I *was* straight, her age alone would be a nonstarter. Besides, she's missing the number one thing I'm interested in."

He couldn't keep the smirk off his face. "A dick?"

I snickered at his suggestion. "More important than that."

"What's more important than that?" He pulled into the driveway of his parents' home. It was a beautiful two-story brick house with a wide courtyard in front of the three-car garage.

I waited until he parked to make sure he was looking at me. "She's not you."

While Orion looked moved, he remained silent.

"Look, I understand you're overwhelmed with trying to figure out what's going on between us."

He smiled faintly. "That's an understatement."

"I have no intention of outing you to your family when you're still processing everything. I don't want to cause problems for you by being overt in my interest in you, okay? You have my word. I won't make out with you in front of everyone to thank you for passing the mashed potatoes."

He laughed with relief before he looked down in embarrassment. "I'm sorry I'm being ridiculous."

I tilted his chin up to force our gazes to meet.

"You don't need to feel bad. In your defense, I haven't been subtle about my interest in you."

His smile broadened into a grin. "Not even a little."

"I won't apologize for that, either. But I promise I'll behave myself. I don't want to hurt or upset you, Cherry. All I want to do is have a nice time with you and your family. After that, we'll go back to my hotel together, where I'll make you moan until dawn."

My words sent a visible shiver through him. "Fuck, Ias."

"All night long." I gave him a flirty wink for good measure.

It surprised me when he leaned over and hungrily kissed me. I enjoyed the burst of passion, although it left me wanting more.

"I'm not ashamed of you, or us, or whatever this is. I just don't understand this enough yet to explain it to them right now."

"I respect that." His words comforted me. "I have no problem with going at your pace. If I do something that makes you uncomfortable, tell me, and I won't do it again."

"Thank you." He hesitated before leaning over to give me a sweet kiss.

I melted into the tenderness, wishing I could pull him closer. When we parted, I caressed his cheek with a fond smile. "Now, let's go eat. I worked up quite an appetite this afternoon."

"Imagine that." His grin betrayed how amused he was.

After we got out of the car, I couldn't resist the urge to sneak in one final tease before I had to behave for the rest of the night. I wrapped an arm around Orion's waist, then pulled him back against my chest so our bodies were flush. He squeaked in surprise as I nuzzled against him. "I can't wait to make you my dessert later, Cherry." I nipped at the shell of his ear for good measure.

He whimpered before he jerked away. "You promised you would behave!" He rubbed his ear where I had toyed with it.

"In front of your family," I reminded him. "It's still just us out here."

He lost the fight against holding back his grin. "Come on."

I made myself behave as I followed him. Well, I might have snuck an appreciative glance at his ass, but who could blame me? He looked great in those jeans.

He took a deep breath before ringing the doorbell. His mother answered the door with a bright smile as she welcomed us inside. She wore a black fit-and-flare dress that was covered in metallic silver-and-gold foil stars of various sizes. It matched her star hair clip and earrings she had on from earlier in the day. Now that Estelle was barefoot, it stunned me how short she was. I was over a foot and a half taller than her.

She went up on tiptoe to greet each of us with a kiss on the cheek before she sighed in exasperation at her son. "We have a guest over and *this* is how you dress?"

He looked down at his long-sleeve black shirt and jeans with a shrug. "I'm no different from the way I normally am."

I wasn't sure why she was fussing over his outfit. I certainly hadn't had any complaints about it when it was on my hotel room floor.

She put her hands on her hips as she chided him. "That's the problem."

"Sorry, I wasn't aware this was a black-tie event that required a tux." He gave her a pointed look. "Besides, *you're* wearing black, too. Why is it an issue that I am?"

Estelle did a cute twirl to make the stars on her dress shimmer in the light. "Yes, but at least *mine* is covered in shiny." She was barely five feet tall, but her colorful personality made her seem larger than life.

"Do you own anything that *isn't* shiny?"

"Why would I ever wear anything without a little sparkle?" She gave a disdainful sniff before laughing brightly. "All I'm saying is that you're so handsome, but your entire wardrobe is the color of a bruise. It wouldn't hurt you to wear bright colors sometimes, you know?"

I was used to having a mother criticize my every

choice, so I spoke up in Orion's defense. "I think he looks nice."

She wagged her finger at me with a playful admonishment. "Now, don't you go encouraging him. It wouldn't have killed him to put in a little effort for you. You're company, after all."

"I don't want anyone going to trouble for my sake. I'm just happy to be here tonight."

"Oh, you're so adorable!" Her exclamation reminded me of Lyra's exuberance. "Please, relax and enjoy yourself. Come on in."

Orion looked tortured as we followed her. I wanted to reach out and comfort him, but I resisted the urge.

As we passed by the living room into the kitchen, it struck me how homey the space was compared to my parents' house. Theirs was filled with furnishings picked out by an interior decorator, which were there more for aesthetics than comfort. The Donati home exuded warmth and coziness, which invited you to come and stay for a while. It was obvious a real family lived there, with pictures everywhere of their happy memories, unlike my parents' empty house, which had never been a home.

Lyra set the table with silverware, while her dad worked on preparing salads. My father's face was stuck in a permanently stern expression, so it surprised me how kind he looked. Dressed in black slacks and a red button-down shirt, he looked right at home in the kitchen. I had never seen mine in the kitchen for anything other than grabbing a beer from the fridge.

"Don't mind your mother, Cherry. You know she's not happy unless everyone is decked out in glitter," he said with a sympathetic expression.

"Life is dreary enough as it is." She headed over to her husband to assess his work. "It's up to us to bring a little fun to it. And nothing is more fun than glitter and sparkles."

"You bring fun into my life every day, no matter what you're wearing, Peaches." He leaned down to give her a kiss that made her giggle.

The casual affection stunned me. I had never seen my parents act that way with each other. As Estelle smiled up at her husband, genuine adoration shined in her eyes. It was beautiful and so different from the cold indifference I was used to. I couldn't help but be a little envious of what it must have been like to grow up in a home full of unconditional love.

"Hi, I'm Neil." He came over to give me a firm handshake and a friendly clasp on the shoulder. "Welcome home."

The sentiment made me warm all over. "Thanks. I'm Iason."

"Trust me, son. There isn't a person in this house who doesn't know who you are." It affected me more than I would have expected to be called "son" by him, although I knew he didn't mean it that way.

"*Dad*!" Lyra looked mortified. "Don't be embarrassing!"

Estelle grinned at her teenage daughter. "Baby girl, if your daddy wanted to embarrass you, he'd tell Iason he knows all the words to his songs because of how loud you blast it when you're singing along in the shower."

His grin was ornery. "No, if I *really* wanted to embarrass her, I'd start singing one of his songs to prove it."

Lyra looked like she wanted the ground to open up and swallow her whole. "You promised you wouldn't embarrass me!"

"You're a teenage girl, sweetie," Estelle reminded her daughter. "You think *everything* we do is embarrassing."

I knew I shouldn't laugh, but I couldn't hold back my chuckle. Sympathetic about Lyra's situation, I tried to take some of the attention off her by thanking them. "I appreciate you having me over tonight."

"We're glad you're here. I hope you brought your appetite. We'll start off with salads to pretend that we're healthy, before we have lasagna smothered in a ton of cheese that proves we're anything but," Neil said with a laugh.

It sounded like the perfect meal. "I love Italian, so

that sounds heavenly. There's no such thing as too much cheese."

"Ha! Pay up, Sugar!" Estelle crowed, nudging her husband with a Cheshire cat grin. "You, sir, owe me twenty bucks."

Neil rolled his eyes as he playfully groused. "Yeah, yeah. Just add it to my tab, lady."

"What did you bet on now?" Orion asked in exasperation.

"Your father assumed Iason would be vegan since he lives out in LA, so he thought I was nuts for making lasagna," she explained, causing me to laugh. "I won that round."

Lyra gave her mom a disapproving scowl. "How is that fair when Iason told you he'd eat anything without pine nuts?"

Estelle's voice was full of laughter. "Shush, you. I've got to take my wins where I can get them."

"My mother is *extremely* competitive," Orion warned me.

"Hey, I'm just glad we're not starving the boy with rabbit food." Neil picked up some of the salad bowls to bring them over to the table. "Besides, it was a sensible assumption. I've seen the pictures of Iason on your walls. People with bodies like his don't subsist on stick-to-your-bones lasagna, thank you very much."

Orion hurried over to carry the remaining bowls, but I didn't miss the flush on his cheeks.

"I've always been of the mindset that a good meal

is worth the extra time at the gym." I walked over to the table. "Where should I sit?"

Estelle took a seat at one head of the table, then gestured toward the chair on her left. "Right here, next to me and Cherry."

I wouldn't complain about that.

"Jason, what would you like to drink?" Neil asked as I sat down. "We've got sweet peach tea, water, soda. Pick your poison."

"Sweet peach tea?"

Estelle grinned, making her accent thicker. "In case you haven't noticed, I'm a bona fide Southern belle, straight from Georgia. Of *course* there's home-made sweet peach tea."

"I'd love to try it, thanks."

When Neil brought over the drinks, Estelle beamed at him. "Thanks, Sugar."

"No problem, Peaches." He kissed her on the fore-head before taking his seat. Their easy affection filled me with a longing to have that kind of life with Orion.

I took a sip of tea and fell in love with the flavor. It was sugary, but that was fine with me since I had a sweet tooth. "This is amazing!"

"I'm glad you like it!" Estelle looked pleased with herself.

As we ate, I tried to include Lyra in the conversation. "With Cherry, Peaches, and Sugar, do you have a food nickname?"

"Yes, but I pretend I don't."

"She's my little Apricot," Estelle answered for her daughter, "not just because she's sweet, but because she was the fuzziest little baby ever."

Lyra scowled down at her salad, spearing the lettuce with more force than necessary.

"I think it's adorable," I told her, hoping to ease some of her embarrassment.

"Do you have an embarrassing nickname you want to fess up to?" Estelle asked.

Does Mommy's Little Disappointment count? I didn't want to bring the mood of the room down, so I stuck with a more benign answer. "Just Ias."

"Iason's your real name?" Neil asked in surprise.

I grinned at the response. "Yep, it's on my birth certificate and everything."

"Huh, I always assumed it was your stage name," Orion said, sparing a glance my way. "It's so unique, I thought it had to be made up."

"My parents intended to name me Jason, but the nurse who did the paperwork at the hospital that night typed it with an *I* instead of a *J*," I explained. "My folks decided they liked it enough not to bother with the hassle of legally renaming me. Plus, they liked how 'Yay-son' sounded as a name."

His amusement was clear. "Are you serious? You were named by a sleep-deprived nurse's typo?"

I held my hand up as if I was testifying. "God's honest truth." It was further evidence of how little regard my parents had for me to make an effort to change my birth name to the correct one.

The sound of his unrestrained laughing made me grin. It was nice to see him enjoying himself after he had been anxious.

"I'm sorry, I know I shouldn't laugh, but—" He dissolved into laughter again, with the rest of the table joining in. "It's too funny!"

I wasn't offended by the reaction. How could I be when he had such a big smile on his face? "Yeah, yeah. Go ahead and laugh it up, Cherry."

"Hey, at least that's not my legal name." He wiped away the tears that had gathered in the corner of his eyes from laughing so much.

"No, you were named after your mother went through every star in the sky to decide which one you were going to be." Neil's eyes were full of fondness as he looked at his son. My father had never once looked at me that way in my entire life.

"Every star in the sky?" I skeptically repeated. That was quite the claim.

"I'm an astronomer turned astrophysicist, so yes, every damn star in the sky," Estelle said with pride.

"I felt like I won a war the day I got her to agree to limit her choices to the International Astronomical Union list of approved star names. When she started considering constellations instead, I knew we had finally made progress."

"My name means 'star,' plus they're my passion

and profession. There was no way my kids weren't going to be named after them."

"Why Orion and Lyra?" I asked.

Estelle got excited as she answered. "When I was a kid, the first constellation I ever learned how to find in the sky was Orion. It always held a special place in my heart because of that. Lyra contains the Vega star, which is one of the brightest in the sky."

"Translation: you chose it because it's one of the shiniest stars in the universe."

She grinned at me. "Now you're catching on."

"Your commitment to the star aesthetic makes more sense." It made her wardrobe all the more charming.

She reflexively touched her wedding ring, drawing my attention to it. Her engagement ring diamond was cut in the shape of a star, with the wedding band featuring two smaller pronged stars to flank it on either side. All three of the stones glittered in the light, matching her dangling star diamond earrings. Her ring had so much meaning in it, which said a lot to me about their marriage. My mother's only consideration when choosing hers had been if it was big enough to outshine her best friend's.

"Sometimes I think she only married me because I have the same first name as Neil Armstrong. I would have been out of luck if I was named Steve or something she couldn't link to space." He chuckled in amusement.

"Your last name being Donati would have been enough. You were obviously meant to be mine." She beamed at her husband with so much love it took my breath away.

"What's the significance of Donati?" I asked.

"It's a long-period comet, named after the Italian astronomer Giovanni Battista Donati. It was first seen in 1858, making it the first comet ever photographed. How could I not fall in love with a wonderful man like you with a name like that?" She radiated happiness and joy. "I told you the day I met you that you were stuck with me. Almost thirty-five years later, and here we are."

"And I'm grateful for it every day." He smiled at her with so much adoration, it took my breath away. Never in my life had I seen such a beautiful marriage. It was like watching a perfect TV family.

After finishing our salads, we brought our dishes over to the sink. Neil opened the top oven to check the lasagna while Estelle had to go up on her tiptoes to peer into the deep pan.

"Yeah, it looks good," she told him. "You can take it out."

"I love how you say that like you can actually see to tell." Neil chuckled, since it was obvious she was too short to assess the food in the upper oven.

He took the lasagna out and set it on a large trivet. To my delight, he hadn't been lying when he said it was smothered in cheese. It looked like a heart attack on a plate with all that oozing, cheesy goodness, but my mouth was watering at the sight and smell of it.

"Now *that* is lasagna," I complimented.

"It tastes even better than it looks," Estelle promised as Neil dished it out onto the plates.

"That's really saying something." I couldn't resist poking Orion in the side to tease him. "How is it your parents cook like this and yet you're still this skinny? I'd seriously be the size of a house."

He scoffed with a laugh. "I doubt that."

"I'd have to live at the gym, but it would be worth it."

We returned to our seats with plates in hand. Neil told me, "Try to save room for dessert."

I couldn't hide my excitement for my favorite meal of the day. "What's on the menu?"

"Why, cherries jubilee, of course," Estelle answered in gleeful delight.

"Cherries for dessert?" I couldn't keep the grin off my face as I glanced over at Orion, who was flame red. "Mmm, that's my *favorite*."

"I had a hunch." Estelle's teasing comment caused me to glance at her with an arched eyebrow. My other brow went up when she winked at me. What was *that* about?

"I wish someone would set *me* on fire," Orion muttered, causing his parents to laugh. His sister gave him a sympathetic look of commiseration.

Since I couldn't say anything else without

pushing it too far, I took a bite of the lasagna. "Wow, you weren't kidding! It's amazing. Thank you so much!"

"Much better than room service, if I do say so myself," Estelle proudly told me.

"That's the absolute truth. I'm envious of you, Lyra. You get to eat like this every night."

She grinned at me. "It *almost* makes up for the constant teasing I endure."

I couldn't keep the wistfulness out of my voice. "You're lucky."

"Spoken like a son whose mom burns everything she touches in the kitchen," Estelle joked, trying to keep the mood light.

I grinned at the comment, sounding impressed. "Oh, so you've already had the misfortune of tasting my mother's cooking, then. I'm so sorry."

She laughed at my joke before reaching over to pat my arm. "You're always welcome here, sweetheart. I'll make anything you want."

Overwhelmed by how genuinely kind and accepting she was, I bowed my head. "Thank you."

She gave my arm a light squeeze. "I mean it. Although fair warning, you'll end up with a nickname if you keep coming over."

"I'm amazed you haven't come up with one already," Neil said.

"So am I," Lyra agreed, causing them all to laugh.

"These things take time." Estelle shrugged. "I'm

still trying to figure it out. Is he a Honeydew? Maybe he's a Kumquat."

"Plum?" Neil suggested.

Lyra wrinkled her nose at the idea. "He can't be a Plum," she protested indignantly. "Those turn into gross prunes."

Neil held his hands up in surrender. "Hey, this is why your mother is the expert at this kind of thing. I gave it my best shot."

Estelle studied me with the utmost seriousness as she tried to figure out a name for me. "You're definitely not hairy enough to be a Kiwi." I didn't miss the way Orion's blush reappeared at the comment. "And you're way too tall to be a Peanut."

He snickered, causing my lips to curl into a perverse grin.

Estelle turned her attention to her son. "What's *your* suggestion, Cherry?"

Orion ate a bite of his lasagna to buy time before he had to answer. He then took a long drink of his tea, causing his mother to groan at the intentional delay. After another pause, he suggested, "Star Anise?" He seemed surprised he wasn't immediately shot down. "I mean, he *is* a star, plus being nick-named after food is a prerequisite for being a part of our family."

Hearing him say he wished I could be part of his family moved me. I wanted to lean over and kiss him to show him how much it meant to me, but I had made a promise to Orion to behave myself. I'd have to wait until we were alone later.

She tapped her chin as she considered it. "Damn, look at that. My son beat me at my own game. That's perfect, Cherry. Has 'star' in the name and everything. Why didn't I think of that?"

"Think you can handle being called Anise for the rest of your days?" Neil asked. "Because once my wife decides on something, absolutely nothing will change her mind. You'll be stuck with it forever."

It didn't matter what name Orion had picked. He had chosen a special name to give me a sense of belonging, which meant everything to me. "Yeah, I think I can live with that."

Orion looked over at me with uncertainty. "Are you sure?"

"You can call me anything you like, as long as you call me."

The happy smile on his face warmed me to the core of my being. Damn, I was already so head over heels for him. Somehow, it felt like we had known each other forever instead of only a few days. I had never felt more at home in my life than I did in the moment.

"Anise it is," Estelle pronounced, looking at me with more motherly affection than my own mother ever had. "Welcome to the family, Anise."

"It's good to be home." I tried not to get choked

up by how overwhelming it was to feel like I belonged somewhere.

She once again reached out and squeezed my hand before we continued on with the rest of our meal. The unexpected comfort of being accepted into their family stayed with me long after dinner was over.

Chapter Nine

ORION

I HAD BEEN SO worried about everything going wrong at family dinner night that it hadn't occurred to me it might go perfectly. As my parents always did, they adopted Iason as one of their own. It seemed to mean something to him. He looked at them as if he couldn't believe what he was seeing. Based on a few of his comments, I suspected he didn't have the warmest relationship with his folks. It made me even happier that mine embraced him with open arms.

Once dinner was over, we moved to the living room to chat until it was time to have dessert. Iason sat on the end of one of the sectional couches. I knew it probably seemed suspicious when I sat close enough to him that Lyra couldn't squeeze in between us. But it was my subtle way of claiming him, just like giving him a nickname was. My sister looked put out, but she sat on the other side of me without too much fussing.

"I can't thank you enough for such a wonderful dinner," Iason said once my parents sat down together on the other side of the couch. "It was one of the best things I've eaten in I can't even tell you how long."

"A good home-cooked meal is better than any of those froufrou fancy restaurants where they serve you a tiny bite of food and charge you top dollar for it," Neil said. "You spend a fortune and you're still hungry after you're finished."

"You're not wrong about that." Iason chuckled as he stretched his arm out over the couch behind me. "But a home-cooked meal for me meant a frozen dinner cooked in the microwave. This was wonderful, thank you."

Mom looked at him like she wanted to hug him tight and never let him go. "You are welcome over here anytime you want, Anise."

"You've made yet another convincing argument for why I need to leave Manhattan behind and come back here for good."

I glanced over at Iason in surprise. "You're planning on moving here?"

"I've been thinking about it for a while. But since I've been back this time, I've found more and more reasons to stay." He held my gaze, letting me know without saying that he meant me. My heart skipped a beat at the possibility of not having to do long-distance with him.

While I felt like I couldn't comment on it without

sounding suspicious, Lyra had no problem voicing my secret feelings. "Oh, that would be *amazing* if you moved here for good! You could come over here every week if you wanted!" She looked at him with hearts in her eyes as she dreamed of a fantasy life where he became a permanent member of our family.

"I can promise you that's much more tempting than returning alone to my empty apartment back in the city."

"You're from here originally, right?" Dad asked.

Iason nodded. "I grew up here, but my parents moved to Florida after I graduated from high school. I stayed here to go to Sunnyside University, then worked for a few years before I relocated to Manhattan after I signed a deal with my record label. I've always made it a point to stop here during my tours to recharge for a week with my friends before continuing the second half of my tour."

"But you don't have any dates for Florida on your tour," Lyra said with a puzzled expression. "Wouldn't you do that to visit your parents?"

"Our schedules never seem to be on the same page, so it's tough trying to book around their plans." Iason shrugged like it wasn't a big deal, but it made my heart hurt that they wouldn't make time for him. It was hard to smother the urge to reach out and touch him in physical comfort. However, I couldn't do it without raising suspicions. "My found family is here in Sunnyside, so that's good enough for me."

Based on Mom's expression, she understood what he wasn't saying. "Sometimes found family is closer than blood. It's good you have loved ones to take care of you while you're on the road. Being on tour for so long must be exhausting."

He ran his fingers through his hair to ruffle it. "It is, especially by the end when I'm running on fumes. But touring with my friends in the band is awesome. I give them this week off to go home to visit their own families before we all meet up again in San Francisco."

"That's nice that you do that for them. I bet they appreciate it." Mom smiled at him. "You're so thoughtful."

He bowed his head with the closest thing to a bashful look I had seen. "I do what I can for them. They've always been so supportive of me, so I enjoy helping them, too."

"It's good you take care of the people who take care of you," Dad said with an approving nod. "I'm sure a lot of folks would think it was enough that you gave them the time off to stay here."

"I wouldn't have the career I do without them." Jason's smile was so beautiful I forgot how to breathe. "I owe so much of my success to them."

"You're such a sweet boy." Mom cooed at him as she gazed at him with affection.

"I'd actually like to invite all of you to come to my San Francisco concert this coming Friday and Saturday. I can have tickets ready for you at the box office."

"Oh my god! Yes, yes, yes!" Lyra squealed as she bounced with joy. "They sold out in a hot second, so I couldn't go. Seriously? We can see you both nights?"

He smiled at her, making her swoon hard. "I'd love that."

Mom's expression was remorseful. "I would love to go, Anise, but we're hosting a conference at the university Friday through Sunday. I'm so sorry, honey."

"And I'm in Dallas all week on business," Dad said in an apologetic voice.

Lyra looked panicked as she stared up at me in desperation. "Please tell me you can take me! Please, Rion!"

There was no way I was missing the chance to see Iason. "Sure, I'd be happy to take you. Since traffic is a nightmare, I'll reserve a hotel so we can stay in the city." Selfishly, I wanted to stay in the hopes of seeing him after the show.

She launched herself at me in a tight hug. "You're the best brother ever!"

I hugged her back. "Even if I make you go to the Legion of Honor Museum with me on Saturday morning?"

"I will look at all the dead-people pictures you want if it means I get to see Iason live on Friday *and* Saturday!" Her declaration made everyone laugh.

"Thank you for your sacrifice," Iason teased her, making her blush.

"I'd do anything for you!" The way she stared at him with the utmost adoration made me wonder how I would ever tell her the truth about my relationship with him.

But that was a problem to worry about for later. For now, it was enough that Mom didn't seem suspicious of me and Iason. Either she was a better actress than I thought, or she really hadn't figured out there was something going on between us.

Chapter Ten

IASON

IT ASTONISHED me how easily the conversation flowed with the Donati family. It felt like it was my fiftieth visit instead of my first. I couldn't get over how much I felt like I was at home—in a place where I belonged. Not once in all my life had I ever experienced such loving kindness in my own parents' house. They were far too selfish to foster a family dynamic. I would never understand why they bothered to have a kid when they were so self-centered.

As I watched everyone joking with each other, it was like watching a movie about a perfect family. Neil sat on the other end of the couch, his arm draped around his wife's shoulder, who was nestled against his side. Although they were about the same age as my parents, they looked at each other like newlyweds madly in love with each other. It was the kind of romance I never dreamed I could have.

How could I be okay with my fractured, fucked-up family when I had finally experienced being a part of something so real and beautiful? What did I have to do to have that kind of life with Orion?

"Well, now that we've settled that, how about dessert?" Neil offered.

Everyone got up to make their way to the kitchen. It surprised me when a hand tugged on my wrist to stop me. Estelle gestured with her head for me to follow her. She took me into her office down the hall. Her enormous L-shaped mahogany desk was covered in piles of papers haphazardly strewn everywhere. The books on the shelves weren't alphabetized but were stuck anywhere there was space for them. Some were stacked horizontally, some sideways, and others had fallen over. There were three telescopes of different sizes throughout the room, with strings of winking star lights around the ceiling. The always organized Orion must have hated the chaos, but I loved how it was the embodiment of Estelle.

"I'm sorry. I shouldn't have made the joke about your mother's cooking earlier." She looked concerned that she had offended me.

It took a moment for me to remember what she was referring to. "You have nothing to apologize for—especially because it's a fact. My mother can't cook worth a damn, and my father isn't any better. If we weren't eating out at a restaurant, we were doing takeout or microwaved dinners."

"It was wrong of me to make light of something when you were being so genuine."

"Please don't feel bad." I hated the thought that she had been regretting her comment the entire time. "Tonight has been wonderful. I'm in complete awe of your family. I can't tell you what it means for all of you to make me feel so included."

The smile returned to her face. "I'm glad you're a part of our family now, Anise."

It was a strange thing to say. "I don't understand. You've only just met me, so why?"

"Because you're in love with my son."

It seemed Orion had been right about her sixth sense. Her statement knocked the air out of me. For his sake, I knew I should deny it, but I couldn't lie to her. "That's—how did you…?"

She looked at me with so much understanding that I choked up a little. "I've known since the minute you got on the phone with him. It was all over your face how much you love him. Not to mention the dead giveaway when you told him your room number. That's not exactly part of the street address."

"I…"

She smiled at me with a knowing look. "I see how he looks at you when he thinks nobody notices. And I *might* have seen you two kissing before coming in here tonight. Your interest obviously isn't one-sided."

The thought that he could feel the same way as

me was overwhelming. I didn't know what to say as I struggled to stay in control of my emotions.

She reached out and took hold of my hand, giving it a squeeze. "All I ask is that you be good to him and please be patient with him. He can struggle with love sometimes, bless his heart. He'll get there, but he might need a little time to understand everything. But something tells me you won't have to wait long."

I debated the wisdom of confessing the truth to Estelle. But if anyone would believe me, it would be her. "I have a friend who joked he wished on the Northern Lights I would meet my soul mate at my live show. I was skeptical, so I told him I'd only believe the cosmic universe if the man showed up with a name worthy of the stars he wished on. With Orion's name being a constellation, he was made out of wishes on stars."

She didn't bat an eye at something that sounded so ridiculous. "See? It was clearly meant to be. The mystical abilities of the *aurora borealis* are no joke." It was a surprising thing to say for someone who believed in science.

"It doesn't make sense, but I already love him."

Her smile was brilliant. "I know you do, sweetheart. Give him a little time to catch up with you. He'll get there."

"Thank you." Her quiet confidence in the situation touched me.

"Besides, don't worry so much about the fact that you've only just met. That doesn't matter."

"It's literally been three days," I told her with a wry grin.

She laughed. "The first time I saw Neil, he was sitting by himself reading in the library. I still remember how the sunlight filtered through the window, as the dust motes floated in the air. Even though I hadn't talked to him yet, I *knew* that he was it for me. I wanted him to smile at me the way he did at his book. So, I marched over there and informed him he was taking me to dinner that night."

It was such an Estelle thing to do that it was hard not to laugh. "What did he do?"

"He laughed and told me I was bonkers," she replied with a cheeky grin. "I knew right then and there that he was the man I was going to love for the rest of my life. I said he was stuck with me, so he better get used to it."

"What happened?"

Her expression softened into a sweet smile. "He took me to dinner, even though he spent the whole time questioning if he had lost his mind agreeing to go out with me. He needed some time to figure out we were supposed to be together, so I'm sorry Cherry takes after him there instead of me. But it was worth waiting for him. I haven't regretted or doubted it for a single second."

"Thank you for telling me." I felt better after speaking with her.

She gave me a fierce hug. I dwarfed her by over a foot and a half, but it amazed me how she was tiny but so strong. I couldn't help but wonder what it must have been like to grow up with someone like her as an ally who had nothing but endless love to offer. Just like with Orion, although I had only known Estelle for such a short time, I already adored her.

Orion interrupted with an annoyed huff. He hissed under his breath, "Mom, what the hell are you doing?"

Stepping back, she looked up at me in amusement. "I love how he blames me first." Her expression turned impish as she faced her son. "Jealous much?"

That telltale blush crept over him again. It surprised me he didn't deny it. "I had to lie to Lyra that you were in the bathroom and he was on the phone with his manager." He was careful to keep his voice quiet enough not to be heard in the kitchen. "She would lose her shit if she saw you hugging him."

"You're not doing much better, dear." She walked over to him, ignoring his protests. "There's no need for you to get your panties in a twist over me hugging Anise when he's part of the family now, Cherry." With those words, she walked away, winking at me over her shoulder as she left.

He threw his arms around me in a tight hug. Although the door to Estelle's office was still open, I embraced him closer. A sense of relief and rightness flooded through me.

"Not being able to touch you is torture now." He huffed in annoyance. "I don't understand."

"I can't tell you how many times I've almost pulled you into my lap tonight."

"Damn it, I can't believe I was jealous of my *mom* hugging you." He groaned, causing me to chuckle. "What's wrong with me?"

I tilted his chin up to meet his gaze. "Maybe you're actually falling for me?"

His reaction delighted me. "Probably."

"If I kiss you, we'll get caught in a very compromising position."

Orion pulled away from me with a pout. "Only because I have to, not because I want to."

"I understand." I blew him a kiss, since that was the best I could offer under the circumstances.

His smile was so beautiful that it took every ounce of control I had not to pull him back into my arms and kiss him senseless. Instead, I followed him out of the office and into the kitchen, where his family was prepping dessert.

Estelle had a knowing twinkle in her eyes as she innocently asked, "Is everything okay with your manager, Anise?"

"Yeah, I wanted to touch base with her to make arrangements for Lyra's and Orion's tickets to the show. I'm sorry that took so long."

"It's not a problem at all," Neil said as he started measuring out the liquor he needed.

"Thanks." I felt a little bad for lying, even though it had been worth it to talk with Estelle and have a stolen moment with Orion. "Mind if I try a cherry?"

Neil gestured at the box of them where they were still on the stems. "Help yourself."

I couldn't stop myself from being mischievous. Making sure I held Orion's gaze, I brought the cherry up to my lips. I let it rest there before sensuously sucking on it, drawing it into my mouth with my tongue, then popping it off the stem. I made an appreciative sound as I chewed. "Wow, I *love* cherries. I can't get enough of them."

Orion blushed so hard that even the tips of his ears were red. However, there was a determined glint in his eye as he held out his hand. "Let me take care of that for you."

I gave it to him without question. When he put it in his mouth, I knew I was in trouble. He teased me by sticking out his tongue, revealing a perfectly tied cherry stem. Thinking about that talented tongue on my dick made me harden, despite being in the company of so many people. "Neat party trick."

He was the picture of perfect innocence, save for the challenging gleam in his eyes. "I thought you might like that."

His sudden boldness aroused me further. I wanted to feel his tongue dancing against mine and moving against my cock. Those thoughts would cause my semi to turn into a full-blown hard-on if I didn't stop, so I mentally checked myself.

Estelle gave me a sassy wink. "You can thank me for teaching him that little trick."

God bless that wonderful woman. She really was my new favorite person. I wanted to buy her all the stars the world offered to give them to her as a thank-you. I gave her a grateful look, which she clearly understood based on how her grin widened.

Lyra was oblivious to what was happening between me and Orion. "I suck at doing that. I can never get it to knot."

"Maybe when you're older." Estelle's joke caused everyone to laugh as her daughter pouted.

After finishing preparations, Neil prepared the cherries in the liquor on the stove. I had never had the dessert before, so it fascinated me to watch him make it, especially when he caught the fire on the side of the pan, resulting in a roaring flame.

"If my dad ever tried that, he'd burn down the entire house," I said with a laugh.

"Don't let his practiced ease fool you. He almost did that once." Estelle snickered at the memory.

Neil defended himself with the air of a weary man who had clearly had the same discussion on more than one occasion. "Hey, it's not my fault that Paulette went to the bathroom. She wouldn't let us light it until she came back, and by that point, they had absorbed so much of the liquor that the flame almost caught the cabinet on fire. That's on her."

Everyone laughed as he finished cooking the cherries and poured them and the sauce over vanilla ice cream in small glass bowls. We took our desserts over to the kitchen table.

"Why is everything you make delicious?" I asked, loving the rich flavor. "This is incredible!"

"He can also do it with bananas if you like that kind of thing." Estelle's perverse grin she couldn't quite smother made me laugh.

"I'd *definitely* be interested in that."

Neil gave me a jovial smile. "Consider it incentive to come back— provided we haven't scared you away yet."

"There's no chance of scaring me off." I caught Orion's eyes, holding his gaze. His radiant smile once again filled my heart with affection for him. I wanted to hold on to that moment forever. Hopefully, he would let me.

Chapter Eleven

ORION

AFTER WE LEFT MY PARENTS' house, Iason remained quiet as I drove to his hotel. He was lost in thought as he looked out the window at the scenery passing by. Having him over had been a lot of fun, but there had been a few times throughout the night where he had almost seemed a little sad. Those moments were brief flashes that were gone as soon as I noticed them. I also burned with curiosity about what he had talked about with Mom when she snuck off with him before dessert. The look she had given him when she hugged him goodbye as we were leaving felt like something was being said between them, but I didn't understand what.

"I hope you had a good time tonight," I said.

"It was *amazing*. I can't put into words what this evening has meant to me."

"Meant to you?"

Instead of answering, his tone turned wistful. "You have such a beautiful family, Cherry. You're so lucky." He had that haunted expression again.

I wanted to make that pain go away. "I am lucky. Both of my parents mean well, even if they go too far with their teasing sometimes."

"They're so in love with each other." His voice was filled with awe. "I've never seen two people more harmoniously balanced than your parents. It's the stuff movies are made of."

"They really are that way all the time. Sure, they've had their disagreements over the years, but I've never once heard them raise their voices at each other. My best friend Vince's parents went through an awful divorce at one point, so the amount of yelling in their house was scary. The weird part was that he didn't seem to notice."

"When that's all you hear, that's all you know." The heavy sadness of his words broke my heart.

I hesitated before I dared to ask a follow-up question. "I take it you speak from experience?"

"Yeah." His laughter was bitter. "When the yelling stopped, that's when it was bad."

"How was that worse?"

"At least when they were yelling, it showed they still gave a damn," Iason said. "When the fire went out of the fight, that's when things would go from bad to worse. But like clockwork, the shouting would return as some new thing set them off. It was always something."

There was so much pain in his words. I wanted to hug him, but I couldn't do it while I was still driving. I realized I didn't know a lot about his personal life. Although my sister had memorized every detail about him, she never mentioned anything about his parents or being romantically linked to anyone. Now, I knew why.

"That must have been so rough." I couldn't imagine living that way.

He shrugged. "I laid low and stayed out of it as best I could. I used to wonder why they didn't get divorced, but I realized they both fed off the drama of fighting with each other. They enjoyed being able to have the power to make the other miserable."

I wasn't sure how to respond to that, so I switched topics. "What did you talk to Mom about?"

"She was worried she offended me earlier in the evening."

"Offended you?" I repeated in confusion. "How?"

"That's what I asked her," he said. "She thought she went too far when she joked about my mom's shitty cooking, even though she was stating a fact. I told her she didn't need to worry herself and thanked her for tonight. I told her how much it meant to me to be included."

"It felt like you had always been a part of our family."

"I've never felt that sense of being home anywhere." His soft voice tugged at my heartstrings. "That kind of familial love was completely new to me. It was beautiful."

As we waited at a stoplight, I looked over at Iason as I whispered his name. He reached over and caressed my cheek with such fondness that it took my breath away.

"Thank you for showing me what it's like to be part of a real family." He brushed his thumb against my cheekbone. "Feeling like I belonged with you means more to me than I can express."

I wanted to lose myself in the depths of his emotional blue eyes that looked glassy with unshed tears. But the light changed, giving me no choice but to continue driving.

The heaviness of the moment made me try to lighten the mood. "Mom's already adopted you."

"Nothing would make me happier. She looked at me with more motherly affection tonight than my own mom. It was amazing." It was one of the sweetest and saddest things I had ever heard. "Your mom is an incredible woman. I hope you're not jealous that she's officially my new favorite person."

The comment made me laugh. "I feel like I should be offended."

"How her tiny body can house that much love for people is amazing." He shook his head. "I admire her headstrong determination to live life according to her rules. It gives me hope."

"Hope?" I almost missed my turn in my distraction.

He sounded amused. "She told me about how she met your dad."

"When you were in her office?"

"Yeah."

The story of how my parents met was legendary. It also put my meeting with Iason in a whole new light. When combined with his comment about hope, a sudden realization hit me that spiked my anxiety. "She knows, doesn't she?"

"About?" He feigned innocence, but it didn't fool me.

"About whatever this is between us." I tightened my grip on the steering wheel. "She figured out there's something going on, didn't she?"

Iason caressed my hair to comfort me. "I love how you say 'us.'"

"Oh, god. Of course, she knows." I groaned. "How does she *always* figure out this kind of thing?"

"Motherly intuition?"

"What did she say?" I demanded. "What were her exact words?"

He didn't give me the answer I wanted. "Let's leave it at she implied that she's aware and fine with the fact that there's something between us."

"Please tell me so I don't drive myself crazy."

He hesitated. "Perhaps that's a conversation best had when you're not driving."

"We're two minutes from the hotel," I argued. "Tell me."

"I'll tell you when we get there. You have my word."

It annoyed me he was right. I huffed in annoyance. "Fine."

As soon as we were in the room, I resumed my questioning. "Will you please put me out of my misery now?"

He led me over to sit on the edge of the bed. "I asked her why she was so insistent on me being a part of your family. She said it was because I was in love with you."

"I'm sorry, she said *what?*" My jaw dropped at the information. No wonder he hadn't wanted to tell me while I was driving. I probably would have wrecked the damn car.

"She knew the minute I got on the phone with you at the restaurant, not to mention that giving you my room number was a dead giveaway." He seemed a little sheepish over the last part. "She saw how you looked at me when you thought no one else was looking."

It was too much information to absorb at once. I held my hand against my forehead to steady myself. "What did you say?"

"The truth." His answer caused my pulse to

skyrocket. "She asked me to be patient with you because you take after your father with matters of romance, bless your heart."

Although the information made me reel, the way Iason affected a Southern accent for the last part caused me to laugh before I groaned. "Ugh, that's the ultimate Southern insult."

He reached out, once again caressing my cheek. Although his touch was gentle, it sent electric thrills running through me when combined with the open look of affection in his ocean-blue eyes. "I promised her I would be good to you and that I would wait as long as it takes."

His words overwhelmed me with what he was implying. I realized at no point had he denied being in love with me. That couldn't be true, right? Could he *actually* be in love with me? But that was absurd, wasn't it? We didn't even know each other!

He withdrew his hand. "She told me she didn't think I'd have to wait long."

Several fractured sounds came out of me, but none of them formed complete sentences. Had Mom seriously implied that I was close to falling in love with Iason? When she was usually right, it made my heart race with all kinds of questions.

As he hesitated for another moment, his voice was barely louder than a whisper. "I told her I was aware it didn't make sense when we hadn't known each other long, but I already love you somehow."

The world screeched to a halt. Iason Leyland—the internationally famous Iason Leyland—had openly admitted that *he was in love with me*. My head spun from the overwhelming information. How was it possible for *him* to love *me* already—or at all? It had to be a joke. There was no way that somebody like him, who had legions of adoring fans all over the world, could love someone as ordinary as me, right?

He pulled me from my internal flailing when his lips turned up in a slight smile. "She assured me you would love me, too. You just needed a little more time."

My jaw dropped again at his words. I didn't know which was more outrageous: that she would say such an outlandish thing or that there was more truth in her claim than I was comfortable with.

When I had given myself over to his passions earlier in the afternoon, I had experienced a connection with him and a hint of that love I was too scared to believe could be true. Was that even something I wanted? I wasn't sure, but then I remembered how perfectly he had fit into my family.

"Then she told me how she met your father. As I said, it gave me hope. I thanked her for telling me. That's when you saw us hugging."

The last three days with him may have been confusing, but they had also been an amazing gift. It was hard to be afraid when I remembered how Iason had spent the afternoon worshipping me with tender caresses and kisses. It didn't scare me now. I wanted it —and more.

I reached out and took his face in my hands, holding his gaze as I searched it for answers. He didn't hide his vulnerability or his fear that I would reject him. I realized I was the one who was in control of the situation, since I was the person who had the power to break his heart.

He wasn't hiding from me, nor was he playing games with me. All he wanted to do was love me, although he wasn't sure if it was allowed. It was up to me to decide whether to accept or refuse his feelings.

For once in my life, I trusted my emotions instead of overanalyzing myself into indecision. I leaned forward and pressed my lips to his, pouring all of my emotions into the kiss. He pulled my body against his in a crushing hug, allowing me to feel him trembling. I did my best to express myself in a way I couldn't do with words yet.

It became more demanding, fueled by our need for each other that built to a fevered pitch. Our clothes came off as we hurried to be bare. His naked body pressed against mine was divine. I softly moaned into his insistent kiss. I burned with my need for him, too far gone to care if I looked desperate.

He checked in with me. "What do you want?"

I hesitated for a moment. Selfishly putting myself out there was something I wasn't used to doing.

He caressed my hips with his thumbs to encourage

me. "Tell me what you want, Cherry. I'll deny you nothing."

I took a steadying breath, needing to collect myself. The afternoon had been him giving me pleasure, so I hadn't had the chance to touch him very much. Never having been with a guy before, I was curious. I worried it might seem weird to ask, although he had been understanding about letting me go at my own pace.

He remained patient with me as I tried to find my courage. "I want to explore you. If that's okay."

His smile lit up his beautiful face, taking my breath away. "I'd enjoy that." He repositioned himself onto his back, holding his arms out to me.

I moved over him as I kissed him with gentle tenderness. It was a stark contrast to our earlier frenzied need to claim each other. Some of my nervousness returned as I moved down his neck. His breathy sigh encouraged me to keep going.

My tongue dipped into the hollow of his collarbone. Why was that arousing? I didn't resist the urge to place a lingering kiss on the small mole there. Why did that turn me on so much?

Deciding it wasn't the time to figure it out, I pushed my questions aside. I mapped out the expanse of Iason's smooth chest with my fingers, admiring his pecs, before building up the nerve to kiss him there. When I was brave enough, I ran my tongue over his nipple. If his reaction was any indication, he liked it.

It gave me the courage to suck on the raised peak, then lightly tug on it.

"So good." He ran his fingers through my hair in a soft caress.

The verbal confirmation helped reassure me, so I repeated the action on his other one before kissing down his pronounced abs. He was cut like a beautiful Grecian statue of a powerful god, whereas I was all softness. It made me self-conscious, wondering how someone who was so muscular could ever find my scrawniness attractive. I sat back as I traced the outline of his ab muscles with my fingertips. God, his body was spectacular. How was he real?

"What's wrong?" Iason asked.

"Nothing." I continued running my fingers along the ridges of his sculpted stomach.

"You're frowning. That's generally not the reaction I get when someone sees my body."

The corner of my mouth turned up in a smile, but it didn't change the fact I felt inadequate in comparison. I bit my lower lip, worrying it with my teeth. "How am I enough?"

"What do you mean?"

"You look like an angel carved you out of marble, and I'm this." I gestured at myself as an example.

"Orion, look at me." He waited until I made eye contact before continuing. "You don't need to be a gym rat to keep me interested. You're perfect just the way you are."

It was too hard for me to believe. "Yeah, but——"

"No, no buts. Do you think I've been faking how much pleasure I get from being with you?"

"Well, no." I realized how silly it sounded when he put it that way.

"This is because of you." He wrapped his hand around his erection and stroked it for emphasis.

The sight of him touching himself short-circuited something in my brain. I could only stare as he worked his hard length.

"This is because being with you gives me so much pleasure. I can't wait to be inside you again." He rubbed his thumb over the head of his cock, spreading the precum that had gathered.

Between the show he was putting on and the words he was saying, his very convincing argument overwhelmed me. "But what did I do to deserve this?"

"You're you. How do I convince you that you're everything I want?"

"I don't know. But can you blame me for having a hard time understanding that my normally boring life is now an amazing fairy tale with an impossibly perfect Prince Charming?"

His smile turned teasing. "I'm really looking forward to our happy ever after."

The comment took away some of the worries that had caused my arousal to wane. "Me, too." I ran my hands along the pronounced V of his hips before I used my fingers to follow the path of his happy trail.

The soft hair under my fingers made my cock twitch with interest. How had I gone so many years without knowing that turned me on?

I took a deep breath as I continued my explorations down to his neatly trimmed pubes. His cock was hot and heavy in my hand. I traced the line of his underside vein, moving up to where more precum had beaded at the tip. I smeared it with my thumb, stunned by how much it made me want to feel him inside me again. How did I go from a lifetime of being straight to wanting to get fucked by a guy?

"What are you thinking?" Iason prompted me, keeping his voice gentle.

"I'm wondering how the hell I've gone all my life not knowing I want this." I stroked his erection as I continued mulling over the issue. "What am I supposed to do about how much I ache to feel this inside me again?"

"I'm more than happy to help make that happen."

"Not yet." I wasn't done with my explorations. Seeing him up close made me want him more than I had wanted anything in my entire life. All my fears were quiet in the face of how much I longed for him.

With shy fingers, I trailed down his perineum to run over his entrance. I wondered if he would ever be willing to let me take him. As curious as I was, I needed him inside of me more.

"Lube is on the nightstand if you want to keep going." He gestured to it just beyond his reach.

A hint of a blush came to my cheeks. "Please tell me you didn't leave that there for housekeeping to see."

He laughed at my reaction. "I'm sure they've seen it all. A bottle of lube is nothing." My expression must have looked more scandalized than I realized because he grinned at me. "It's not like I left out a monster-size dildo, a whip, and some chains for them to find."

The thought of it made me chuckle, despite being embarrassed by it. I grabbed the lube, but I handed it to him instead of using it.

His blue eyes lit up with excitement. "Does this mean it's my turn now?"

"Yes." I rolled onto my back to allow him access to my body. "Not that I don't want to with you, but—"

"I'll take you any way I can get you." He positioned himself over me, allowing him to kiss me senseless. His erection brushing against mine drove me to rock against it. He wrapped his hand around both of our cocks and stroked them together. I keened as I surrendered to his masterful touch.

All too soon, he stopped so he could shift positions. I mourned the loss, but he gave me something new to focus on when he slid a lubed finger inside of me. He worked me while kissing me all over, once again worshipping my hips.

"What is it with you and hip bones?" And why did

I now find it arousing when he lavished them with attention?

I shivered at his puff of amusement on my skin when he laughed. "Fuck if I know, but they drive me wild." He ran his tongue along my right hip bone, then sucked on it. "Especially yours."

As Iason continued covering me everywhere in kisses, he added another finger to help get me ready for what was coming next. It still felt odd, but I couldn't focus on anything other than feeling good.

"Every inch of you is perfect, Cherry." He said it with so much awe and admiration that I trusted without a doubt that he meant it. I may not have understood how someone who looked like him could feel that way about me, but I challenged myself to trust him.

By the time he had worked a third finger into me, I was more than ready to move on. Just when I was about to plead for respite, he withdrew his fingers. As he applied a condom, my sense of anticipation mounted.

However, instead of penetrating me, he lay down beside me. "Get on top of me."

Desperate to have him inside me, I straddled myself over him without question. He helped guide me onto his cock. "Go easy. You don't need to rush, okay?"

With a nod of understanding, I let his erection spread me open. It was still awkward as I lowered myself, but I didn't want to go too fast and hurt myself. The process felt agonizingly slow as he filled me inch by inch until I had taken all of him inside me.

I adjusted my seating as I got used to the position. There was something intimidating about my body being on full display, with nothing hidden from his eyes. However, as his gaze roamed over me, all I saw was his naked desire for me. It was a heady feeling seeing Iason, of all people, looking up at me like I was his entire world.

When I tensed my muscles as a test, it earned me a sharp inhale as his hands gripped my hips. I kept my movements small as I adjusted to his thick cock moving inside me. As I built up a rhythm, I gained more confidence on my downward bounce. When he thrust up with more strength, I couldn't hold in the soft cry that escaped from me at the red-hot pleasure it sent streaking through me.

After that, there was no holding back. I braced my hands on his firm abs, getting turned on from how his muscles tensed under my fingertips. It gave me the leverage I needed to steady myself as I started dropping down more forcefully on each pump of his hips. I tossed my head back, my eyes sliding shut for a moment as I rode him hard.

Every time he growled my name, it felt like a physical caress. When he grabbed my ass to help me take him in deeper, I thought I might lose it. I loved the sound of our bodies connecting. Aggressive and primal, I took what I wanted from Iason's body, which he willingly gave me.

My pace grew sporadic as I neared my end. Iason reaching out to stroke my cock had me almost shouting his name. Everything became a buzzing white heat in my mind as I raced to my climax. I came with a loud cry, shaking with the effort. The sight of his beautiful body covered in my cum appealed to the animalistic part of my brain. It purred that it made him *mine*.

I faltered, almost disoriented from how intense my orgasm had been. In the blink of an eye, he had me flat on my back. He kissed me like I was the only thing giving him life. The fevered need calmed into a gentle passion before he pushed into me again.

Everything was hypersensitive from my release. I expected him to resume the harder pace from before, but he rolled his hips against me, sending me even higher despite being incapable of physical arousal yet. He touched me everywhere, worshipping me as he made love to me. He whispered his affection in between kisses and caresses.

I had never felt so treasured and loved in my entire life. Without words, he told me he cherished me as we moved as one. I never knew until that moment that it was possible to be so close to someone. As I lost myself in his beautiful eyes, it felt like I had known him forever instead of a few days. I had bared my soul before him, with all of my secrets on full display. He accepted everything about me without hesitation.

When he came, moaning my name as if it was the most sacred word ever spoken, I heard the echo inside of me whispering, *His*.

The connection between us was almost a tangible thing. He saw all that I was, and he still loved me, anyway. The enormity of the experience brought tears to my eyes. It was the most pure and beautiful moment of my life, something I never dreamed could be possible.

"I love you," he whispered against my lips in between soft kisses.

All of my doubts, all of my fears, all of my concerns paled in the face of his open declaration of feelings. It freed me to say the words I understood the true meaning of because of him. "I love you, too, Anise."

Chapter Twelve

IASON

I WOKE up curled around Orion. There wasn't anywhere else in the world I'd rather be. I wanted every morning to start with me holding him in my arms. Instead of getting up, I enjoyed the closeness of having him near me.

When I placed a lingering kiss on his shoulder, he sighed in his sleep as he pressed against me. It made my dick harden with interest. I rocked it against his ass to encourage him to wake up.

While his body moved against mine, his breathing stayed steady as he slept. I reached around to stroke his cock to get his attention. It rose to the occasion, but he remained deep in dreams. *Seriously?*

Torn between not wanting to take advantage of him while he slept and needing relief, I took advantage of the king-size bed to ready myself. I moved away from him, which earned me the cutest little whimper at the loss of my heat against his body.

I worked myself open with lubed fingers with a patience I didn't possess. It made me eager to move on to the fun part, provided I could get Orion to wake up for it. I couldn't believe he was sleeping through what I was doing.

Once I was ready, I rolled him onto his back and straddled over him. I took a moment to enjoy the sight of him beneath me, looking like a sweet angel. He was beautiful, inside and out. I didn't understand why he had so many self-confidence issues when everything about him was wonderful. I'd do my best to build him up.

When a kiss failed to stir him, I attempted to entice him into waking up by feathering teasing touches all over his body. Other than shifting, there was no reaction. What would it take to wake him up? A bomb going off?

Stroking his erection earned me a breathy sigh as he stirred, but he was out like a light. Maybe trying his sensitive ears would be the thing to inspire him to join the land of the living?

I tilted his head to the side, allowing me to capture his earlobe in my mouth. I sucked on it, which drew a soft moan from him as his body arched against mine. Finally, some progress.

Not satisfied with that, I tugged on his ear with my

teeth. It caused him to startle awake with a confused noise that was laced with sexual desire.

"You'll want to wake up for this part, Cherry."

"Huh?" He looked adorably dazed.

I rolled a condom onto him, then stroked it with lube to get it ready for me. Moving into position, I slid his cock against the crack of my ass. "Trust me, you don't want to miss this."

His hands glided up my thighs as he tried to make sense of what was happening. "What?"

Rather than explaining with words, I guided his stiff erection into me with a relieved sigh.

His grip on my thigh tightened. "Anise, what?"

Having him filling me was incredible. "I want you so much, Cherry."

"Yeah, but—" Orion interrupted himself with a groan when I clenched my muscles around his hard length inside me.

"Do you have an objection?" I stilled my movements, not wanting to continue if he had a complaint.

He shook his head. "No, but—"

"But what?"

A cute blush graced his cheeks. "I didn't think that you would…"

"Bottom?" My guess earned me a shy nod. "I love everything. The fun is only getting started."

He seemed bewildered. "Okay."

Figuring a demonstration was more effective, I moved with purpose. His next sentence disappeared into a swear as I built up a satisfying rhythm. I reveled in the magic of having him inside me.

"Holy shit, you're so *tight*." He groaned with pleasure as he thrust up on my downward bounce.

"Feels good, doesn't it?" I once again contracted around him, making him gasp.

"Fuck *yes!*" He stared up at me with awe.

He was so damn precious that my heart almost couldn't handle it. Words became scarce after that. I picked up speed as I bounced down, crying out when he thrust up to meet me. It sent my lust spiraling out of control as I chased the sensations. I tossed my head back as I rode him hard.

It surprised me how much noisier he was compared to yesterday. His moans and gasps drove me wild as he called out my name. I enjoyed having his hands roaming all over as he tried to touch me everywhere he could reach.

It pushed me to my limits, so I took myself in hand to jerk off to the beautiful sight of Orion, lost in his intense pleasure. I grinned when it caused him to grip my ass hard. "Oh, fuck! Ias!"

"Come for me, Cherry."

He arched under me as he came, almost shouting my name as he emptied into the condom. Having him climax inside me was enough to trigger my own orgasm with a cry. Seeing my cum splattered on his stomach felt like I was marking him as mine, a thought that pleased me in a way I didn't have the wherewithal to process.

We panted from the effort, still lost in the aftershocks of satisfaction. I moved first, pulling off him so I could bend down and kiss him. "Good morning, Cherry."

His unrestrained laughter delighted me, as did the unguarded look of happiness on his face. "I'd say it's a good morning. *Wow*."

"You certainly made me work for it. You sleep like the dead."

He grinned sheepishly. "Sorry, I'm a pretty deep sleeper."

"That's a hell of an understatement." I snorted in amusement. "Thankfully, I managed to get you up."

We shared a laugh at the innuendo. I loved this glimpse of the unrestrained side of Orion, who wasn't bogged down by his insecurities yet.

"You have my permission to start every morning that way." He reached up to caress my cheek. "That was incredible."

"Yeah, it was." I nuzzled into his palm before kissing it.

A worried look darkened his face. "Did I hurt you?"

I reached down and smoothed away the furrowed wrinkle of his brow. "No, you're covered in proof of how much I loved having you inside me." I took the condom off him to toss into the nearby trash can. "You clearly enjoyed yourself."

The reminder made him blush. "Yeah, but I don't know what I'm doing."

"I wouldn't say that. You've had sex before."

"Not with a man." His blush deepened. "I was just reacting and—"

"And it was perfect."

His embarrassment was precious. "You're always so dominating, so I never thought that you'd be okay with doing that."

I smiled down at him. "I'm a hedonist who enjoys pleasure in all its forms with you."

"Really?"

"Absolutely." I kissed him with a little more heat this time to convince him. "Come on, let's get you clean."

After getting out of bed first, I held my hand out to Orion. He accepted my help, interlacing our fingers as we headed into the bathroom.

I let go to start the shower, but I kept an eye on him as he studied his reflection in the mirror. He reached down and touched the mess on his stomach with a thoughtful expression.

"What's wrong?" I hoped he wasn't regretting what we had done.

He once again touched the cum on his skin. "I feel like I'm supposed to be grossed out by this, but I'm not."

"That's a good thing."

"But why am I so okay with it? Why do I want to taste it?"

His second question shocked and excited me. "Do it."

"But that's weird." He wrinkled his nose.

"No, it's fucking hot." I reached out and gathered some on my finger as I held it up to him to try. "It's no different from when I swallowed yesterday after blowing you."

He hesitated long enough that I thought he would refuse to do it. However, he moved closer and took my finger into his mouth. He ran his tongue over the tip to lick the cum off, then sucked on it in a way that made my dick want to perk up again with interest. "I don't hate it? At least, I don't think I do?"

"Fuck, you're too precious." I captured his lips in a passionate kiss as I backed him against the sink counter.

He responded for a moment but jerked back once he realized what he had done. "But I just—your cum."

"It didn't stop you yesterday."

"Yesterday?" He sounded confused until realization dawned on him. "Shit, I was so caught up in how incredible everything was. I didn't think about that."

"Then don't overthink it now." I pulled him closer for another kiss.

He moved away from me, looking at me with stunned disbelief. "Wait, did that make you hard?"

My cock was desperately trying to rally after his erotic display. "You sucking my cum off my finger while imagining you doing that to my dick did that."

The blush returned to his cheeks. "I don't know if I can do that."

"You never have to do anything you don't want to do, Cherry. I'll never push you for more than you're comfortable giving."

"Did you forget the part where you relentlessly pursued me, even after I told you I was straight?" he asked in a humored tone.

Although he was joking, I needed him to understand where we stood. "I'm serious. I never want you to do something sexually with me you don't want to do. The last thing I want is for you to be uncomfortable or pressured into anything."

"I appreciate that." He looked away from me in embarrassment. "I'm afraid I'll be bad at it and humiliate myself. I mean, you're *so* great at it, and I've never been with a guy before."

"You don't need to put that kind of pressure on yourself," I told him in a gentle voice. "I'm not expecting you to be an instant expert. I just want you to feel good."

"Everything has felt amazing."

Unable to resist, I reached around to grope Orion's ass, earning a gasp as he pressed closer against me. I let my fingers dip into his crack to tease his tight hole I was dying to be inside of again. "Even this?"

"*Especially* that." A current of sexual frustration colored his voice. "Please get in the shower and stop teasing me."

There wasn't a chance I'd ever turn down the opportunity to be naked under water with Orion. As soon as we were inside and closed the door, I embraced him under the spray of water cascading from the waterfall showerhead in the ceiling. Our slick bodies moving against each other stoked my lust. It was like kissing in the rain, which I had never seen the appeal of until that moment.

I let my hands traverse the same path of the water sluicing down his body, pleased when he mimicked my touch. Although it was light and teasing, it made me desperate for more.

Unable to resist, I dropped to my knees in front of him, ready for another taste.

"You don't have to—" I shut him up by taking him in all the way. He threw out his hand to steady himself against the wall, banging his head against the tiles as he thrust into my wet heat. "Fucking hell, Anise!" His fingers carding through my hair heightened my enjoyment. Best of all, he once again forgot to smother his needy moans. Every noise he made drove my arousal to new heights as it echoed in the shower.

I swallowed while groping his ass with one hand. The other held his dick steady. When I could tell he was getting close, I dipped a finger inside of him and moaned around the length in my mouth.

It had the desired result of making him come. The sight of him overcome with bliss made me come without touching myself. I leaned back on my haunches to gaze up at him with a smug expression.

He sank to the floor, his breathing shaky as he stared at me with wide eyes. "I swear you just sucked my soul out of my cock."

His reaction made me chuckle. "I told you yesterday: it's worth getting on my knees and worshipping."

"What about you?"

I ran my fingers over my spent member with a grin. "Obviously, I enjoyed myself."

Realization dawned in his eyes. "You got off from blowing me?"

"What can I say? You make me feel like a teenager all over again. Seeing you blissed-out is enough to do it for me. Especially in here, where the acoustics make your moans echo so beautifully."

"Oh, shit! The neighbors!" He slapped his hand over his mouth with a wide-eyed expression.

I laughed at his reaction, amused by how long it took him to remember that we had people who could have been listening. "If they haven't banged on the walls yet to tell us to be quiet, I don't think we have to worry about it." Although I didn't want to move, my knees protested being on the hard floor. "Let's get out of here before we turn into prunes."

I got up to shut off the water as Orion also stood. When I started to leave, he took hold of my wrist to stop me. He hesitated before he leaned closer to brush his lips against mine. I let him build up the courage to taste himself in my mouth. He kissed me with such intense passion that I was breathless when he pulled back.

When he didn't say anything, I prompted him. "What?"

"I want you so much it scares me." His fear showed on his face.

"Don't be afraid. Take me. Make me yours."

Instead of the protest I was expecting, he surprised me with another soul-searing kiss. I melted into with a moan as I held on tight, never wanting to let go.

His stomach grumbled, causing me to laugh. "How does room service sound?"

"Like a great idea."

We returned to the bedroom to get dressed and place our order. As we waited, I realized I needed to tell him about my plans for the evening.

"While I would happily spend every second of my time here in Sunnyside with you, I'm supposed to have dinner with my best friend tonight. Duke's my old college roommate who owns the Hurly-burly Bar and Grille."

I saw a flash of Orion's cute pout before it disappeared as quickly as it had appeared. "That's okay. I actually was going to meet up with my friend, Vince."

"Will you come back here when you're finished?" I hoped like hell he would say yes.

"As long as you want me to."

"Every day and night," I told him with all sincerity. "Always."

His answering smile was one of the most beautiful things I had ever seen. How was it that every little thing about him made me fall for him more?

IT HAD TAKEN a monumental effort to tear myself away from Orion long enough to meet with Duke for dinner. He had been my best friend since we were roommates in college. I loved him like a brother. Although I didn't get to see him as much now that I lived in New York, he was still one of the most important people in my life. Whenever I came to Sunnyside, I would spend almost all of my time hanging out with him and his wonderful husband, Early.

Duke had always been a proud hit-it-and-quit-it kind of guy, but that changed when he had met Early. His transformation from an unrepentant playboy into a devoted husband had fascinated me. I never thought he would be the type to settle down with anyone, but after I met Early, it made sense. He was all things sweet and loved Duke with all of his heart. Becoming close friends with Early was yet another reason I was grateful to have Duke in my life. I had always envied their close relationship.

It was something I never imagined I would find for myself, but Orion had changed everything. I had never been so glad to be proven wrong. Although I was getting ahead of myself, I loved the idea of the four of us hanging out together. It would be even better if Duke's younger brother, Fitzy, could join us. Thinking about the fun we could have made returning to my tour and back to New York City even more unappealing. After being with Orion, I was ready to leave Manhattan for good. The move would be worth it to bring me closer to him.

The sight of Duke approaching my table pulled me from my thoughts. He was a tall and imposing man, with huge muscles and chiseled masculine edges. His slate-gray eyes and black hair, which was tousled as if he had just finished a good fuck, made him a striking figure. Dressed in tight black jeans and a leather jacket with belts hanging off it, he screamed sexy bad boy and had the dark baritone voice to match. It made it even more amusing to see him with Early, who was sunshine and rainbows personified. They were a strange couple, but that was what made them perfect for each other.

"Shirley Temple? Really?" Duke asked as he

approached and saw what I was drinking. "Since when?"

I couldn't keep the grin off my face. "Since I developed a taste for cherries."

He slid into the booth across from me, his enormous body making the space seem a lot smaller. Besides their delicious food, the high booth walls were one of the best things about *Bueno, Bonito, y Barato*. I wore glasses to disguise myself to be on the safe side, but I wasn't worried about getting recognized in the dimly lit place we had been hanging out at since our college days.

"There's a joke in there I'm not understanding." His flinty eyes assessed me for some kind of clue.

"Never mind. I'm being silly."

He continued studying me. "You look pleased with yourself."

"That's because I am."

"You finally wrote the song that's going to make you go quadruple platinum, huh? Good for you."

I laughed at his comment. "No, better than that."

"You've decided to move back to Sunnyside?"

It was something I had talked with him about several times over the past year, so his insightfulness didn't surprise me. "I now have a *very* convincing reason to."

"What does that mean?"

The server interrupted to take our order before leaving us alone once more.

"I have a boyfriend who lives here that I don't want to live a country apart from," I said.

It was almost unheard of to stun Duke into silence, but he looked gobsmacked at my news. "*You* have a *boyfriend*? You don't *do* boyfriends."

"Neither did you until you met Early. I've found my Early, Duke."

He ran his hand through his black hair with a shocked expression. "A *boyfriend*, Ias? *You?* Wow."

"Tell me about it. I'm still trying to wrap my head around the fact that I fell in love."

"You fell in love?" His jaw dropped at the revelation. "Not just a boyfriend, but *you fell in love?*"

"Head over heels."

He floundered at my news. "Like, *fell in love* fell in love? Not falling in lust with someone you want to fuck more than once?"

I couldn't blame him for being skeptical. The entire time I had known him, I had never once had a boyfriend. I preferred no-strings-attached hookups over getting entangled in a messy relationship like my parents' god-awful marriage. Sex had always been easier, but Orion had changed that for me. "I want him forever, Duke. He's it for me. He's the happy ever after I didn't know I wanted."

Duke leaned back in the booth with an amazed expression. "Holy shit. Who is this magical man who tamed you?"

"His name's Orion. He's an assistant curator here at the Sunnyside University Museum of Art."

"How did you meet?"

I kept it vague. "At one of my concerts."

"If he works for the university, shouldn't he have been at your show at my bar?"

"He was."

Duke gave me a disapproving frown. "And you didn't think to introduce us that night? What the hell, man?"

I hesitated before I confessed the truth. "We weren't dating at that point."

"You still could have introduced him to me."

"I couldn't, because that was the first time I had met him." I braced myself for his reaction.

"*What?*" His deep baritone voice boomed loud enough to draw some attention to our table. "Wait, is this the same guy you told me about that night? The cutie who 'was made out of wishes on stars' and ran away when you tried to make a move on him?"

"It is."

He became more dubious. "Are you telling me you met *your boyfriend* this past *Thursday?*"

"Yeah."

"Today is Sunday." He looked at me as if I had lost my mind.

I took a sip of my drink without saying anything.

"You met him four days ago." He said that as if I wasn't aware of how ridiculous the timeline was.

"Thursday, Friday, Saturday, Sunday. Four fucking days ago. *Four*."

"Yes."

"And you're in love with him?" Duke hissed at me.

I nodded. "I am."

"Have you lost your goddamn mind?" He forced himself to take a calming breath. "Are you being serious? You're not fucking with me as a joke?"

"Do you think this is something I would joke about? Come on, you know me better than that."

He massaged his temples with a deep breath. "So, let me get this straight. You met a man four days ago —who you're not only dating, but you've *fallen in love with*. Now, you're planning to move across the country to be with him because you're convinced Kieran Aiello wished him into existence on some stars. Do I have that right?"

"I know what it sounds like."

"It sounds like batshit insanity," he told me in a harsh tone.

Our server came over at that moment and brought our dinners, along with drink refills, before disappearing again.

Duke still looked overwhelmed by my news as we started to eat.

I tried to defend myself. "Look, I felt the same certainty with him that I did about committing to my music career. It was risky to quit my job to move across the country for a shot at one of the hardest industries to make a living in. But I also had unwavering conviction that it was the right decision. You thought I was nuts then, too, but look where that's gotten me."

He sighed. "This is different, though."

"If you met him, you'd understand."

"*You've* barely met him," Duke reminded me. "For fuck's sake, you haven't known him a full *week* yet!"

It was a fair point, but I refused to back down. "Are you forgetting that you went home with Early the first night you met him and knew by the morning that he was different? That you wanted more than one night with him?"

Duke scowled at the reminder. "I wasn't ready to marry him four days after I met him."

"You were married less than three months later. Most people would consider that an unusually accelerated timeline."

"My mom had just died." Duke's dad had never been in the picture, so he had always been extremely close to his mother. Losing her so suddenly had wrecked him for a long time. "I didn't know what the fuck I was doing."

"Do you think you made the wrong decision?"

He nudged his enchilada with his fork. I regretted invoking the memories of a time in his life that was still hard for him. However, I didn't know how else to make him understand what Orion meant to me.

"Losing Mom made me realize I couldn't live another day without Duchess," Duke said, using his pet name for his husband. "I'll never regret marrying him, but it would have been better under different circumstances."

"I know, and I'm sorry. I wasn't trying to—"

He sighed as he looked at me apologetically. "No, you're right, Ias. All of my other friends told me I had lost my mind for wanting to marry Duchess when I did. They outlined all the reasons it was a terrible idea, but I didn't listen to a single one of them. You were the only person who told me to do it because you understood what he meant to me."

"It was obvious the first time I met Early why you had fallen in love with him. You were meant to be together."

The corner of Duke's mouth turned up in a smile. "Yeah, that shit was written in the stars or something. I don't know how I got so lucky."

"That's how I feel about Cherry."

"Cherry?"

"He's *very* prone to blushing bright red like a cherry. Trust me, it's an appropriate nickname."

Duke chuckled at that. "Your Shirley Temple makes a hell of a lot more sense now." He took a deep breath before looking at me. "Well, if anyone can make love at first sight work, it would be you. There's nothing you can't make happen when you put your mind to it."

"Come meet him tomorrow. He has to work, so I'm meeting him at the Brewhaha Café for lunch at noon. He said that's his favorite place to go, so surely that counts for something."

Duke rubbed his chin. "If he's a regular, I bet Duchess knows him."

"Probably." Early was friendly with a lot of his customers.

"You better hope he's not one of Duchess's dicks."

"Trust me, there's no chance of that," I assured him. "I'd bet anything Cherry is one of his favorites."

Duke finally relented. "I've never heard Duchess mention an Orion before, but if he says this guy is great, I'll stop worrying. I don't want to see you hurt."

"Which I appreciate. You've always had my back, even when nobody else did. But I'm telling you, Cherry is the one. You'll see."

"I can't wait to see what kind of man stole your heart." Duke raised his glass in a silent toast. "He must be one hell of a guy."

I clinked my drink against his. "He's the best."

Duke's gaze softened as he looked at me. He realized in an awed voice, "Shit, you really are in love with him."

My smile said everything.

Chapter Thirteen

ORION

I CHECKED my phone notifications while I waited for Vince to return from the bathroom after dinner. To my delight, I had a text from Iason. I grinned at his picture of a Shirley Temple full of cherries.

"Wow, it seems you forgot to mention something important," he said as he sat down at the table across from me once more.

We had been best friends since I had moved in next door to him in second grade. He was a little taller than me, with a broad build that dwarfed me. His sandy-brown hair was short, but it was growing out at the top. He looked handsome in his flannel shirt and jeans. We had been through everything together, through all the good times and heartbreak.

I turned off my phone screen to return my attention to him. "What do you mean?"

"You seem to have a new romance."

He was too astute at picking up the little details. It was what made him such a stellar attorney. "What makes you say that?"

Vince looked amused by my question. "Because you're grinning like a teenage girl whose crush texted her." I couldn't help but laugh at his description. "Plus, I saw on your screen that her name is Anise."

He never missed a single detail. "You're right. I met someone special."

"Tell me everything!" He leaned forward with eager interest.

I wasn't worried that he would judge me for being with a man, but it was weird to say out loud. "We met at a concert."

"When you went to Iason's live the other night?"

I nodded but didn't add any details.

"Ugh, now I'm even more annoyed I had to miss out because of that stupid deposition I couldn't get out of." He scowled in annoyance since he was a big fan of Iason's. "What she's like?"

"Talented, kind, gorgeous, and somehow interested in me."

He shook his head as he gestured at me. "Who wouldn't be into you? You're cute!"

My stomach fluttered with nerves as I hesitated. "He definitely agrees with you."

His eyebrows shot up in surprise. "I'm sorry, but did you say *he* agrees with me?"

"I did."

"Anise is a *guy*?" Vince questioned in disbelief.

I nodded. "It's a nickname."

"No shit. You're dating a guy now?" There was no trace of judgment in his tone, only curiosity.

His question made me realize I had never talked with Iason about the official status of our relationship. Was he my boyfriend? Although we hadn't discussed it, I felt confident enough to confirm. "I am."

"I need details!"

It was hard to put into words. "When he looks at me, I get lost in him. He makes me feel things I never imagined were possible."

He heaved a dreamy sigh. "That's so romantic."

"It's confusing, but being with him, it's the first time since Nyla that I've been happy."

The news pleased him. "Good for you, Rion. You deserve it. You've been alone for too long after leaving her."

"Thanks."

He pressed for more details. "What's he like? He must be one hell of a guy to get you to switch teams."

I knew revealing Iason's identity would explain everything, but I was torn. On the one hand, I wanted to maintain his privacy. On the other hand, Vince was my best friend. He would never betray me by going to the media with a salacious story about Iason. "This has to stay between us. Consider this as sacred as attorney-client privileged information."

He seemed surprised by my request. "Why the need for secrecy?"

"Promise me you won't tell anyone, not even your family."

"I promise."

After a quick glance around, I lowered my voice to make my confession. "It's Iason."

"*What?*" His shock was almost comical. "You're joking, right? *Iason Leyland* is your new *boyfriend?*"

"I met him backstage because Lyra is a member of his street team. Things just sort of happened."

"How? You're straight, and he's never had a partner of any kind!"

It was embarrassing to confess the truth. "He was interested in me at first sight, but it took me some time to understand everything. It was a lot to process when I've never felt that way about another guy before."

"Are you okay with it?" His expression grew concerned. "I can't imagine how I would handle falling for a girl when I've always known I'm gay."

"Honestly, I'm baffled by my reaction. But when I'm with him, everything feels right somehow."

Vince took a sip of his drink as he studied me. "Are you guys doing the long-distance thing since he lives in Manhattan?"

It was something I was worried about, but we hadn't talked about it yet. "He seems serious about me, but we haven't had an official conversation about where this is going."

"Where do you want it to go?"

I shrugged with a sigh. "As much as I want to be with him, I'm not sure how that works."

Vince looked confused. "What do you mean?"

"Do I tell him I want to be his boyfriend?"

"Well, do you?"

My cheeks colored with embarrassment. "I want him, so I guess that means as a boyfriend? But we don't live on the same side of the country. How would that work?"

"You should talk to him about what you want."

"Something tells me we'll get distracted." I could easily imagine Iason's sexy attempts at distraction leading right to bed. It was entirely too tempting a thought, so I pushed it aside.

Vince was in awe. "You lucky bastard."

"It's so weird." What I was about to admit was embarrassing. "I don't understand how I've lived thirty years without knowing how great it feels to be with a guy."

"I mean, you had to have *some* inkling." Vince chuckled at my comment. "You've gone to gay clubs with me before. I've lost count of how many times you've been hit on by men there while they're grinding their erections against your ass as you dance together."

"Yeah, but it never aroused me." My face was on fire from talking about my experiences. "I never wanted what came next."

"You also weren't disgusted by it. Most straight guys aren't fine with having a hard-on pressed against them."

It was true, but I had never thought about it. "That was harmless dancing. It never made me curious or turned on. Whereas with Anise, I ache for more."

"Have you two…?"

Although he didn't finish his question, it was obvious what he was asking. My cheeks flushed a bright scarlet, saying everything I was too embarrassed to admit.

Vince grinned at my reaction. "Way to go, Rion. I'm proud of you." He sighed with a woeful expression. "Damn, I'm jealous. I'm out here striking out with basic guys, and you land a god on your first try."

"He pursued me! I wasn't trying to seduce him or anything. I don't even know how to do that."

"You've never understood your own appeal," Vince told me. "I blame Indra for filling your head with all those awful doubts."

It was true a lot of my insecurities stemmed from my ex-girlfriend's treatment of me over the years. "No one would look at me and assume I could be with somebody as flawless and famous as him. *I* certainly wouldn't."

"I'm glad he sees the real you." Vince smiled at me. "It makes me a bigger fan of his than I already am."

"You would think he'd have a colossal ego and be an asshole. But he's so down-to-earth. Not to mention really sweet."

Vince never missed a thing. "If he was a jerk, you wouldn't be interested in him."

"True." I'd never be able to date that kind of person. "He's nothing like I imagined, but so much more than I ever hoped to find."

He gave an impressed whistle. "Wow, you've got it for him *bad*, don't you?"

I hid my face in my hands with a groan. "Ugh, I know."

"Why is that a problem?"

"Because he's famous, he lives on the other side of the country, and I'm not going to survive this without getting my heart broken." I sighed with frustration at the reality of our situation. "We live in two different worlds, Vince."

"Is he worth fighting for?"

I didn't need to think about how to reply. "Yes."

"There's your answer. Fight for him, Rion. Stop worrying about all the things that could go wrong. Focus on what's right."

It helped to hear. "Am I stupid for thinking I might really love him? It's only been a few days, but why does it feel so right?"

"Don't be afraid of being happy. You deserve it more than anyone I know."

"Thanks." I was relieved after telling my best friend about my unexpected romantic situation. "By the way, how are things going with Jacob? I haven't heard you mention him in a while."

His grin turned wry. "That's because we broke up yesterday."

"Shit, I'm so sorry."

"I'm not," Vince replied with a laugh. "He was *awful* in bed. The absolute worst."

"But I thought you liked him?"

He shrugged. "I liked looking at him, but I drew the line at him asking me to 'butt dial' his ex, so he could hear us fucking. I'm not into that petty shit."

"Wait, he wanted you to do that?"

"He *begged* me." Vince sighed with a rueful expression. "So yeah, good riddance to him. At least now I know to ignore a call from him in the future, unless I want to laugh at the reminder of how terrible he was in bed."

Vince's reaction amused me, but I still hated he had gone through yet another breakup. "I'm sorry he turned out to be a jerk."

"Eh, it is what it is."

I hated hearing him be so defeated. "The right guy is out there for you."

"Until then, I'll enjoy living vicariously through you." Vince held his glass up in a toast. "Maybe I'll take up a hobby or something. I always wanted to learn how to play guitar, so perhaps that can be my new thing."

I picked up my drink to clink against his. "Cheers to that." We shared a laugh as we continued hanging out until I had to go back to the hotel with Iason.

Chapter Fourteen

IASON

AFTER RETURNING to the Luxurian Suites Hotel after my dinner with Duke, I saw Orion inside the elevator, holding the doors for me. I stood next to him as I hit the Door Close button. "Fancy meeting you here."

He smiled as he pushed the button for our floor. "Sorry I'm late. I stopped home to grab clothes."

It made me notice the black bag slung over his shoulder. Any excuse to keep him with me one more night was fine with me. I longed to lean down and kiss him, but the risk of the security video kept me from acting on my desires. It was disappointing to have to behave.

We exited the elevator and went to our hotel room. I grinned when he took out his suits to hang up in the closet so they wouldn't get wrinkled. He was always so fastidious, but I couldn't wait to see that suit crumpled on my floor tomorrow night after he got home from work. I also loved his initiative of bringing multiple outfits, implying he planned to stay with me for the rest of my time in Sunnyside.

I sat down on a chair near the window. "How was dinner with your friend?"

Once he finished, he took the seat opposite me. "It was fun! We haven't been able to meet up a lot recently because he's been doing a lot of overtime on a case that's about to go to trial. I'm glad we could finally catch up with each other."

"Did you meet in college?"

He shook his head. "No, I moved next door to him during second grade. We've been best friends ever since." He grew anxious. "I wasn't sure if it was okay that I told him about you. I realized I should have asked before I left for dinner. But he figured it out pretty fast."

"I don't mind. If he's your best friend, he has to be a good guy. Not to mention that being a lawyer, he understands the importance of attorney-client privilege."

"Vince would never tell anyone. He was obviously shocked, but he was thrilled for us. And maybe a tiny bit jealous since he's a huge fan of yours."

I loved hearing him use "us." It was such a simple thing, but it made me so happy. "It's nice to have friends that support you no matter what."

"How was your dinner?"

I ran my hand through my hair with a sigh. "It was great once Duke finished lecturing me."

"Lecturing you?"

"He's the protective type." It was a hell of an understatement. "Given my history, he was concerned."

"What do you mean?"

I crossed my leg over my knee. "I've never been the boyfriend type, so hearing me talking about how serious I am about you so quickly worried him. After I reminded him he fell hard and fast for his husband, he understood."

Color crept to his cheeks. "I wasn't sure if I was allowed to refer to you as my boyfriend or not."

"Do you want to call me that?"

He turned shy. "Obviously, I never thought I'd have one, but if it's okay with you, I'd like that."

I took advantage of the fact that our chairs were close together by grabbing Orion's hand and tugging him into my lap. "It's more than okay. Especially since that's how I referred to you when telling Duke."

His pleased smile was adorable. "You called me your boyfriend?"

"I did." I finally gave in to the urge to give him a tender kiss.

When we parted, he hid his face against my neck. "I never want to wake up from this dream."

"It's not a dream, Cherry. Against all the odds,

this is real. I don't care if it's madness to fall at first sight. I love you."

He pulled back, looking deep into my eyes with a trace of fear I hated seeing. "But what happens when you leave?"

"You'll come see me in San Francisco on Friday through Sunday. Afterward, I'll see you in LA the following week. I'm free after finishing the three weeks left on my tour."

"What am I supposed to do when you go home to Manhattan?" The pain in his voice hurt my heart.

"I won't let anything stop me from being with you, Cherry."

He frowned at me. "There's literally an entire country separating us once you're in New York."

"Temporarily."

His expression became puzzled. "What does that mean?"

"It means I'm talking with my manager soon about moving to Sunnyside."

He fought hard to keep the hope off his face. "Permanently?"

"It's something I've talked about before, but now that I know it'll bring me closer to you, nothing will stop me."

"Are you serious?" He looked like he wanted to believe me but was too afraid to.

"I can't do anything about finishing the rest of my tour, but I'll be damned if I'm going to live almost three thousand miles away from you when I can do something about it. I've been flirting with the idea for the past year. With my career where it is, I don't have to be in New York anymore to do what I need to do. I miss being near my friends out here. I love this town, and with you here, why would I keep living out there?"

He threw himself on me in a fierce hug. "Are you serious?"

"There's no reason to settle for long distance with you when it's not necessary."

Orion surprised me when he pulled back and showered me with appreciative kisses. I let him take what he wanted, even as my desire built up for the man who had changed my life for the better.

When he took off his sweater and threw it aside, the rare show of initiative pleased me. I encouraged it with teasing touches over his bare skin. He pulled off my shirt next, then slid to the floor. My cock stiffened at the sight of him on his knees between my legs.

As if reading my mind, he licked his lips as he gazed up at me. "Can I?"

"You can do anything you want, Cherry."

He reached for the button on my jeans. "I want to try."

It was almost too good to be true. I lifted my hips to undo the zipper of my pants, allowing him to pull them and my briefs off to be cast aside. My erection stood up, eager for some attention. It twitched under his touch as he held it steady. I loved watching him lean forward and slide me into his mouth.

Orion was tentative at first, but he grew bolder at working my length as he built up confidence. I stroked his hair in encouragement, careful not to guide his head and make him take more than he could handle. I hated it when guys did that. No, I was content with letting him go at his own pace. Watching my length slide along those plump lips and into his slick heat was more than enough pleasure for me.

He moaned around my cock, sending a shudder through me. Considering it was his first time sucking a dick, it was a promising start. I whimpered his name when he swallowed, racing toward my climax. Not wanting to take him by surprise, I warned him, "Cherry, I'm so close."

Instead of pulling off and finishing me with his hand, he stunned me when he showed me just how talented his tongue was. Not only could he tie a stem with it, but he could make me come undone with teasing rolls and flicks of it against my cock. My toes curled from the intense pleasure as I came.

It was hot as hell when he swallowed and licked his lower lip to catch the last trace of me. I pulled him up and kissed him hard, moaning at the taste of myself in his mouth. My voice was ragged as I ordered, "Bed. *Now.*"

"Does that mean I wasn't awful?"

It was beyond me how he could look self-conscious after what he had done. "You were so great that if I didn't know any better, I wouldn't think it was your first time."

"You're being nice."

"No, I'm serious," I insisted. "That tongue of yours can work some magic, Cherry. I want you to show me what else you can do."

My answer must have satisfied him, because he scrambled off me and shucked off his pants and underwear before pinning me down on the bed.

"I can't even with how sexy you are in those glasses." It delighted me when he kissed me hard.

I had forgotten I still had them on from my dinner with Duke, but I loved the reaction they inspired in Orion. However, as my lenses fogged up, I took them off and tossed them onto the nightstand.

He placed a kiss on the mole on my collarbone with a breathy moan. "Why is this so hot? I've never cared about moles in my life."

I laughed as I ran my fingers through his sandy-colored hair in a caress. "I'm not judging."

He looked up at me with a hint of smugness. "You think hip bones are sexy, so you're not in any position to judge."

"Everything about you is sexy. Your hip bones are just extra special."

His laughter delighted me. "I'm so glad I'm not the only weird one."

I didn't bother replying as he set about working

me back into full arousal with kisses and teasing flicks of his tongue. That mouth of his was sinful. I couldn't get enough of him.

When it was time to move on, he looked up and scowled when he saw the lube on the nightstand. "You need to quit leaving that out for housekeeping to see," he muttered as he leaned over me to grab it and a condom.

I was unconcerned. "They already know it's here, so what's hiding it going to do now?"

He restrained himself to rolling his eyes as he dispensed some before pressing against my entrance. "Is this okay?" he asked, hesitating to act until he had consent.

"Once you enter me, it will be." I lifted my hips in encouragement.

It was a relief to have one of his fingers sliding inside of me. He made a strangled noise at watching it disappearing in and out of me as he worked me.

"This is so obscene." An appreciative moan escaped him when he added another finger.

I rocked under him with a breathy plea. "Give me more."

He whimpered my name as I contracted around his fingers.

"I need you inside me before I lose my mind, Cherry."

The command inspired him to move on as I

hoped it would. He pulled out, then reached for a condom. I stopped him. "You don't need that."

He made a confused noise. "Why not?"

"Because I want you to come inside me with nothing between us." It was something that had never appealed to me until I met Orion.

His eyes went wide. "Are you sure?"

"Absolutely. I want you to make me yours in every sense of the word. I was tested before going on tour, so I'm not putting you at risk."

"*Oh.*" His eyes were wide with surprise. "My tests after Nyla and I broke up were negative, too. Is it really okay?"

I arched up as I stretched out on the bed to tempt him. "*Please!*"

My deliberate show inspired him to slick his cock with lube and push into me.

The slow pace tortured me, although feeling him without the condom was better than I had dreamed. "You can't break me." I enjoyed the fullness of having him inside me, but it still wasn't enough. "Fuck me, Cherry!"

There was no stopping him after that. He set a hard rhythm that gave me what I craved. I writhed under his touch, luxuriating as he took me forcefully. It was a side of him I hadn't seen yet, but I loved it.

He shifted his angle, making me arch off the bed with a gasp at how it let him hit deeper inside of me.

"So good!" My body kept pace with his as we chased the sensations. "So fucking good, Cherry!"

It was everything I wanted and then some. I wrapped my arms around his shoulders, embedding my fingers in his hair as I held on while our bodies moved in sync.

When he stroked my renewed erection, I cried out his name, uncaring of the neighbors. Nothing mattered to me in that moment except for Orion and the pleasure he gave me. Each plea for more was met with vigorous attempts at satiating my lust. I tensed up as I neared my second release.

It caused him to hiss. "Shit, you're so tight! You feel so good, Anise."

Hearing him call me by the nickname drew my orgasm. I climaxed with a protracted moan as my back arched from the effort. It got even better when he pushed in deep and came. His cum spurting inside me made my toes curl with pleasure. Feeling it leaking out of me when he pulled out satisfied me in a whole new way. It made me feel like I was his in the best of ways.

He leaned down and kissed me tenderly. I surrendered myself to him with a soft moan because my everything was his.

Chapter Fifteen

ORION

THE NORMALCY of sitting in my office on Monday was surreal. Everything seemed so *ordinary* now. I was back in the real world, where nothing exciting ever happened to me. It was a place I didn't know where I fit anymore.

I kept expecting people to notice that I was different. Surely, everyone would be able to tell that I was with Iason. But all I received were a few comments about how it looked like I had a good weekend. It was an understatement that didn't come close to describing the incredible sex. Yet again, the memories were enough to make me hard.

A knock on my open office door startled me back to the present. Mom came in with a wave and a sunny smile. "Hi, honey!" It wasn't unusual for her to drop by for a visit since she worked for the university.

My heart hammered in my chest as my arousal

died a quick death in her presence. "Hey, Mom. What are you doing here?"

She shut the door behind her, which did nothing to calm my anxiety. "I wanted to see how you were doing after the weekend."

I cleared my throat as I tried to get into the right headspace to have a conversation with her. "Great, thanks."

"Dinner with Anise was so much fun, wasn't it?" When I answered with only a nod, she continued talking. "He's such a dear boy. I could just eat him up, couldn't you?"

I gave her a pointed look. "What are you implying?"

Rather than answering, she pivoted questions. "Is there something you want to say to me?"

I took the coward's way out. "Thank you for inviting him over. It meant a lot to him."

"He could come over every night as far as your father and I are concerned." She smiled at me. "We enjoyed having him over. Something tells me we weren't the only ones."

"Yes, I'm sure Lyra died a million fangirl deaths of joy that her idol was in our house."

"And what about you?"

I blanched as she shifted the focus onto me. "It was fun."

"So, are we going to talk about Anise or keep dancing around the truth?"

I hung my head with a sigh. "What's there to say when you already know everything?"

"Since I know, that should make it easier on you, right?" Her expression softened into sympathy. "I think it's important for you to say it out loud."

She was right because she always was. I took a deep breath as I made myself use my words. "Fine. Iason and I are dating. Happy?"

"Ecstatic, actually." She beamed at me with so much joy that it lessened my anxiety over the strange situation. "You didn't let your fears stand between you and the best thing that could have happened to you."

"Aren't you supposed to warn me I'm moving too fast and I shouldn't love a celebrity who's out of my league?"

She waved away my concerns. "That's nonsense. I'm an excellent judge of character, and that boy is madly in love with you. He's not interested in breaking your heart. He wants to treasure you. And if you were smart, you'd let him."

I held my head in my hands with a groan. "But Lyra is going to kill me when she finds out. She worships him like a god. She even has a shrine to him built in her room." It wasn't an exaggeration when she had posters of him on every wall of her bedroom. "Do you have any idea how weird it is that my *boyfriend* is plastered all over my sister's walls and watching her sleep at night?"

Mom laughed hard. "Admittedly, that is a strange

predicament. But I don't think you're giving your sister enough credit. Yes, she adores him. She wants him to be happy. If that means being with you, she'll get over her crush."

"There's no way. She'll be devastated that I betrayed her by making her idol fall in love with me and not her."

"Maybe for a few minutes while she processes the news. But she's bright enough to understand that as a fifteen-year-old girl, she does not have what it takes to make a thirty-something-year-old gay man happy."

I wanted to believe her, but I couldn't imagine Lyra accepting my relationship with Iason when she was head over heels in love with him. The reality of the situation made me sigh. "She'll never understand or accept it."

"I'd place money on the fact that him dating you will only make her love him even more." Mom's gaze softened. "Honey, she worships you just as much. Having her two favorite people be together will send her over the moon with happiness, especially since it means she gets to see Anise in private."

"Can you at least appreciate how strange it is to have my baby sister lusting after my boyfriend?" I scowled at the thought. "It's super awkward."

"Welcome to the joys of being a teenager." She giggled at her own joke. "I promise she'll be fine once she's had time to process everything. What are you really worried about?"

"That I'm getting into a deep relationship with Iason way too fast?" I ran my fingers through my hair with another sigh. "He says he plans on moving to Sunnyside, but I'm scared to trust him."

"Because it'll mean he's actually serious about you." Once again, she hit the nail on the head.

"But what if he regrets moving here for me?"

"He won't." She said it with such conviction that I couldn't help but want to believe her. "Talk to him about your fears instead of letting them run wild. Don't talk yourself out of the best present the cosmic universe could have gifted you."

I worried my lower lip with my teeth. "It doesn't bother you he's a man?"

"Why would it?" She shrugged at me. "Gender is just a construct, anyway. All I care about is that he loves you with all of his heart and takes care of you. And from everything I've seen, he does both of those things."

Her words brought a smile to my face despite myself. "He does. It's amazing."

"I know Indra and Nyla did a number on you when it comes to trusting your partner, but you can't bring that baggage into your relationship. It's not fair to him." Her eyes pleaded with me. "Give him a chance to prove himself before you talk yourself out of loving him. He's a good man, Cherry."

They were wise words. I wanted to do my best to embrace them. "I'm trying to be brave."

"Because you love him."

"I do." It felt like a weight had been lifted off me after admitting the truth. "So much, Mom. He's amazing."

"He is, and so are you. Be happy with him, Cherry. You deserve it."

Although I was pretty sure of the answer, I still had to ask the question. "Does Dad know?"

"You probably shouldn't have shown off your stem-tying skills in front of him if you didn't want him to figure it out." I facepalmed hard with a groan as she laughed at me. "He's happy for you, too. We both would love for him to come over more once he's settled. He's always welcome in our home."

"Thank you. I appreciate you embracing him with such open arms and being supportive of us, despite how suddenly it's happened."

"Your father and I have no room to judge on fast relationship timelines." She reached out to give my hand a reassuring squeeze. "As long as you're okay, that's all that matters. We'll always support you, no matter what."

"I keep feeling like I should be freaked-out by what's happening, but when I'm with him, everything feels so natural that I forget to be scared."

"Well, you've always been open-minded and curious, so I'm not sure why it's so surprising to you." Her knowing snicker made me blush hard. "Plus, I'm confident he's a wonderful teacher who has taught you many interesting and exciting things."

"*Mom*." I huffed in annoyance over the innuendo.

"What?" She tried to look innocent, but I didn't buy it for a minute.

I glanced at the clock and realized I was going to be late for meeting him at the Brewhaha Café if I didn't leave soon. "Sorry to cut this short, but I'm meeting him for lunch."

The news delighted her. "Oh, that's wonderful!" She got up and gestured for me to come give her a hug. When I did, she squeezed me extra tight. "I'm so proud of you, honey. And so very happy for you."

"Thank you. I'll keep trying to be brave."

She patted my cheek with a fond smile. "Then you're guaranteed to have your happy ever after. I'll talk to you soon."

"Love you."

She gave me a final parting hug. "I love you, too. Tell Anise hi for me and that we can't wait to have him over again."

"I will."

After she left, I sent off two quick emails before I headed out to go meet Iason with a flutter of excitement in my heart.

Chapter Sixteen

IASON

THE SIGHT of Orion entering the Brewhaha Café in his stylish black suit, violet shirt, and lavender paisley tie was stunning. His bright smile when he spotted me brought sunshine to my soul. I'd give anything to kiss him hello, but the last thing I needed was the paparazzi descending on us while we were building the foundation of our relationship.

"Sorry I'm a little late." His expression turned remorseful. "Mom surprised me by stopping by the museum. She says hi, by the way."

"A worthy reason." I gave him a reassuring smile. "I'll always wait for you."

His cheeks flushed with that blush I loved so much. "Thank you for that, and for wearing your glasses. They suit you."

I adjusted them further up my nose. "I'm happy to oblige your nerd fantasy."

He laughed hard. "You're too kind."

Our server approached the table, a tall man who had striking amber-colored eyes. He was handsome with an amiable smile, looking amazing in his jeans and white button-down shirt with the sleeves rolled up to expose his beautiful forearms.

Orion seemed excited by his appearance. "Welcome back, Wolfie!"

"Thanks. It's good to see you as always, Rion. Hopefully, you didn't miss me too much while I was gone." Rather than being threatened by the man, I loved their easy camaraderie.

"I did, although Brinley took great care of me in your absence. How was your visit home with your mom?"

As Wolfie filled Orion in on his trip, I fell more in love with my boyfriend. It was clear he treated Wolfie as more than a regular server who didn't matter. He cared enough to remember minor details, which spoke to how big his heart was.

"I'm so glad you had a wonderful time," Orion said after Wolfie finished talking.

"Speaking of wonderful, we have your favorite three-cheese panini as today's special."

I loved Orion's delighted reaction that he didn't hide. "That's great! I'll have that."

"I'll have the same thing with tea." I handed over my menu with a word of gratitude.

"Awesome." The server accepted the menus and

put them under his arm. "I'll get those right out for you."

"Thanks, Wolfie."

The man flashed a charming smile. "I'm happy to help."

After he left, Orion turned to me with bubbling excitement. "I promise you'll love this panini. It's probably my all-time favorite thing here, which is saying something since everything here is excellent."

"I've certainly never had a bad meal here. I stop here whenever I'm in town."

I loved how happy he was that I supported his favorite café. The joy he derived from such simple things made me treasure him even more. "The food is always delicious and everyone is super nice. You can't ask for more than that."

Wolfie brought our drinks over. I noticed he gave Orion a strawberry lemonade, although he hadn't ordered one. It spoke to his status as a regular, which made me happy that he was supporting Early.

"How's work?" I asked after he left again.

Orion's expression grew sheepish as he nudged the ice around in his drink with his straw. "Painfully slow when all I wanted to do was come here with you."

"I know the feeling. I couldn't focus on working at all this morning once you were gone."

He perked up with excitement. "Were you writing a new song?"

"Trying to." I gave him a wry grin. "I didn't get very far when all I could think of was how much I wished I was with you instead."

His eyes went wide at my open declaration. "*Oh.*"

Before I could say anything further, Wolfie brought our sandwiches over. It was an unusually fast turnaround time on an order, but I realized he must have sped it up because Orion was on his lunch break. He also left the check at the same time.

We continued making small talk as we ate our meals. I loved the normality of being able to have lunch with my boyfriend, something I had never done before. As much as I enjoyed the experience, I wanted Duke to come soon to meet Orion before he had to return to work.

When we had finished eating, a girl of about fifteen came over to our table, her cheeks flushed as she apologized in a rush of words. "I'm so sorry to interrupt your lunch with your friend, Iason, but I'm such a huge fan, and I would love it if I could ask for your autograph, please."

Although I resented the interruption—and her calling Orion my mere "friend"—I smiled at her. After all, I wouldn't have the meteoric career I did without superfans like her. "Sure, no problem."

The girl squealed in excitement, reminding me of Orion's sister. I accepted the pen and paper that she handed me and signed it with a flourish before handing it back to her.

She made another excited noise as she stared at my signature before she clutched it to her chest while profusely thanking me. "Iason, thanks *so* much! I can't believe you're here and would do this for me! I love you and your music, so thank you!"

"You're most welcome." I gave her a kind smile, hoping that she would leave now that she had gotten what she wanted.

With another rambling thank-you, the girl raced back to her table, where her parents were sitting. They waved at me with grateful smiles. I tilted my head in silent acknowledgment before returning my attention to Orion to judge his reaction. He had a thoughtful expression on his face, causing me to ask, "What?"

His gray eyes studied me. "Sometimes, I forget you're you. Spending so much time with you as Ias, it's like I somehow forgot that you're *the* Iason Leyland."

I grinned at him. "I'm never happier than when I'm your Anise, though."

My comment made Orion smile. "Same. Too bad your glasses don't hide you all the time."

Before I could say anything, Duke entered the cafe, looking like a total badass in black leather and faded jeans.

"Hey," I greeted him when he came over to our table.

"Hey yourself." He chuckled before he turned his

attention to Orion, sizing him up with a critical gaze. "So, you're the boyfriend."

"I am." Orion seemed to shrink back from nervousness. It was understandable since Duke was an intimidating presence.

My friend dragged the moment out into an uncomfortable silence as he continued staring before he extended his hand and introduced himself. "I'm Duke Morrow. Nice to meet you."

Orion shook his hand. "Likewise."

Duke grabbed a nearby chair and turned it backward so he could sit, resting his massive forearms against the back as he leaned on it. "I've got to say, you're nothing like I imagined." The comment caused Orion to blush, making Duke laugh. "I get why your nickname is Cherry, though."

He sheepishly rubbed the back of his head. "Yeah, being so pale and easily embarrassed is a terrible combination."

"It's cute." Duke seemed to realize something. "You were with that woman in a corset at the bar the other night. Does she hit on everything that moves, or am I special?"

Orion laughed a little awkwardly. "Nyla can be very flirty. I'm sorry if she offended you."

"She's nothing I can't handle."

"I believe that being handled by you was probably her goal," he retorted with a rueful shake of his head.

"My husband would have some objections to that." Duke's retort caused me to chuckle with him as Orion's eyes went wide.

"Speaking of which, where is your better half today?" I had also assumed Early would be at the café.

Duke frowned as he looked around the restaurant. "I'm surprised he's not here."

"Oh, does your husband work here?" Orion asked.

"He owns the place."

The shock on Orion's face was downright comical. "Wait, you're *Early's* husband?"

"Yeah. You know him?"

He blinked again as he stared at Duke. "*You're* Early's *husband?*" he repeated with shifted emphasis.

A hint of defensiveness crept into Duke's tone. "Is that a problem?"

"No, no, no, not at all! But he's always described his husband as being cute, and you look like—I mean, not that you're *not* cute, but…"

I tried to help him out. "No, it's true. Duke looks more badass than cute."

He looked relieved that I understood. "Well, yeah. I don't mean any disrespect—"

"Relax, I'm just fucking with you," Duke told him with a smirk. "It's the classic opposites-attract situation. I'm a Rottweiler next to an adorable bunny like Early."

"It's why you work so well together." As if summoned by us talking about him, Early appeared. With his soft blond features and boyish face, he was a ray of sunshine compared to his dark storm cloud of a partner. "And speak of the devil."

He hurried over to our table with a puzzled expression. He wore a plain black shirt with jeans, clearly about to start his shift—late, as per usual. Good thing he opened the place and was his own boss. Otherwise, he'd *so* be fired for his attendance issues. He stood next to Duke and gestured at us sitting together. "How did this happen?"

Duke wrapped his arm around Early's waist to pull him closer. He nodded his head in Orion's direction. "This is the boyfriend."

"Seriously?" Early looked over at Orion with a broad grin. "And suddenly, everything makes so much sense."

It wasn't the response I had expected from him. "How do you figure?"

"Because he's the best." Early reached out and squeezed Orion's shoulder with a fond smile.

Duke seemed confused. "If he's the best, why have I never heard you mention him before?"

It was Early's turn to be baffled. "What are you talking about? I talk about Rion all the time."

"Wait, you're saying that he's *milkshake* Ryan?" Duke asked in confusion.

"Yeah, but it's *R-I-O-N*, not *R-Y-A-N* like it sounds."

Understanding dawned on Duke. "Ohhh, so he's *that* guy."

While he may have understood, I was still lost. "Milkshake?" I repeated, noticing how the question caused Orion to blush again.

"Years ago, I was having the worst night ever," Early explained, causing Duke to hug him closer. "Anything that could go wrong turned into a catastrophe. I was barely holding my shit together after a long double shift, when Rion brought me a peanut butter milkshake with extra whipped cream at the end of the night to make me feel better. It was the sweetest thing a customer had ever done for me. I was so touched that he had noticed I was having a horrible day. I hadn't been able to talk to him when he came for lunch earlier that day."

"That's how I knew something was wrong," Orion said with a small smile. "You always find time to say hello, even if it's only for a quick moment."

"Duchess thought it was sweet, but I was convinced that 'Ryan' was trying to make a move on my husband."

Orion shook his head. "I would never do that! Since I was having a milkshake to make myself feel better after a shitty late night at the office, I figured maybe it would help Early, too. I didn't have any ulterior motive or anything."

Early laughed. "*I* understood that, but my caveman husband sometimes gets paranoid that I'm too tempting."

Duke frowned as he continued staring Orion down. "The only reason I let it go was because Duchess swore up and down that Rion was straight. And now you're with Ias, so something isn't adding up."

I wanted to groan as he hit on the issue I had been hoping to avoid. We both had been hurt by straight guys before, but he still held a fierce grudge against them.

Early nudged his husband with a chiding look. "In case you forgot, people are allowed to like more than one gender."

"Yeah, but you said he was straight, not *bi*." Duke's stubbornness made me want to bash my head against the nearest wall.

"I had met his last two girlfriends, so I made an assumption about his sexuality I shouldn't have. That's on me, not him. Besides, none of that matters. Rion continues to be a wonderful friend to me, and now he's making Ias happy. You have nothing to worry about, so let it go, caveman."

Duke grumbled. "You can't blame me for worrying."

"Not everyone is out to get me, contrary to what you think." He leaned down and gave his husband a kiss. "You're not in any danger of losing me, so calm down. All you're doing is upsetting yourself and everyone else."

He sighed with a contrite expression. "Sorry."

"It's sweet that you care so much." Early caressed his hair lovingly. "But I promise all Rion is going to do is make Ias the happiest man alive."

"I really want to." Orion's quiet conviction touched my heart. "It may be new to me, but I want to make things work."

I reached under the table to squeeze his hand. "You've already made me happier than I've ever been. You're doing fine."

He squeezed me back but didn't say anything.

"Why don't you both come over tomorrow night?" Early suggested. "I'll cook dinner."

And that was why I loved him. He always knew the right thing to do.

"Is it really okay?" Orion hesitantly asked, although I could see he was excited about the possibility.

Early smiled at him. "Absolutely. And I promise my guard dog will be on his best behavior."

I answered for us. "We'd love to come over."

My answer pleased him. "Then that settles it. Does tomorrow night at 6:30 work for you both?"

Orion looked so happy that it was precious. "That sounds great, thanks. Should I bring anything?"

"Just your appetite." Early gave him a playful

wink. "I've got to go handle work, though. Brinley had to call out, so they're swamped."

When he tried to walk away, Duke tightened his hold on his husband. "Aren't you forgetting something, Duchess?"

"Never." He gave his husband a final kiss. "Now, play nice if you want more of where that came from."

I glanced over at Orion to find him smiling at their interactions. It made me curious about what he thought of my friends, but that talk would have to happen later.

After Early sauntered off, I teased Orion. "Duke's not so scary now, is he?"

He relaxed a little. "Not *quite* as scary, although I wouldn't want to get on his bad side."

"He may seem like the tough guy, but Early is his weakness."

Duke hummed with interest. "So that's how you intend to play it? Should I tell Rion some of the dumb shit you've done in the past and see if he wants to get out while he still can?"

I held up my hands in surrender with a laugh. "Fine, I deserved that."

"But I have so many great stories about weird stuff you say when you talk in your sleep." Duke clearly was loving getting back at me.

Orion leaned forward with interest. "Really?"

"I don't do that." Crossing my arms over my

chest, I pretended to give a haughty sniff of disdain. "You're making all that nonsense up to make me look like an idiot."

"You can do that all by yourself without my help." Duke grinned at me. "You absolutely talk in your sleep."

Orion looked amused by our banter. "Now, I *have* to hear."

"My personal favorite was when Ias was dead asleep during finals week and said in the most indignant tone, 'You can't cook *pancakes* in an *igloo!*' He made it sound like the worst offense in the world." I begrudgingly had to admit that Duke's impression of me was pretty decent.

"Please, I've never said anything that stupid in my life."

"Just like you never said, 'The bodacious bodega has Bordeaux for our beautiful bungalow,' huh?" Duke was nonplussed by my attitude since this was an ancient argument.

"Nope, never said that either." I shook my head. "You're making that up."

Orion's amusement over our antics made Duke's stories less annoying. "He seriously said that?"

He held up his hand to swear. "God's honest truth."

Orion's peals of laughter disarmed my ire. "Yeah, yeah, laugh it up," I groused good-naturedly. "Wait until I get payback by telling him about *your* misadventures, Duke."

"As much as I can't wait to hear that, I need to return to work now," Orion said in a disappointed tone after a quick glance at his watch. "Maybe later? And how much do I owe?"

"I've got it," I told him. "See you back at the hotel."

"Thank you." He gave me such a sweet smile that I wanted to lean over the table and kiss him, but my fame made it impossible. "Duke, it was very nice to meet you. Please give my regards to Early."

Duke tilted his head in acknowledgment. "See you tomorrow night."

Orion stood up to leave. "I'm looking forward to it."

"See you soon, Cherry."

His shy happiness was too cute as he said his last parting words. He left with a wave at Early behind the counter, who was in the middle of taking an order.

Once we were alone, I turned my attention to Duke. "I told you he'd be one of Early's favorites."

"I can't believe you're dating the milkshake guy." He shook his head. "I at least feel gratified I was right about him not being straight."

"See? Cherry is a total sweetheart."

He gave me a suspicious look. "What about that woman he was with at the bar?"

I didn't want to answer that question, but I had no choice. "She's his ex-girlfriend that he's still friends with."

As I expected, the truth raised his temper. "Are you shitting me? He's 'friends' with his ex-girlfriend and you aren't the least bit threatened by that?"

"No, because I trust him. She left him to explore her polyamorous urges, and he refused to be a part of that. What do I have to be threatened about?"

He frowned. "Fine, but what happens when she goes running back to him and tells him she made a huge mistake and only wants to be with him?"

"It won't happen."

His stubborn streak asserted itself, again. "You don't know that."

As if summoned on cue, Nyla entered the restaurant in sunglasses and another fabulous outfit that earned her many appreciative stares from the straight men. She looked around and did a double take when she saw me, hesitating only a moment before coming over.

I said a silent prayer that she didn't make a scene. Doing my best to sound casual, I greeted her. "Hi, Nyla."

She took off her sunglasses, allowing me to see the relief on her face. "Oh, it really is you! Thank god. Hey, I'm sorry to interrupt, but can we chat for a minute?"

I gestured for her to take the seat Orion had vacated, while giving Duke a warning look to not say a damn word. "What did you want to talk about?" When she glanced uncertainly at my friend, I realized why she hesitated. "It's okay. He knows about Orion. Nyla, this is Duke, my best friend and owner of the Hurly-burly Bar and Grille."

"Oh, trust me, I remember Mr. Tall, Dark, and Handsome. It's not every day I get shot down by someone as gorgeous as him." She laughed into her hand before her expression turned remorseful. "I wanted to apologize for the other night. I didn't mean to fuck everything up. But I was so surprised that I didn't know how to react. I mean, it's *you* and *Rion*. That was quite a what-the-fuck to wrap my head around in an instant."

"I'm as much at fault for assuming you were his girlfriend." It was something I still regretted. "I'm sorry I overreacted."

"I never would have forgiven myself if I had ruined things between you." Her eyes pleaded with me. "Please believe me when I say from the bottom of my heart, I'm so happy for you both. Rion is a good man who deserves someone who loves only him. Don't break his heart like I did."

Before I could answer, Duke spoke up. "You really mean that, don't you?"

She shifted her gaze over to him, giving him an

assessing glance-over. "I do. All I've ever wanted was for Rion to be happy. Unfortunately for me, he would never be happy if we stayed together. But he has enough love in his heart to support me living my truth, although it hurt him to let go. He deserves someone to treasure that about him."

"And I do. It says a lot about both of you that you stayed friends." I hesitated before I laid it all out on the table. "I'm not threatened by your friendship with him."

"You have no reason when his heart is yours. It was obvious even on that night when I talked to him after you left."

While the situation had obviously worked out for the best, I still hated how I had overreacted. "Why did you say it explained a fuckload of things?" I had never gotten the chance to ask Orion about that comment.

She grinned sheepishly. "I might have assumed you were looking over at *me* during the concert because I was convinced you wanted me. When I saw you two together, it made me realize you only had eyes for him. It also explained when he was all blushes and flustered cuteness after meeting you backstage and after the show."

"I had a story built up in my mind that catching us together was proof he was secretly gay and why your relationship wasn't working." My stupidity was astounding. "I'm sorry I jumped to the wrong conclusion."

"And I really wish my dumbass mouth hadn't ruined everything. He was so upset after you left. I felt absolutely awful about it. Thankfully, you were smart enough to give him a second chance and not hold my idiocy against him."

Since it was obvious she still cared about him, I wanted her to understand I was serious about him. "I will always take care of him. As soon as my tour is over, I'm moving back here to be with him."

"In that case, I'd like it if we could eventually be friends, too." She gave me a hopeful smile. "I'll understand if that's not something you're interested in, though."

I gained nothing from driving a wedge between Orion and her. "Something tells me we'll get along like fire and dry grass in August once we get to know each other."

"That would be awesome. Thanks for giving me a chance and for making Rion so happy." She stood up to leave. "I don't want to take up any more of your time. Congrats on falling in love with the biggest sweetheart in the world. Take good care of him for me."

She left with a wave to walk over to the counter to order something to go. Duke watched her with narrowed eyes as she laughed and flirted with his husband.

I sighed. "What?"

"Do you have any idea how irritating it is that I want to believe her sincerity?"

I had to laugh at that. "If she was a bad person, Orion never would have fallen for her. I'm inclined to trust her."

He watched her as she joked with Wolfie while waiting for her order. "You aren't uncomfortable with her hanging around?"

"She won't stop being poly, and Cherry will never accept being anything less than someone's whole heart. I have nothing to be threatened by when there's a fundamental incompatibility in their romantic needs. Alienating her when they're still friends is a surefire way to lose Orion's trust, so I gain nothing by acting like the caveman you are."

Rubbing his temples, Duke lowered his voice to warn me. "It never works out with straight guys. You're setting yourself up for heartbreak."

"He's not like George." I was referring to the straight guy I had developed feelings for freshman year, only to have my heart crushed by him when he slept with me and then quit returning my calls. After that, I had sworn off boyfriends until I met Orion.

Duke persisted. "He's straight, and he's going to break your damn heart."

I refused to believe it. "Oh, I assure you that Cherry is *far* from straight when he's moaning my name in bed." I sighed when he refused to accept my reassurances. "Look, I understand why you're concerned, but I promise that he's not like that."

He remained unconvinced. "You haven't even known him a full week. *You* don't know what he's like yet."

I wasn't interested in rehashing our argument from last night. Before I could get back into it, Early appeared with coffee for Duke.

"Here." He held the cup out for his husband to take. "Drink this and stop giving Ias a hard time."

"I don't care how nice this guy is—he's *straight,*" he growled as he accepted the coffee. "We all know how that's going to end."

Early chimed in as the voice of reason. "You suspected Rion wasn't straight from my stories about him, so why are you so hung up on this?"

Duke scowled as he waited for his drink to cool down. "Why are you acting like I'm the bad guy for being worried about my best friend getting hurt?"

Early caressed his black hair to soothe him. "As the person here who has known Rion the longest, I promise you he's not the villain you're trying to make him out to be. He's a great guy."

"You don't think it's suspicious that he's friends with his ex-girlfriend? I saw her flirting with you and Wolfie. Hell, she flirted with me the other night."

Early sighed as he shook his head. "Yes, Nyla is a playful flirt. But she's not Rion's girlfriend, so it's allowed. She's a sweetheart and a good customer.

What I want to know is why she was over talking to Ias."

"She walked in on us in Orion's apartment after my first date with him. I assumed she was his girlfriend and stormed out."

Duke scowled. "She *was* his girlfriend."

"Fine, I assumed she was his *current* girlfriend. It was only once I was back at the hotel and cooled off that I realized she hadn't been pissed about catching us. She had just been surprised." I shook my head at how much I had screwed things up. Thankfully, Orion hadn't held it against me. "She was apologizing for causing chaos."

"See? She's a sweetheart, just like Rion." Early gave his husband a look that told him to get his act together.

"If you don't believe me, you should at least trust Early's judgment. He's never wrong. You know that better than anyone," I reminded Duke.

He conceded with a sigh. "Please be careful. I don't want you to be hurt because he doesn't understand his new feelings and rejects you when he gets scared."

"He won't," Early and I said at the same time.

"You'll see tomorrow night when you spend more time with him," Early promised. "I wouldn't approve unless I believed they were good for each other."

It was the best argument I had at the moment.

Everyone knew he had a weird ability to read people. He was never wrong about that kind of thing.

Duke still looked uncomfortable. "Fine, I'll keep an open mind tomorrow."

"That's all I can ask." Early kissed his husband's forehead, then left with a final reassuring smile at me.

"I'm not trying to be a dick." Duke frowned after taking a sip of coffee. "I'm just worried."

"Which I appreciate," I said. "You always look out for me, but I promise, Cherry is it for me."

"I want that to be true, Ias. You deserve that."

"Straight thing aside, what do you think of him?" I asked.

He stroked his chin. "I never thought 'quiet nerd' was your type, but he looked good in that suit. It makes sense why he reminded you of Duchess."

I grinned at his comments. "In fairness, I didn't know it was my type either, but I'm enjoying his shy cuteness."

"Want to hit the Record Exchange with me while you wait for him to get off work? I've got time to kill before I have to go to the bar tonight."

I recognized the peace offering. It was a used CD, DVD, and vinyl store that we had spent countless hours and dollars in while students at Sunnyside University. "Sounds good." I put my credit card in to pay while Duke finished his coffee.

Wolfie came over to collect the bill. It felt right to

tell him, "Rion's sorry he had to go back to work without saying goodbye."

"No problem, I'll catch him next time." He gave a charming half-smile before leaving to run my card.

After he returned, I gave him an extra-generous tip as a thank-you for always taking such good care of Orion. With a final farewell to Early, Duke and I left to go hang out at the used record store like old times.

Chapter Seventeen

ORION

DUKE AND EARLY lived in a quaint two-story blue house with navy shutters. It was surrounded by large trees everywhere and had a beautiful garden of flowers. While I looked forward to spending more time with Early, I was still nervous about Duke. I couldn't tell if he liked me or not, but I wanted his approval because I knew how much it mattered to Iason.

"It'll be fine." He gave me a quick kiss before he led the way to the front door.

Tightening my grip on his hand, I drew strength from his certainty. I was out of my depth, but I reassured myself that it would be okay since Early and Iason were both on my side.

Thankfully, I had changed at the hotel into a black sweater and jeans before coming over. Being the only one in a suit would have made me uncomfortable.

Iason was similarly dressed in a light gray argyle sweater and jeans, but he looked like he had just stepped out of a photo shoot. I couldn't compare.

Early opened the door with a welcoming smile. "I'm glad you could make it!"

"Thanks for having us over," I said shyly.

"There's no need to be so formal." He ushered us inside with a warm smile. "We're all friends here."

As he led us into the kitchen, I took a calming breath to steady my nerves. I experienced a surge of appreciation when Iason once again squeezed my hand in silent reassurance.

Duke stood in front of the stove, watching a boiling pot as if it held the mysteries of the universe within it. He looked so out of place, with his massive muscles, which were even more impressive now that he was wearing a plain black T-shirt that showed off his impressive biceps. Iason was fit, but Duke was *jacked*. I felt three inches tall next to him.

Early shooed his husband away from the pot. "I know you're starving, but it'll be just a few more minutes." Duke moved, which was surreal watching that giant wall of muscles obey someone who was shorter than me by quite a few inches. "I hope pierogies are good."

"I *love* pierogies!" It was impossible to tone down my excitement. "They're seriously one of my favorites."

Early smiled at me. "That's why I made them

special tonight. Potato and cheddar seemed right up your alley."

"You know me so well." The show of consideration touched me. "We've talked about it before, but I never thought I'd get the chance to try them unless you added them to the menu."

Duke hugged Early from behind, dwarfing him. "I like them too much for him to get sick of them at the café." He kissed the dimple on his husband's cheek when he grinned.

Early dropped the homemade pierogies to the boiling water, clearly used to cooking with his huge hulk of a husband holding him at the same time. It was such a sweet sight, filling my heart with warmth at how wonderful their relationship was. I had heard stories over the years about how Duke was the perfect doting spouse, but that had been difficult for me to reconcile with the man I met. However, seeing them moving so in sync, I understood.

Early nudged his husband with his elbow as he stirred the pot. "Drinks."

It was obvious how hard it was for Duke to pull away from him, but he obeyed without complaint. "We've got beer, cider, milk, and water."

"Cider sounds nice," I said.

"You'll love it." Early took out the plates as he talked. "We get it from a local brewery that makes it on their farm."

Duke handed a glass bottle to me while grabbing

beer for him and Iason. He then grabbed another cider for Early and carried them over to the table, which was already set with silverware.

"This is the real reason he loves pierogies," Early continued as he pulled them out of the boiling water with a slotted spoon to dish out. "They're ready so quick he doesn't have time to get impatient for them."

"That, and they're delicious." Duke carried the prepared plates over to the glass table, where there were small bowls of sour cream and cinnamon applesauce for each of us.

As we sat down, Iason thanked Early. "I'm so glad you made these tonight. Duke isn't the only one who loves them."

"It's nice to be loved." Early gestured for us to start eating. "Please, enjoy."

I used a generous helping of the sour cream and applesauce before taking my first bite. It took effort to restrain myself from moaning in delight at how good it was. "Early, this is delicious! Thank you!"

"Even better than I remembered," Iason added.

He was clearly pleased with the praise. "I'm glad you like it."

"Love it," Duke corrected, causing us to laugh.

Early took the opportunity to segue. "Speaking of love, spill it. I'm tired of hearing everything second-hand through Duke."

I had no idea where to start. How could I possibly explain what I was still trying to understand?

Iason surprised me when he didn't answer but asked a different question. "When did you fall for Duke?"

"When I saw him across the club grinding against a twink and knew that needed to be me instead," Early answered with a laugh. "I marched right over, got in between them, and made him mine."

"That's how you fell in love with him?" I asked in surprise.

Early's gaze softened with fondness. "No, that was when I woke up the next morning with his muscular body curled up around me like I was his favorite teddy bear. It was so unexpectedly adorable from a guy who could bench-press me with one hand. It made me want to learn more about the real side of him that his badass attitude was hiding."

I had heard Early refer to his husband as cute countless times over the years I had known him, but it was hard to reconcile because Duke was nothing like I had imagined. Then again, it *had* been cute seeing him hugging Early while cooking.

"I knew for certain when he attempted to sneak out that morning and I told him no." Early grinned as he shared a look with Duke that said so much. "Challenging him was the most thrilling thing I had ever experienced."

"*No one* tells me no," Duke said in a dark rumble. "It was infuriating."

Iason laughed at the memories. "I had to listen to

Duke fume for *hours* afterward about how he couldn't believe the nerve of that guy who dared to tell him *no*."

"Once I calmed down, I had to deal with the fact that I didn't want to leave, anyway." Duke shrugged as he ate another pierogi. "I could tell he was different, but I couldn't figure out why at first."

"I loved Duke from early on, but it took him a while to catch up." Early reached over and squeezed his husband's enormous forearm. "But it absolutely was worth waiting for him to sort his shit out."

It was weird realizing that I had more similarities with Duke in this situation, when I never expected to have anything in common with him. Hoping it wasn't out of line, I asked him, "How did you know?"

He surprised me with his openness. "I wanted more than just one night with him. I wanted him to be mine and mine alone forever."

"More caveman logic," Early joked. "It's *so* romantic."

We all laughed, even as Duke defended himself. "Hey, I can be romantic."

"Yes, you can, baby." Early blew him a kiss. "My very own knight in shining armor."

"When you know, you know," Iason insisted.

My cheeks grew warm from how he gazed at me with all the love in his heart. I wasn't sure how it was possible, but I wanted that kind of life with him.

Early gestured between himself and his husband with his fork. "We're living proof of that. Everyone thought we were nuts for getting married less than three months after we met, but it was right for us. Love doesn't come with a timeline. I wish more people understood that. Sometimes it's love at first sight, and sometimes it takes twenty-five years to realize you're in love with your best friend."

I appreciated Early's support, despite Duke still looking concerned. "Even though I don't understand everything, I don't want to lose out on love because I was too scared to take that chance."

Iason reached over and took my hand to give it a light squeeze. It sent a small thrill through me as I smiled at him.

"Well, I think it's great." Early's show of gratitude touched me. "I'm glad you're not letting your past hold you back from happiness anymore."

"Never again." I refused to let myself ever get into the same situation.

Duke frowned as waves of disapproval rolled off him.

"Say it," Iason told him, squeezing my hand once more before pulling away.

I found it interesting that Duke's gaze darted over to Early, almost as if looking for approval to share his thoughts. He didn't seem like a guy who would ever ask anyone for permission to do anything.

Early sighed softly. "You may as well say it. I'd rather you get it out in the open than stew on it all night and be a dick about everything."

Scowling at being ganged up on, Duke looked at me. "Can you honestly say never again?"

"I'm never going to put him in that position," Iason vehemently promised.

"That's not what I meant." Duke returned his attention to me. "Are you sure you'll never want to be with a woman again?"

The question caught me off guard. I hadn't thought about it before. Although it embarrassed me, I made myself be honest. "I've never felt this way about anyone else, man or woman."

"But is that enough? Can you be content with him when you've spent your whole life interested in women?"

"Are you seriously asking him if he'll get sick of me and crave women again?" Iason incredulously demanded.

Duke held his hands up in surrender. "Hey, you said it, not me."

"There's a difference between being protective and being an asshole." Iason's growl sent an unexpected jolt of arousal through me. What was *that* about?

Early said Duke's name reproachfully.

While it was hard for me, I forced myself to speak. "No, it's okay."

"It really isn't," Iason disagreed with a frown.

I assumed Duke was aware of everything from Early and Iason, which made it easier for me to talk. "No, he's your best friend. He's just looking out for you. I can't blame him for being suspicious over how someone who has only dated women suddenly has a boyfriend. I understand why he's concerned, because in his defense, it sounds ridiculous."

Iason still looked angry, while Duke seemed stunned I was taking his side. I drew strength from Early's encouraging gaze and attempted to verbalize my feelings. "I'm still figuring it all out, so I won't sit here and pretend I have all the answers. What I can promise you is I'm not after his fame, money, or whatever you're worried about. None of that matters to me."

"I'm more concerned about how you go from being straight to gay without having a single issue," Duke argued.

"That's fair. It's something I've been struggling to understand myself. All I can say is that when it feels like I've found the other half of my heart, I don't care if Iason's a man or a woman. I only care that it's him, and he makes me happier than I've ever been in my entire life."

Iason gave Duke a pleading look. "You didn't know why you wanted Early in the beginning, but you knew that you did. This is the same thing."

"I've also known my whole life that I'm gay," he

shot back. "If I suddenly fell in love with a woman, I'd have a hell of a lot of problems with that."

"As would I," Early joked, keeping the mood light.

I was pretty sure my flaming red cheeks said everything I was too embarrassed to fess up to. "Being with Ias, I understand now why none of my relationships with women ever worked."

"You were gay and didn't know it?" Duke questioned skeptically.

"Maybe I'm bi or pan." I shrugged since I wasn't sure what to call myself. "Maybe it's just Iason. I wish I had a better answer because it would reassure us all. But I'd rather embrace what I feel for him than talk myself out of the best thing that's ever happened to me and hurt both of us."

Early smiled at me. "That's wonderful, Rion. We don't always have to know why. We just have to know."

Duke seemed to waver on the matter. "You're seriously fine with everything that comes with being with a man?"

"He's *more* than fine with it," Iason answered for me. His voice was filled with so much innuendo that it made me shift uncomfortably in my seat.

My face was on fire. "Yeah."

"It doesn't gross you out at all?" Duke persisted.

"Why should it?" Acting nonchalant, I shrugged and tried not to die of embarrassment.

Duke frowned. "It's one thing to mentally be cool with two dudes hooking up when it has nothing to do with you. It's totally different when you have a dick up your—"

Early interrupted with a sharp "Not your place, hon."

"Would *you* be fine if you had to eat out some chick after a lifetime of loving dick?" Duke asked, causing Early to roll his eyes. "That's harder to wrap my head around than anything."

Iason howled with laughter, which made my humiliation worse.

Ever the diplomat, Early took the tactful route. "While I personally couldn't do it, I applaud the fact that Rion is open-minded enough to explore his sexuality without judgment. It says a lot about who he is as a person."

Early's comments touched me. "Thank you."

"You've seriously never thought about being with a guy before Ias?" Duke questioned, clearly still hung up on the issue. "Never?"

"I've danced with some guys at a gay club with my friend Vince, but it never did anything for me, even when they hit on me. I've never fantasized about guys before, though."

Duke leaned back in his chair with a shake of his head. "That's wild."

"Are you done grilling him about something that's

none of our damn business?" Early asked, a slight frown on his face. "Because I invited them over to have a good time, not to get interrogated."

"You can't tell me you didn't have your reservations about this whole thing."

Early gave his husband a chiding look. "As I mentioned earlier, given that I'm the person who has known Rion the longest and Ias almost as long as you have, it makes perfect sense to me. I'm happy they found each other. I couldn't have picked better partners for them if I tried."

"At least Early gets it," Iason said in a playful tone. "You need to work on helping convince your man."

"That'll have to wait until after you guys leave." Early's grin turned flirty. "Don't worry. I'm quite confident I can get him to see things our way."

"Thank you for caring about Ias enough to worry about him," I said.

"I told you, didn't I?" Early patted his husband's arm. "Rion is a good bean."

"Yeah, he is." Iason gave me a fond smile that sent my butterflies into flight. He leaned over and caressed my hair, sending fire racing through my veins even as it comforted me.

"I bet a remodeled kitchen they're married within the year," Early confidently predicted. The certainty in his voice startled me.

The love in Duke's eyes for his husband was clear

to see. "I learned long ago not to bet against you, Duchess. You win every time."

"Damn right I do."

With the heavy topic out of the way, we moved on to more pleasant small talk. I felt more at home as the evening continued. The easy relationship between Duke and Early awed me, making me long for that same kind of partnership with Iason. The thought warmed my heart instead of scaring me away.

I DISCOVERED a new type of happiness as I nestled against Iason's side on the couch with his arm around me to hold me close. After our talk at dinner, Duke had slowly warmed up to me. I stopped being so afraid of him and his disapproval. The sight of him cuddling his husband across from us helped make him seem less scary.

While he was a foreboding, huge wall of man, he was all things gentle and adoring when it came to Early. I never would have expected someone like him to be so soft and doting. Their relationship made me envious, even as I realized that Iason and I were developing a similar bond.

"Ias, can you come with me for a sec?" Early requested when there was a lull in the conversation. "I need your help in my office real quick."

"Sure." He kissed the top of my head before untangling himself from me to leave.

I didn't miss the look Early shot his husband as he left the room. Left alone with him, my nerves returned as I waited for him to say something.

Duke ran his hand through his black hair with a heavy sigh before apologizing. "Sorry, I was out of line earlier."

"No, it's okay. I understand why you have your concerns about me. You're just looking out for Ias." I couldn't get mad at him for being worried about his best friend.

"Yeah, but I was prying into shit that's none of my business."

"I get it, though. If Vince showed up with a new girlfriend and told me he was straight, I wouldn't be taking it nearly as well as you." I shook my head at the imagined scenario. "Don't get me wrong. I love him like a brother, but he has a tendency to pick partners that are bad for him, so I would have a lot of questions."

Duke hesitated before continuing. "Ias and I have both had our hearts broken by straight guys who got scared off by their feelings. I don't want that to happen again. I just can't wrap my head around how you can go from spending a lifetime thinking you're straight to being totally fine with gay sex? Not to mention what your folks will think."

"They accept our relationship and adore him."

The information stunned him. "What do you mean?"

"They think it's wonderful that we found each other. Both of them were ready to adopt him from hello."

"No offense, but is your whole damn family nuts?" He stared at me incredulously. "How do you go from dating only women to having your family being cool with you bringing home a boyfriend?"

"Because they raised us to believe that love is love. All they care about is that my partner loves me for who I am and makes me happy."

He leaned back against the couch. "That's unreal."

It was important to me he understood where I was coming from on the matter. "All I want to do is love him. I promise I don't have any ulterior motives here."

"Duchess has always liked you." Duke's shift in the conversation confused me. "You make his day better, and for that, I'm appreciative."

"I'm grateful that we've become friends over the years." One of the biggest reasons I went to the Brewhaha Café so much was because I loved having the chance to chat with him.

Duke grinned at me. "I seriously thought you were in love with him. I mean, what straight guy brings a man a milkshake to make him feel better?"

"I promise, it's never been about that. Early is a good friend, and I'm kind of weird."

Duke's grin softened to a smile. "I see that now. You don't look at Duchess the same way you do Ias."

"I always loved hearing him talk about you because you have such a great relationship. If I'm being honest, I was envious."

"He wished you could find a partner who would make you happy like us," Duke said. "If you can deal with the hang-ups that come with his fame, Ias could be that guy for you."

"I hope so."

Early and Iason returned to the living room. He asked his husband, "Did you make nice?"

Duke reached out and pulled his husband onto his lap to nuzzle against him. "I apologized for being a dick."

"Good." Early kissed him on the cheek in reward.

Iason sat down next to me on the couch once more, holding his arm out to allow me to snuggle closer to him. I rested my head on his shoulder, sighing in happiness. It felt so right being held by him.

"You left out the part where his *parents* are already cool with you guys," Duke said to Iason, who grinned in response.

"That was surreal. I never in a million years would have expected his mom to tell me I was in love with him before I told him myself, let alone be supportive."

"You've always had a way with charming women," Early teased. He leaned closer to Duke when he wrapped his arms around his waist. "It's such a waste to have all those screaming lady fans and not wanting to do anything with them."

Iason's grin was wicked. "The only person I'm interested in making scream in bed is Cherry."

I flushed as I tried to ignore the waves of arousal crashing through me. When everyone laughed, I hid my face against his shoulder in embarrassment.

The doorbell ringing interrupted us. When Early tried to go answer the door, Duke pulled him closer and refused to let him leave. "If that's who I think it is, he can use his damn key."

A male voice called out. "Are you fucking, or is it safe for me to enter?"

"There's a wild orgy going on," Early shot back with a cheeky grin. "Come if you dare."

The person laughed as he entered the living room. He was in his early twenties, wearing ripped jeans with a white shirt and a black leather jacket. Although he wasn't as physically imposing as Duke, I could see the family resemblance in the man's square jaw and his gray-blue eyes.

He shook his head with mock disappointment. "What kind of orgy involves everybody wearing all their clothes?"

"A disappointing one," Iason answered, causing everyone to laugh as the man sat down on the single chair. "It's good to see you again, Fitzy. This is my boyfriend, Orion Donati."

He looked me over. "Wow, so it's true that you're dating someone. And he's cute to boot. Nice job, Ias." He reached over and held out his hand to me. "I'm Duke's younger brother, Fitzgerald, but everyone calls me Fitzy."

I shook his hand. "Nice to meet you."

He made himself more comfortable on the chair as he leaned back. "Sorry I missed your concert the other night. Rena called out of work, so I had to take over her lessons."

Iason looked concerned. "Is she okay?"

"We're not sure." He frowned as he shrugged out of his jacket. "She's been having severe migraines for over a week now, so we're all worried about her. She promised to go to the doctor, so hopefully they can figure out what's going on with her. She's bitter that she picked a hell of a time to stop drinking coffee."

"Did she go from being a heavy coffee drinker to stopping cold turkey?" I asked.

"Yeah, how did you know?" Fitzy asked in surprise.

"The migraines are probably from caffeine withdrawal because she quit so suddenly," I suggested. "My mom had the same problem when she swore off coffee, but as soon as she started drinking it again, they stopped. She eventually managed to gradually cut down on how many cups she drank a day without giving it up completely, so it didn't trigger the same migraine issues."

"I'll definitely mention it to her. Thanks."

My curiosity got the better of me. "What do you teach?"

"I run the Sunnyside Music School here in town. I teach guitar and drums, but we have instructors for all kinds of instruments."

It was a place I had driven past quite often on my way to and from work. "That's really cool."

"When they told me Ias had a boyfriend, I had to come see for myself. I didn't believe it, but here you are." He gestured at me with amazement.

"Here I am." I appreciated Iason squeezing my shoulder in support. Thankfully, Fitzy didn't seem to harbor the same objections as his older brother.

"I lost a dollar to myself, because I assumed Ias would end up with a muscle bro like Duke."

"Nah, he likes being the big guy too much," Early disagreed.

Duke chuckled. "And this is why I say never to bet against Duchess."

"It's funny." Fitzy continued studying me thoughtfully. "I never thought I'd see the day where Ias ended up with a sweetheart. Then again, I thought the same thing about my brother, and look at how that turned out."

"I love proving people wrong," Early joked. "Is everything still woeful on the dating front for you?"

"You would think a soulful, good-looking musician would be in higher demand," Fitzy said with a dramatic sigh. "Apparently, being a relationship-only guy instead of a love 'em and leave 'em type is a real problem these days."

"My friend Vince has the same issue, minus the musician part. He's an attorney here in Sunnyside, so his free time is pretty limited. He would rather invest in a relationship, instead of wasting time with meaningless sex."

He seemed surprised. "You would think it would be the other way around and he'd want meaningless flings since he doesn't have time to invest in building a relationship."

"Vince has always preferred serious relationships, but he hasn't had much luck. It's a shame because he's a nice guy."

"In my experience, nice guys are never as nice as they think they are," Fitzy said with a frown.

"Admittedly, he swears like an angry sailor when he gets cut off in traffic," I conceded with a laugh, "but the rest of the time, he's a hopeless romantic who would do anything to help out someone in need. He's the best kind of friend you could hope for."

Duke looked baffled. "He's all that and you still didn't fall for him?"

I wrinkled my nose at the thought. "No way. He's handsome, but that would be like dating my brother."

"Do you have a picture?" Fitzy asked, sounding intrigued.

I pulled my phone out of my pocket and found a recent one of Vince from his social media page to hand over for Fitzy's inspection.

He accepted it and made a hum of interest as he studied it. "Damn, he's actually pretty hot and looks damn good in that suit." He passed the phone to Early and Duke for them to see. "I certainly wouldn't say no."

"Oh, *that* Vince! He's been to the café with you before," Early realized as he looked at it with Duke. "He's an absolute doll."

"Early likes him, so that's already another point in his favor," Fitzy said.

"He's been talking about taking up guitar as a hobby. Maybe I can convince him to go to your school," I offered, wondering if Vince would be interested.

Early passed my phone back over to me, and I showed Iason the picture before pocketing it once more. He teased Fitzy, "Just imagine what other kinds of lessons you could teach him besides guitar."

After we laughed, Fitzy changed the subject. "Did I make it in time for dessert?"

"Yep, we're having peanut butter pie," Early informed him.

"Hell yeah! Is now too soon?"

"Now is good," Iason agreed. "Early's pies are the best."

Early slid off Duke's lap. "Then now it is."

We all began to head into the kitchen, with Iason holding my hand. As someone who was shy and awkward, it amazed me how natural it felt to be with him and his friends. It was one more sign that we were meant to be.

Chapter Eighteen

IASON

"THANK YOU FOR TONIGHT. I had so much fun with everyone," Orion said on the drive home.

"I'm glad. I wish Duke hadn't been such a dick in the beginning, but sometimes he can't help it."

Orion chuckled. "I would have been more upset if I hadn't understood where he was coming from."

"He didn't have to be so crude about it." I scowled in annoyance.

"Please don't take this the wrong way, but is it a concern you have?"

"That you'll want to be with a woman again?" I asked in surprise. He nodded in response. "I'm quite confident in my ability to keep you more satisfied than any woman ever could."

To prove my point, I leaned over and captured his earlobe in my mouth, sucking on it as I ran my hand up his inner thigh toward temptation.

He swerved a little in the lane. "Fuck, Anise!"

I never tired of hearing him call me that. To show my appreciation, I tugged on his ear with my teeth before murmuring, "Pull over."

"Do not make me crash this car!" Orion swore when I cupped his arousal.

"That's why I told you to pull over." I laughed when he forced my hand off him.

"Look, I don't want to ruin a wonderful night by getting arrested for indecent exposure," he growled, which turned me on more. I loved the rare show of rough Orion. It made me want him to do untold things to me.

Overcome by a mischievous impulse, I leaned over and moaned in his ear. "But I need you inside me now, Cherry." His grip on the steering wheel tightened until his knuckles turned white, making me grin. "Or do you want me inside you, showing you why no woman will ever be able to satisfy you the way I can?"

We stopped at a light, giving him the opportunity to pull me closer for a desperate, heated kiss. It was rough and aggressive, which had me hard as a rock in an instant when I thought about him taking me like that. Our tongues dueled against each other as I gave myself over to his demanding passion.

A horn blared from behind, making us jerk apart. Orion drove, but I could see how flushed his cheeks were and how hard he was breathing after our fierce kiss. Fuck, I wanted him so much I didn't know how I was going to last until we returned to the hotel room.

When I reached over to get access to his pants, he knocked my hand away. "I said stop."

"And I said pull over." I slid my hand between his thighs again and moved it upward.

He stopped me short of my goal. "We don't have anything to make it possible, so please quit torturing us. We'll be back at the hotel in ten minutes if you quit distracting me."

"I have lube and a condom in my wallet."

He glanced over at me in surprise. "Seriously?"

"I never want anything to stop me from being with you. Pull over."

An interesting whine escaped from him at my command, but he continued to rebuff me. "I'm not fucking you in the woods like a heathen and getting arrested while landing you on the cover of every tabloid. I'm begging you, please don't torture us."

While I knew he was right, I didn't have to be happy about it. I crossed my arms over my chest with a huffy sigh. "Fine, have it your way." My pout turned into a wicked smile as an idea came to mind. "I'll just have to punish you for it later."

The sound of his whimper at my sexy promise made me regret giving up the hope of immediate gratification. I enjoyed watching him struggling to control himself, loving that I could affect him so much with minimum effort. It was further proof that Orion was mine and mine alone.

"Fitzy seemed nice," he said, clearly trying to take his mind off the noticeable tent in his pants.

"He's great." I readjusted my hardness that had yet to abate. "He's the little brother I never had."

"I think Fitzy and Vince would hit it off."

It wasn't a terrible idea. "If he's your best friend, Vince has to be a good guy. Feel free to play Cupid."

"I don't want to give Duke any more reasons to not like me, though."

"He doesn't dislike you. It's his nature to be suspicious. Trust me, if he hated you, you'd know."

Orion laughed. "That's weirdly comforting. I never want to end up on his bad side."

"It's pretty fearsome. Thankfully, I've only been on the receiving end of his anger a handful of times."

"Really?" He sounded surprised while we waited at a light.

"Do you think it should have been more?"

"No, it's the opposite. You two get along so well, I can't imagine him being angry at you."

Thankfully, it was rare that we had fights. "It was almost always deserved, so I don't hold it against him. You might find this hard to believe, but I can be kind of an asshole from time to time."

He laughed, a sound that never failed to warm my soul. "I can't picture it."

"That's good, then. I never want to act like that with you, though."

"Which I appreciate. And I'll do the same."

His comment made me snort with amusement. "I can't picture you being an asshole to anyone."

He grinned. "Wait until someone cuts me off in traffic. Vince isn't the only one who goes off. In my defense, they deserve it for driving like dicks."

"This I have to see!"

"I don't *mean* to do it, but I guess that's what learning how to drive in California does to you."

"Are you saying it turns you into a raving asshole behind the wheel as soon as someone drives like a left-lane dick?"

"That's absolutely what I'm saying." His cheeky grin made me want to lean over and kiss him again, but I refrained since we were close to the hotel.

I switched topics to distract myself from my lust. "Why didn't you tell me you knew Early?"

He answered with a shrug. "I didn't realize you knew him until we were already at the café."

"I can't believe you brought him a milkshake." It tickled me that Orion cared enough about Early as a friend to do something so perfect for him.

"We had talked before about our favorite milk-shakes at some point and agreed they make every-thing better. I figured he'd appreciate it after a shitty day. It never occurred to me it was a weird thing to do."

I reached over and caressed the back of his head. "It was sweet."

"But I never thought that it would make Early's husband uncomfortable."

"That's because you were thinking of it as a friend, which is adorable," I told him. "Besides, that's just how Duke is. He has that whole alpha caveman thing going on with Early."

"But it kind of seems like Early is the one actually in control, doesn't it?"

It was impossible not to laugh. "I love that you've known Duke less than a day and you already figured that out. He's all badass dominance on the surface, but inside, he's totally submissive with his husband."

"Fascinating. He doesn't seem the type."

"Early is Duke's entire world," I said. "The sun rises and sets with him. If it will make Early happy, Duke will gladly do anything. His possessive streak is deep, but he never tries to control his husband. His problem is always with the other people he perceives being interested in Early, but never with Early himself. Duke never wants to smother him with his love."

Orion sounded in awe. "That's amazing. They're so in sync with each other."

We pulled into the hotel parking lot, so I refrained from replying to get to the room faster. As soon as the door swung closed, the fiery need from the car came rushing back as our clothes littered the floor. While I had wanted him to take me on the ride home, my desire to show him why no woman could ever pleasure him like I could took over.

I pinned him down on the bed, my arousal hot and heavy against him as I leaned in close to kiss him. "Cherry, I need you so fucking much."

"Anise." His nickname for me sent fire through my veins.

I tore myself away from his plump lips, allowing me to cover him with kisses and touches all over. I took my time driving him wild with lust. He rubbed his hardness against mine in search of more substantial pleasure.

Not content with that, I moved into position to go down on him. I drew his cock deep into my mouth as I sucked on it with enough pressure to make his body arch off the bed. It didn't take much for him to come with a cry. I swallowed it all before ordering in a rough voice, "Turn over."

"Huh?"

"Hands and knees." I helped him move into position.

The sight of him made my dick ache with the need to bury inside his willing body. But I wanted to make sure he understood I was the only one who could satisfy his every need—including ones he didn't know he had.

I spread his cheeks to reveal his dusky hole I wanted to plunder. Taking advantage of the fact he was still pliant after his release, I leaned forward and ran my tongue over his sensitive entrance. He tensed as he made a startled noise, but I didn't let it stop me from dipping my tongue inside his tight pucker to work him open.

"What the fuck is that?" Orion exclaimed in shock.

"Rimming." That was all I said before I resumed teasing his hole with my tongue.

Swears fell from his lips as he hid his face against his forearms. He grew louder the longer I tortured him with teasing flicks. It reduced him to fragmented syllables, his body shaking from the overload.

When I sat back on my haunches, his groan of loss made me smirk. I reached around to pump his returned hardness. "Looks like somebody enjoyed his first rim job."

Orion could only make fractured sounds as he rocked against my hand with a lusty moan. He groaned when I moved away, allowing me to slick my fingers with lube, then plunge them inside him. His body rocked against me as he cried out. Since I had primed him for what was about to happen, I didn't prolong the process.

When I reached for a condom, he stopped me. "No, don't."

Something primal within me purred with antici-pation. "Are you sure?"

He hid his face against his folded forearms. "We're both safe. I want to know what it feels like."

He really was the gift that kept giving. I slicked myself and then pressed my tip against his entrance. Rather than pushing in, I waited until he begged. "Please, Ias!"

That was what I wanted to hear. I took my time sliding into him, relishing his body opening to welcome me. The feeling of his slick heat without the condom filtering the sensations was *incredible*. It took my breath away from how different it was.

Not satisfied with that, he pushed back to force me into him. He almost shouted from being filled, echoed by me from having his tight channel clenching around me. I couldn't restrain myself when he was making such sexy noises, begging for more.

He kept up with my rhythm, sending white heat flaring through me as I took him aggressively. While I had considered slowing down and drawing out his pleasure before speeding up again, I couldn't make myself stop.

Before long, he shuddered as he came a second time with a cry. It drew my orgasm as I pushed in all the way and climaxed with a satisfied growl. When I pulled out, I watched in fascination as some of my cum leaked out of him. It made something in me rampage wildly and wish I could plunge back into him for another round. I loved that it was further proof that he was all mine.

He was shaking from the intensity of his release and the effort of holding himself upright. I took pity on him and helped him roll onto his back before I laid down on top of him. He embraced me as we lazed together, lost in the afterglow, uncaring about the mess we had made. I had everything I wanted in that moment, and nothing else mattered more than the beautiful man embracing me.

Chapter Nineteen

ORION

THE IMPENDING APPROACH of tomorrow suffocated me. It barreled down, eager to steal away the beautiful dream I never wanted to wake up from. Nothing could change the fact that Iason was leaving in the morning to continue on his tour. It meant losing the close connection between us, something that physically pained me. I wasn't ready to give it up yet.

At work, I still had residual soreness from the rough way he had taken me the night before. Rather than hurting, that dull ache made me remember in graphic detail how it had felt when he aggressively claimed me as his. Much to my embarrassment, it kept me on the edge of arousal all day, driving me to jerk off twice in the bathroom to the memories. I had never done that before, but it had been exciting, dangerous, and addictive as hell. I had passed the point of no return, where I could never again go back to how life was before Iason had changed it forever.

As much as I wanted to believe my relationship with him would survive the long-distance test as he finished his tour, I returned to the hotel with a heavy heart after finishing work. I let myself in with the key he had given me, but I stopped dead in my tracks at what I saw.

Iason sat in the center of the bed, leaning back against the headboard while playing his blue guitar that made his eyes the color of an endless summer sky. It was like I had stumbled into a dream as I drank in the sight of him wearing only tight black jeans and a white tank that showed off his toned arms. He crooned a new song, keeping time by moving his right foot, crossed at the ankles as he stretched out his long legs. The way his fingers deftly traveled over the fretboard filled me with longing as I remembered him touching me everywhere.

Rooted to the spot in a trance, I watched his lush lips forming soft words. His rich tenor voice wrapped around me in an intimate caress that left me spellbound. Every note he sang made me harder. When his eyes lifted to meet mine, it sent a wild shock of lust ricocheting through me. All of my earlier troubled thoughts fled to the shadows as he beckoned me closer with an inviting look.

Unable to resist the pull of magnetic attraction, I stumbled over to the bed. It was one thing to hear him singing in front of a crowd, but something totally different from a private concert just for me. His honeyed tone suffused me with warmth, enthralling me with every note. I couldn't process the words because I was too lost in the sound of his voice and the color of his ocean-blue eyes.

Seeing him performing so close was a magical experience. Having Iason privately serenading me in bed was probably the stuff my younger sister's dreams were made of, but it was somehow my real life. I was awash in bliss from hearing his mellifluous voice filling such a small space.

When the song ended, he once again met my gaze. There was a burning look of desire in those blue depths, melting me with their fire. I stiffened when his tongue darted out to lick his lips, then bit his lower one as he smoldered at me. My arousal stirred under his intensity.

"Welcome back, Cherry."

Still tongue-tied, I couldn't respond. It wasn't like I even knew what to say, anyway.

"Do you have any requests?"

Everything in me wanted to reply: *Stay with me.* However, I had no right to make such a request, not to mention it wasn't what he meant. That didn't stop me from wishing I could keep him with me, though.

It was a golden opportunity to hear Iason sing anything, but I suddenly forgot every song in the world. I couldn't find my voice to respond, even as I was aware I needed to speak before the silence became uncomfortable.

Rather than being bothered, he smiled at me. He held out his guitar to me and requested, "Would you please put this back in the case for me?"

"Is it okay?" I wasn't worthy to touch it since it probably cost a fortune.

"Yeah." He gestured for me to take it.

I reverently accepted the guitar, taking it the few steps over to place it in its midnight-blue velvet-lined case. I studied it for a moment, admiring the artistry of the bright ombre shading of the wood. It was the perfect guitar for Iason, matching his bewitching eyes and smooth voice. Not for the first time did I envy it for intimately knowing his touch as his fingers danced over its strings.

I came back to the bedside, where he had moved to the edge and stood up on his knees. He reached out and grabbed my suit lapels to draw me closer. He was almost as tall as me.

"Let me welcome you home, Cherry." His voice was a sensuous murmur as he leaned in to kiss me.

It was sweet and unhurried as he delved deeper for a teasing taste. My arms encircled around him, bringing our bodies together as we continued our gentle exploration of each other's mouths. It filled me with desire, while comforting me at the same time.

"I missed you," he confessed against my lips before initiating another tantalizing kiss.

My heart sang at hearing him say that. I couldn't fathom how he felt that way about me, but it made me happy all the same.

He pushed my suit jacket off my shoulders, and I shrugged out of it, letting it fall to the floor. He used my tie to yank me closer as he looked up at me with fiery passion. "I've wanted you all day." His nimble fingers undid the knot and cast it aside. "So fucking much, Cherry."

"I couldn't stop thinking about being with you." I groaned as he made quick work of my buttons next. He ran his hands in tandem up from my waist, along my chest. He pushed off the shirt to join the rest of my outfit on the floor.

His voice deepened with lust. "Were you remembering how good it felt when I was inside you?"

"Yes." My cheeks grew heated as he undid my belt, tugging it free with a sharp crack of the leather.

Iason's lips curled up into a smirk. "You had to jerk off at work today, didn't you?"

I flushed in embarrassment that he figured out my secret. "How could you possibly know that?"

"Because I had to do the same thing." He cupped my hardness with his hand. "I've been on edge thinking about how much I want you."

It was too much for me to handle. With more boldness than I thought possible, I asked, "How do you want me?"

"Inside me."

How was anyone supposed to resist that invitation?

Chapter Twenty

IASON

AS MUCH AS I wanted to take Orion again, I knew he had to be sore after last night. I didn't want to push him too hard and hurt him, plus I selfishly craved that pleasure of him inside me after torturing myself all day.

"Okay." He didn't resist when I undid the button of his slacks and drew the zipper down so he could kick them off along with his briefs. When he toed off his socks, I relished him being bare before me.

I stroked his erection, growling low in my throat at the thought of it inside me again. "Need you so much, Cherry."

Orion responded by tugging off my tank, chucking it aside with the rest of his clothes. He made an appreciative noise as I laid back on the center of the bed. I raised my hips up enough for him to help strip off my tight jeans, followed by my black briefs.

"You're so beautiful, Anise." There was a dark need in his gray eyes as they roamed over my naked body. He moved into position over me, making me sigh as our bare skin came into contact.

I wrapped my arms around his shoulders as he devoured me in an ardent kiss. He started off dominating but soon calmed into gentleness as he trailed soft kisses down my throat. I tilted my head to give him better access, loving how his tongue licked along the sinewy curve of my neck, before he worshipped the small mole on the ridge of my collarbone.

In contrast to our earlier fevered need, Orion took his time as he worshipped me. His fingers mapped out the paths that his lips and tongue then followed. The passionate, slow burn consumed me as I trembled under his careful attention.

As he moved down, I held my breath in anticipation of what he would do next. He didn't disappoint when he licked along the length of my cock before taking it into his mouth. I swore in shock at his boldness, surprised he wasn't holding anything back as he took me deeper. He worked all kinds of magic on my dick. I wasn't sure how it was possible for someone who had no experience with men to be that skilled at giving head, but I wasn't willing to question it. All I wanted to do was surrender myself to enjoying every moment.

He eased off me and moved down to suck one of my balls into his mouth to tease. I fisted the sheets in my hands, not having expected him to toy with me in such a manner. By the time he switched his efforts to the other one, I was ready to beg for a reprieve.

Thankfully, he didn't torture me for long. He once again went down on me, taking my erection all the way to the back of his throat like he had been doing it for years. I about lost my damn mind when he hummed around me. When he inserted his slicked fingers inside me, I came in his mouth with a prolonged moan of satisfaction.

As he swallowed my release without complaint, I wondered how the hell I got so lucky.

"You prepared yourself already?" Orion asked in amusement.

"I didn't want any delays because I need you now."

He withdrew his fingers and wiped them clean on the sheets. "Fuck, that's so sexy."

I spread my legs wider apart to welcome him into my body as he pushed in deep. As he filled me, I whimpered at the perfection of our bodies joining as one with no barriers between us. It was everything I had longed for since he had left for work earlier that morning. Despite already coming, I was greedy for more. It would never be enough with him.

While I had spent most of the day fantasizing about Orion taking me hard and fast like he had the other night, he surprised me by continuing his reverent worship. Instead of fucking me with aggressive need, he made slow, sweet love to me. It satisfied me in a different way.

The buildup of pleasure was gradual as he rocked into me, with each pump of his hips claiming me with gentleness. I braced my hands on his shoulders, loving how his muscles moved under my fingertips. I wrapped my legs around his waist to embrace him completely, crying out when it allowed him to go even deeper at the new angle.

When he leaned down to capture my lips in a tender kiss, I fell in love with Orion all over again. My arousal returned, spurred on by the way he lovingly made me his with every thrust. I lost myself in him as we whispered our nicknames for each other, the quietness of our coupling rendering it even more intimate than normal.

His teasing touch on my cock made my whole body jerk from the overload as he worked it in time with his rhythm. It didn't take much before I climaxed again.

It drew his release as well, making me moan as he came inside me. I couldn't get enough of the feeling of his cum inside me. I felt even closer to him when I could feel his release inside me.

As I whispered how much I loved him, he leaned forward and gave me the sweetest kiss of my life. It overwhelmed me with a myriad of powerful emotions. I didn't care if I had fallen for him hard and fast. All I knew beyond any doubt was that I adored him.

I hated feeling Orion pull out of me when all I wanted was to stay as one with him. But the feeling of his cum seeping out of me was deeply arousing. I held my arms open to him for him to lie down on me. He did so without protest, snuggling close to me as I embraced him. We didn't care about the mess we had made. I nuzzled against him with a kiss on the forehead.

We remained in silence for some time, lost in our thoughts after our intense climaxes. It surprised me when he was the first to speak. "I never want this moment to end."

"Just because I leave tomorrow morning doesn't mean this ends, Cherry." I held him tighter to reassure him. "We're only getting started."

"I don't know how to go back to the way things were before I met you," he admitted in a pained voice. "I don't *want* to."

"You don't have to. We'll see each other for the next two weekends, then after that, I'll be back before you can miss me."

Orion simultaneously broke my heart and made me happy when he said, "I miss you already and you haven't even left yet."

"I feel the same way." Trying to keep him calm, I caressed him with soothing touches. "But we've still got all night and tomorrow morning, then the next two weekends."

He nodded in response, but we lapsed into

thoughtful silence. It came as a surprise to hear him say, "I'll never understand why you picked me out of everybody in that room, but I'm glad you did."

I smiled at his words, kissing his forehead again since that was the closest part of him I could reach. "I'm also grateful you gave me a chance despite it all."

He made a cute noise as he cuddled closer to me. I loved the hot flush of his cheek against my shoulder. We'd eventually need to get cleaned up, but for the moment, I continued basking in our closeness as I held him tight.

LEAVING Orion the next morning was one of the hardest things I had ever done. It was torture having to separate from him, although it was only for a single night.

I texted him as Dylan drove to San Francisco and made fun of me for it. But all I cared about was that Orion didn't think I had abandoned him. I wanted him to understand I was there with him, even if I couldn't physically be next to him because I had to continue my tour.

Once we reached the venue, it was time to focus on rehearsals for the concert the following night. It felt great to reunite with my friends who made up my touring band, although they immediately began busting my balls.

"So, what's this I hear about you falling in love, Ias?" Levi asked as he stretched his long legs out on the couch in the group dressing room. He was my childhood friend who had always stayed with me through thick and thin. His easygoing personality and good looks had won him a legion of fans as my drummer. As usual, he wore ripped jeans and an old tour T-shirt from the band Four Princes. "We were only gone a week!"

"Yeah, what happened to all your claims about how you don't do love?" Sal asked with a laugh. He was a talented keyboardist and a smart-ass who was as skeptical about true love as I had been until I met Orion. He wore a green T-shirt and jeans. "Am I the last cynic left now?"

"Maybe it's time for you to grow up, too," Ferris told Sal with a snicker. He was my bass guitarist who was the most stylishly dressed. It was twice as surprising since he was the only straight one in the band. "There's nothing wrong with believing in love."

Tiago slung his arm over Ferris's shoulder as he pretended to cuddle with him. He was my rhythm guitarist, who was dressed in badass leather like Duke. "Love's everywhere, if you know where to look for it." He pretended to make a kissy face at his best friend.

Ferris snickered as he playfully pushed Tiago's head away from him. "If you're ready to fall in love with me, you've been single for way too long."

"It's perfectly natural for a friend to help a friend

when it gets lonely on tour." Tiago gave him a flirty wink that made us all laugh at their familiar antics. He was never deterred by Ferris's heterosexuality.

Ferris's grin was smug as he taunted him. "One of these days, I'll say yes to you, and you won't know what to do."

"Oh, I can promise you that I know *exactly* what to do with you," Tiago purred, sending a shiver through Ferris.

Levi got us back on track. "Come on, don't leave us hanging. Tell us everything so I don't have to bug Duke for details. That dude scares me sometimes."

I laughed at that. "He scares everyone most of the time."

"That's because he's intimidating as hell," Sal muttered. He wasn't Duke's biggest fan.

It was time to catch the band up on what had happened. "I fell in love with a sweetheart at my live performance at Duke's bar. His name is Orion, and he's literally made of wishes on stars. He's everything I never thought I could find."

Levi seemed impressed. "Huh, so Kieran and Rook weren't just talking out of their asses about asking the cosmic universe to send you Mr. Right? Wow."

"Trust me, no one is more surprised than me." I shook my head in disbelief. "But he's amazing, and you can meet him tomorrow after the concert when he comes backstage. I expect you all to be on your best behavior. Try not to scare off the best thing that's ever happened to me, okay?"

My friend grinned at me. "I mean, we have to bust your balls at least a *little* when we meet him."

"His younger sister, who is a huge fan of mine, will be with him. She doesn't know yet, so I'd appreciate you not exposing our secret before he's talked to her about it." I wasn't sure when Orion was planning on telling Lyra, but I hoped it would be soon. Lying to her was uncomfortable.

"Don't worry, we'll keep your secret," Ferris said. "But man, that's gotta be awkward with her being a fan? She'll probably be hella jealous when she finds out brother dearest is with you."

I could only imagine her dramatic reaction to the news. Hopefully, it wouldn't scare Orion away from dating me. "We'll cross the bridge once we get to it. A little restraint would be appreciated, though."

Tiago gave me a reassuring smile. "No worries. We've got your back, man."

"So, has he survived meeting Duke yet, or are you saving that nightmare for once you're more secure in your relationship?" Sal asked.

I had to laugh at that. "Yes, Orion survived meeting Duke. You guys should be a cakewalk in comparison, provided you don't give him too much shit for having a big enough heart to love me."

Levi reached over to clasp me on the shoulder with a squeeze. "Hey, I think it's great you finally found a muse for your love songs. And if he survived Duke, then he's a keeper. You've got nothing to worry about."

"When the tour's over, I'm planning on moving back to Sunnyside to be with him."

Tiago gave an impressed whistle. "Damn, you move fast. Are you sure that won't scare him off that you're coming on too strong?"

"Not really. I've wanted to move back for a while, so he gave me a reason to speed up that process. It may seem fast, but it's the perfect pace for us."

Dylan came into the room as she clapped her hands to get our attention. "As fun as this little gossip session is, you boys need to rehearse."

"Aww, but we're not done teasing Ias about his new sweetheart," Levi complained with a theatrical groan that earned him an eye roll from my long-suffering manager.

"Save it for afterward." She gestured for us to move toward the stage, where our gear was setup for practice.

My band members followed behind her as she led them away. Levi hung back to stop me for a moment. He looked down at me with a warm smile. "I'm thrilled for you, Ias. I can't wait to meet him."

"You'll love him."

"I'm sure I will. He has to be incredible to melt your heart." He squeezed my shoulder. "We'll talk more after we finish. And you better not leave out a single detail. I want to hear exactly how much Duke flipped out when you told him."

"You won't be disappointed." I chuckled at how he knew Duke well enough to understand what his reaction would be. "Thanks, Levi."

"Anytime."

I headed to rehearsal with a bounce in my step. Practicing our set would bring me that much closer to having Orion back in my arms once more.

Chapter Twenty-One

ORION

ALTHOUGH WE HAD ONLY SPENT one night apart, I hated it. Being alone in bed made my time with Iason feel like a distant dream. I longed to fall asleep in his arms again after the most satisfying sex of my life. With distance between us, it was too easy for the doubts to creep in. If it weren't for the residual soreness of my muscles reminding me of the incredible intimacy we had experienced, it would be hard to trust my own memories.

On the way to San Francisco, Lyra practically vibrated with excitement. I identified with her unbridled joy a little too much for comfort. It had only been twenty-four hours since we parted, but I couldn't wait to see him again. While I wanted to hear his amazing voice in concert, what I really needed was private time away from my sister to reacquaint myself with every inch of Iason's body.

It would be a challenge to mask my true feelings for him around her. I hoped he wouldn't be too overt in his interest in me. It would be awful to have the weekend ruined by Lyra discovering Iason and I were together. We would have to tell her at some point, but I intended to put it off as long as possible. I wasn't ready for my younger sister to hate me yet.

Her voice broke through my thoughts as we entered the amphitheater. "Seriously, thank you *so* much, Rion! You're the best brother ever!"

She wouldn't think that if she knew I would sneak into Iason's hotel room after the concert for some mind-blowing sex later. Rather than addressing that, I told her, "I'm glad we could come here today." Talk about epic understatements.

"Our seats are incredible!" Lyra squealed as we sat down in the center of the front row. She pulled out her phone and started taking pictures of the stage to send to her friends. "We're so close he could sweat on me!"

I laughed at her comment, even as an image flashed in my mind of licking a bead of sweat off Iason's neck in the middle of sex as he arched under me while I thrust into him. It made me shift uncomfortably in my seat. "Yeah."

As Lyra continued her fangirl rambling about seeing Iason again, I turned around to check out the rest of the space. Whereas the Hurly-burly Bar and Grille we saw him perform at in Sunnyside was a small and intimate setting, the amphitheater could seat over ten thousand people. It was impressive when I knew how fast the show had sold out two nights at the venue.

As the crowd started filing in, the din of chatter grew louder. There was a palpable excitement in the air. My heart hammered in anticipation of seeing Iason appear onstage. While I was eager to see him alone offstage, the fan part of me couldn't wait to watch him perform right in front of me.

When the lights dimmed to signify the concert would start in five minutes, the crowd murmur grew louder. It was easy to get caught up in the moment, especially because it had been a few years since I had seen him live at such a big venue.

Before his performance started, his opening act came out first. Mirror Mirror was a band featuring two identical female twins, one who played acoustic guitar while the other used an electric guitar. Their sound was different from Iason's, but I enjoyed the blending harmonies of their alto and soprano voices. However, I was too anxious for Iason to appear to appreciate their performance. I glanced over at my sister, surprised to see her mouthing the words to the moody song the twins played.

After almost forty-five minutes, the twins took their final bows before the curtain fell. A half-hour intermission was announced to reset the stage for Iason's band. Lyra's gushing over Mirror Mirror's performance provided a sufficient distraction, but I grew antsy for the concert to begin.

When the lights lowered, a hush descended over the audience. Everyone held their breath in anticipation of Iason's arrival. My heart rate rocketed up, knowing he was about to appear.

It felt like forever before the curtain went up, revealing the band at their instruments. The world disappeared the instant Iason stepped onstage. He was gorgeous in tight jeans, a white T-shirt, and a black jacket accentuated with decorative silver and gold zippers.

The crowd erupted into wild noise. My sister's ear-piercing screech made me wince as it joined the chorus of the audience losing their minds when Iason waved.

As he approached the center of the stage, our eyes met for a moment, causing my heart to stutter at his small smile meant only for me. It was further confirmation that what had happened was real.

He picked up his blue ombre guitar from the stand and slid on the navy leather strap. The man looked like a god, lording over everyone with perfection. I wanted to bow down and worship him.

"Are you ready to have a good time tonight, San Francisco?" Iason asked the audience, strumming chords on his guitar to check the sound.

A cacophonous roar answered him, making him

grin at the response. I wondered how he could get used to over ten thousand people screaming at him.

"Then let's get started." The random chords morphed into his current single, "In My Arms."

As Iason sang, an awed silence fell over the audience as he captivated everyone with the sound of his voice, which filled the enormous theatre. It washed over me like a physical caress on my body. I wanted to lose myself in the experience, but I was very conscious of Lyra beside me. The last thing I wanted was to get an erection while sitting next to my sister, but he was making it a serious challenge. Watching him performing in his full glory onstage was incredible. He seemed so much larger than life, making it almost impossible to believe that he was my boyfriend for real.

I was lulled into a trance by Iason's magical voice; he hypnotized me with the way his fingers danced over the guitar strings. I watched his lush lips forming such beautiful words, then longed to feel them covering every inch of me in kisses again. Those were dangerous thoughts when his sensuous voice teased me into arousal.

It took a monumental effort to tear my eyes off Iason long enough to glance over at Lyra. She stared up at him like he was her entire world, silently singing along with him. I realized there was no room in her mind at that moment for anything that wasn't him. Since she wasn't paying a single iota of attention to me, I let myself embrace listening to his incredible voice. I could only hope that I didn't look up at him as openly lovestruck as her.

Hearing Iason backed up by the other musicians was a much different experience than seeing him playing alone at the bar. It drove home the fact that he was a famous star, which I kept forgetting somehow. He wasn't just my Anise—he was the global musical phenomenon, Iason Leyland. Although he was mere feet from me, he had never felt further away.

The bassist supplied backing vocals, harmonizing with Iason. They sounded good together, but the bass guitarist didn't have that same smoky smoothness of Iason's dulcet tenor that caressed your soul.

He paused after a few songs to take a drink of water and start talking to the audience during his break. "Thanks for the warm welcome." His words set off a sonic boom of girlish shrieks. He grinned at the reaction. "I've been looking forward to performing here all week, so I appreciate you coming out to join me this evening."

Iason drank again, somehow making the act of swallowing look sensual. Why did everything about him scream sex? He capped the water bottle and set it aside, then began introductions. "I want to thank my amazing band for being here tonight. Sal is rocking it on keyboard. Tiago and Ferris are on guitar and bass with backing vocals. And as always, my man Levi is making magic happen on the drums. Let's give it up for them!"

The crowd applauded and cheered as Iason also clapped for his band members. It was a welcome reprieve, because despite only being a few songs into the concert, I was already hot and bothered thanks to his sensuous performance.

When the applause died down, he began speaking again. "It's amazing how music can take you back to those special moments in your life, isn't it? This next song has a special place in my heart, because it reminds me of the best first date I've ever been on. We'll just ignore the part about this song being about heartbreak." He laughed at his own joke.

It made my soul ache because he had such a beautiful smile on his face. I wondered who he was referring to. Despite feeling a little jealous, I did my best to push it aside. I was aware he had a past, so I kept telling myself that the present was more important. He was mine now, and that was all that mattered.

"This is Jeff Buckley's 'Last Goodbye,' so enjoy." They began playing the song's intro.

My heart thudded hard as I stared up at him in disbelief. Was he talking about me? I would never forget him singing along to that song in my car on the way back to my place after dinner that first night, but Iason couldn't possibly mean me, right? On what planet was it possible that *our* first date was his favorite? I hadn't known we were on a date!

He winked at me, leaving no doubt in my mind he meant me. Hearing him crooning along in my car under his breath was one thing. Him singing it in earnest was something else entirely.

I forgot how to breathe, how to think, how to do anything other than experience every note he sang on an intimate level. When he tossed his head back and opened up his huge voice on the big climax of the song, I almost lost the battle against my body. I experienced the fullness of Iason's voice with the entirety of my being, leaving me trembling and on the brink of release.

When the last note faded, everyone burst into applause and cheers, but I couldn't react. It was too much for me to handle—*especially* knowing he sang that song because of me. His eyes met mine, causing the theatre and crowd to disappear, leaving only us. He smiled just for me, making me swoon.

Iason lifted his gaze to stare out over the audience, allowing me to gasp for air. I hadn't realized I had been holding my breath until that moment. They began playing another one of Iason's songs, but I was still lost in hearing the echo inside my soul of him singing "Last Goodbye" just for me. It suffused me with warmth, serving as further proof that he treasured me in a way nobody ever had before.

He played a single off his last album, pulling me from my thoughts as I got caught up in listening to him. I was still on the brink of embarrassing myself from my body's intense reaction to him. While I had always had sensitive hearing and had been to concerts before, no one's voice had ever affected me on such a sexually stimulating level before.

Now, his voice intimately penetrated me, with every rise and fall of his vocalization a satisfying thrust. The desire pent-up inside me became more unbearable with each song he sang. How would I make it back to the hotel without coming first?

I lost myself in the experience of being surrounded by Iason's magnificent voice, which filled the enormous theatre space with its fullness. I forgot about everything that wasn't him as I let him carry me away with his music.

All too soon, he announced they were doing the last song for the evening. They performed my favorite one, "Midnight Magic." It pushed me to the very edge of my limits, but I reminded myself about my sister's presence to curb my raging desires Iason stoked with every note he sang.

As soon as it was over, everyone jumped to their feet in a raucous standing ovation. I subtly adjusted myself as best I could while applauding with everyone until Iason and the band left the stage. Once they were offstage, the audience chanted Iason's name, begging for an encore. It seemed to last forever before he came out by himself, a big grin on his face.

He picked up his guitar once more, sitting on the

tall chair and bringing his mic closer to adjust it to the change in position. "And so we meet again."

The crowd roared, with many catcalls sounding from the audience. While strumming the strings, he coyly asked, "Did you miss me?"

Several women shouted at the top of their lungs, "I love you, Iason!"

He chuckled at the reaction. "I love you, too!"

That triggered more fevered screams from the ladies. The surreal experience reiterated to me exactly who Iason was. How did a man who was famous enough to have anyone he wanted choose *me*?

"As you all know, I enjoy sharing a special song for my encores. This next one is new, but it's very near and dear to me." He strummed a random melody I didn't recognize. "It's about the magic that brings us someone to love."

I didn't know if my brain was slow to process his words because of my lusty haze, but he wasn't talking about me again…was he?

He fell silent, still playing idle chords. It made me wonder if it was something he did when he was anxious. But why would a pro like him be nervous?

"We should all be so lucky to find that person who gives us the words to our incomplete melodies." The corner of his mouth turned up with the faintest trace of a smile. He was so beautiful in that moment, but there was a vulnerableness there I wasn't used to seeing. I wanted to do anything to soothe away those unspoken worries.

"Hold on to that person who knows how to make your soul sing." My breathing hitched in my throat when our gazes met. "This is called 'Wishes on Stars.' It's dedicated to the person who gave new meaning to my words."

The random sounds Iason played changed into the song he claimed he wrote for me the night we met. It sounded more soulful tonight, filled with a longing that made me want to hug him in comfort. I felt it on a new level as the lyrics resonated within me.

I had given up hope,
Had made myself believe
That love wasn't possible
For people like me.

But then I met you,
My impossible love,
Made of wishes on stars,
And all my hopes and dreams.

I had been incredulous the first time I heard the song, but now I wondered if maybe the lyrics meant more than I could have imagined. It stunned me to realize how much had changed in the week since I had met him and had my whole life turned upside down.

When he finished, the crowd gave an enthusiastic standing ovation. He thanked everyone again as he took his final bows, making my heart leap into my throat when our eyes locked. The moment ended when he walked offstage for good.

The clapping continued like an echoing boom before it petered out as people began leaving. I dropped into my seat, trembling from the overwhelming experience. It startled me when Lyra hid her face against my shoulder and squealed, "Oh. My. *God*! That was *so awesome*!"

"Yeah," I agreed, my voice shaking from how affected I was by the concert.

She stared at me with wide eyes. "How is this real? How is this actually happening, Rion?"

"I have no idea." It was an impossible question to answer when I found it unbelievable that the man we had watched perform was my secret boyfriend.

"Did you see when he looked right at me and smiled? He winked at me! I have to be dreaming!"

It fascinated me that like Nyla, Lyra assumed those looks meant for me were aimed at her. I wasn't risking the fallout from correcting her. Maybe she would be so lost in her joy that she would pay less attention to how Iason and I interacted backstage.

She continued rambling a mile a minute about how incredible the concert was, and I tried my best to keep up with her. It was challenging considering I could still feel Iason's voice intimately filling the cracked places inside my soul. Combined with knowing we were going to be meeting him in a few minutes, I didn't know how I would handle it. I touched the backs of my fingers to my cheeks, embarrassed by how flushed they were from the experience.

Dylan appeared with a wave. "Hey, guys! Did you enjoy the concert?"

I let Lyra's enthusiastic screech speak for both of us.

The manager laughed at the reaction. "I'm so glad! Ready to go backstage?"

Once again, Lyra's shrill response was enough of an answer. I wasn't quite up to forming words yet.

My body reacted on autopilot as I followed Dylan and my sister backstage. Nervousness overtook my desire. What if it was weird between me and Iason? We had only spent a day apart, but I didn't know what would happen with Lyra being present. Was I supposed to treat him like he was a stranger? He had been to our house for dinner, so maybe it wouldn't be strange if I was friendly with him? But what if I was *too* friendly and Lyra figured everything out?

Dylan led us over to where Iason was talking with his band members. The group had such a natural chemistry that it made me wonder how long they had known each other. My sister probably knew the answer.

Iason's face lit up with a beautiful smile when he

saw us. How was he real? "I'm so glad you both made it tonight! Did you enjoy the show?"

"It was the best!" Lyra bounced from her uncontrollable excitement. "I can't believe we were *front row center*! My friends are dying of jealousy!"

"Nothing but the best for you," he replied, but his eyes were on me when he said it. His words sent heat flaring through me.

Surrounded by the band, I felt shy. "Thank you for tonight." It was an epic understatement, but it was the best I could say at the moment without throwing myself at Iason and making out with him like there was no tomorrow. It was so hard to resist when his plump lips were made for kissing.

Iason's pleased smile caused my heart to flutter. He was so beautiful inside and out. How did I get so lucky?

He made introductions. "Guys, meet Sal, Tiago, Ferris, and Levi. Everyone, this is Orion and Lyra, who I told you about from Sunnyside."

We all shook hands, but Lyra held on to Levi's hand as she emphatically said, "Thank you!"

He grinned at my sister's antics. "I'm glad you had a good time tonight."

"I also meant thank you for taking Iason to that open mic night," Lyra clarified, causing Levi's eyebrows to raise. "It's because of your help that he became my favorite singer!"

I marveled at how my sister could say such a thing

without any trace of embarrassment. It also was further proof that her level of fan knowledge was almost scary in its thoroughness.

Levi chuckled at the reaction. "While I'm sure Ias would have been discovered on his own, I'm fine with taking credit for his success. It's nice to be appreciated, thanks."

Lyra talked with the band like they were all old friends, rather than this being the first time they had ever met. It impressed me as I observed, not sure what I could contribute to the conversation. It didn't help that I kept catching Iason looking at me with his expressive blue eyes. Breathing became a challenge as my heart continued doing strange things in my chest. I had to look away, fearing my sister would notice our tension. Thank god me being silently awkward wasn't unusual behavior.

Dylan came back over with an apologetic expression. "I'm so sorry to interrupt, guys. Lyra, could I ask you for a huge favor?"

"Sure, what's up?"

"Some of our street team couldn't come tonight, so we're short-handed at the merch tables right now," Dylan said. "Since you were such a tremendous help in Sunnyside at the show, would you mind assisting us? I normally wouldn't ask, but we're *really* swamped out there."

"Of course! Wait, is it okay, Rion?"

I looked over at Iason, whose lips were pursed as

if he was trying hard to suppress a grin. Something told me he had a hand in orchestrating the supposed emergency. I told my sister with a shrug, "Sure, I don't mind if you want to help."

Dylan sighed in relief. "You are *such* a lifesaver, Lyra!" She then led my sister away, leaving me alone with Iason and the band, but not before she winked at us over her shoulder.

"That's our cue," Iason announced with a cheeky grin, taking my hand and pulling me toward him. It felt like sparks igniting deep inside me at feeling his touch again. "If you'll excuse us, we have some *very* important things we need to discuss privately."

The band snickered, but I was too turned on to care as I let him lead me to his dressing room.

Chapter Twenty-Two

IASON

AS SOON AS the door shut and locked behind us, I pinned Orion against it. I leaned forward, intent on capturing his lips in a passionate kiss. To my surprise, he shoved at my chest to rebuff my advance. "No, stop, stop, stop."

Being refused hurt, but I was more concerned by the reaction. Did seeing me perform cause a problem for him? Was he worried about his sister discovering us? Rather than trying to guess, I asked in a gentle voice, "What's wrong?"

He fisted my shirt in his hand with a pained groan. "I'm too close. We *can't*."

A grin pulled at my lips. "But you want to."

"Of course I *want* to, but we——"

That was all I needed to hear. I dropped to my knees in front of him, undoing the button of his jeans to pull down the zipper.

"Shit, we *can't*." He pushed at my shoulders to drive me back.

"The door's locked, remember?" I yanked down his pants and briefs. It freed his glorious erection, which was glistening with precum and begging me for relief.

While the sadist in me wanted to prolong teasing Orion, I was more interested in making him feel good. I moved forward and took his hardness into my mouth, relaxing my jaw to let him slide in deeper. All it took was for me to moan around his length and apply the slightest suction for him to shoot down my throat with a groan.

I swallowed his release, then rested on my heels with a smirk. He sank to the floor with a whimper, hiding his face against his arms folded over his knees. He was too miserable for someone who had just gotten off.

"Talk to me, Cherry. Tell me what's going through that mind of yours."

His words were muffled when he spoke. "This is *so* humiliating."

"What is?"

He made a pained noise. "I came in like five seconds. It's *embarrassing*."

"Actually—"

Orion gave me a fierce glare, which turned me on more than it should have. "So help me, if you say it was actually three seconds, I'm not visiting your room tonight."

"You have my word that wasn't what I was going to say. I was only going to point out that it wasn't a few seconds. You endured over two hours of vocal foreplay without making a mess of your pants, so if anything, I'm impressed at your stamina."

He grinned at me. "You made it a serious challenge. Your concert was *so* good. You were incredible, Iason. Tonight was…*wow*."

I found it interesting that Orion was using my full first name, but I didn't comment on it. "Did you enjoy your Jeff Buckley surprise?"

"*So* much. Although, it was news to me that was our first date." His reaction was adorable.

"I wasn't lying when I said it was my favorite first date. Every date with you has been the best, Cherry."

He looked overwhelmed and awed by my words. "How did I get so lucky?"

"Because you're the best." It was too much temptation to resist, so I claimed the kiss I had been craving since the moment I stepped on stage and saw him in the audience.

Orion didn't pull away from me. He whimpered when I slid my tongue into his mouth, letting him taste himself. Our kiss grew more heated, but he pulled back with a groan. "Quit torturing us, damn it!"

"We still have time and a locked door," I

reminded him again with a cheeky grin. "I told Dylan to keep Lyra occupied as long as she could plausibly get away with it."

His laughter was music to my ears. "I *knew* you had something to do with that!" Thankfully, he seemed amused rather than annoyed at my deliberate interference.

"I'd do anything to be with you."

I felt victorious when he bit his lower lip as if trying to restrain himself from kissing me again. Everything in me ached for him, but I didn't want to push him further than he was comfortable with. And contrary to my claims, Lyra's return would interrupt us far sooner than we wanted.

He ruefully shook his head. "Out of everybody in that theatre, why am I the lucky one?"

That was an easy answer. "Because you're the only person I love. You're you, and that means everything to me."

His beautiful smile moved my heart. "Hearing everyone screaming for you was downright surreal. Everybody in there wants you, but I'm the one who gets to be with you tonight—provided my sister falls asleep."

"Are you afraid she'll pull an all-nighter?" I hoped like hell that wouldn't happen. We had arranged it so Orion would stay in the same hotel as me, allowing him to sneak up to my room while Lyra was unaware.

I needed him to visit me so I could indulge in him without restraint.

He shook his head. "No, but I'm worried she'll be so excited that she won't sleep until it's too late for me to sneak out."

"Should I tell her to go to bed early tonight so I can visit her in her dreams?" I stood up and held my hand out to him.

"Please don't make me think about my sister having sex dreams about my boyfriend." He looked horrified, but he accepted my help to get off the floor. He pulled up his pants and briefs, arranging himself to decency.

After he finished, I wrapped an arm around Orion's waist to draw him into a tight embrace. I nuzzled against him to murmur next to his ear, "I love when you call me your boyfriend."

"I keep hoping if I say it enough times that I'll eventually believe it."

He was too precious for words. I captured his lips in a demanding kiss, further stoking my lust for him. The way he surrendered to my desires was downright intoxicating. I wanted all of him and more.

Orion stunned me by cupping his hand around my arousal. He looked up at me with wide eyes. "Should I…?"

That was a sinful temptation that was almost too much for me to resist. "We don't have the time right now for how I want to worship every inch of you." I loved the way my words caused him to swallow hard. "After making you survive so much sexy torture, it's only fair that I get a taste of my own medicine."

"Are you sure?"

I covered his hand with my own, cupping it against my hardness. "Don't misunderstand me. I'd love nothing more than to bend you over that vanity and watch in the mirror as I fuck you until your voice gave out from crying my name."

He caressed my cock in response as he keened with lust.

"But I don't trust myself to stop even if your sister walked in. I'm resisting every instinct that is begging me to take you soft and slow, then hard and fast, until neither of us has the strength to move." My voice was almost a feral growl from my dark need for Orion.

He crushed his lips against mine as he backed me up against the door. It tested the limits of my willpower.

While I wanted to let him have his way, we were running out of time. I should have stopped him, but I couldn't pull away from the rare show of aggressive need as he dominated me with rough kisses. When his hands slid under my shirt to caress my bare skin, I groped his ass hard.

A sharp knock caused us to freeze.

"Dylan texted she's walking back with Lyra now," Levi announced. "You better make yourselves decent ASAP."

"Damn it!" Orion made a frustrated noise, resting his forehead against my chest as he tried to calm himself.

"I don't care how late it is, please come to my room no matter what," I pleaded in a hushed tone. I didn't want him to talk himself out of coming if Lyra stayed up past the wee hours of the morning.

"I promise." He stole a last kiss, which had an edge of desperation to it.

It was hell prying ourselves apart, but I did the right thing and forced him back a few steps. I rearranged myself to disguise the fact that I was still hard and wanting. Only then did I open the door, revealing Levi waiting with a knowing smirk.

Countless smart-ass retorts popped into my mind. However, I restrained myself to saying, "Thanks."

Orion sat on the couch, but I remained standing by the vanity, resting my ass against it with one leg crossed in front of me. I got a stick of gum as I tried to will my body to calm itself.

Levi grinned at me as he walked over. "Real subtle, Ias."

"I don't know what you're talking about."

"Sure you don't." He snorted with amusement.

I blew a bubble at him and popped it in response, making him laugh.

He turned his attention to Orion. "Your sister is a trip."

"I'm sorry if she overstepped earlier," he apologized, concern on his face. "She's just a huge fan."

"I meant it as a compliment. But wow, that must make shit really awkward considering you and Ias—"

"Levi," I addressed him in reproach, not wanting him to get into it when Lyra might be within earshot. I had explained our situation to him earlier, but sometimes he got a little carried away without meaning to.

He held his hands up in surrender. "Sorry, that wasn't what I meant to say. You know I'm excited for you, man."

Before the conversation continued, Lyra came bounding into the room. Orion's concerns about her being too excited to sleep became an understandable fear. "Sorry that took so long. There were *so* many fans out there! It was amazing!"

"Thanks again for being willing to help out." I appreciated her effort, even if I had manipulated the situation to steal some much-needed alone time with her older brother.

She looked at me with all the love in her fangirl heart on full display. "I would do anything for you, Iason!"

Levi snorted in amusement, covering it with a cough when I shot him a warning look. Old friend or not, I didn't want him causing problems between me, Orion, and Lyra. We would cross that bridge once we came to it.

I gave her a soft smile. "I appreciate that." The

simple action made her radiate joy like the star she was named after. "As a thank-you, I'd love it if you guys came to my LA show next week."

I didn't expect Lyra's crestfallen expression or her anguished tone. "I'm so sorry, we can't go. I have a stupid gymnastics meet in North Carolina that I can't get out of. Unless I tell Mom that I sprained my ankle or—"

"You can't do that." Orion's eyebrows furrowed in frustration at the unexpected roadblock thrown between us being together.

She scowled. "Even if I did, they'd make me attend to support the team, so it wouldn't work, anyway. Damn it, this sucks! Out of all the days of the year, why did they have to choose next weekend for the national finals? I want to go to LA to see you again!"

"Maybe next time," I offered, although it did little to help the situation.

"Wait, Rion could still go, though!" She brightened at the prospect as she gave her older brother a pleading gaze. "If you go, you can tell me everything about it!"

A weekend alone with Orion? That was even better than I had hoped. "If he comes, I'd be happy to give him a recording of the concert to bring home for you to enjoy the show."

She clasped her hands together as she gazed at me with stars in her eyes. "You would do that for me?"

"Of course." It was a small price to pay for a glorious weekend alone with him. I smiled at her, making her swoon hard before she turned to beg her brother.

"Please, Rion, now you *have* to go! I know it's kind of far away to go by yourself, but——"

He held up his hand to cut her off. "I'll go for your sake."

She launched herself at him with a delighted squeal. "You're the best! Thank you for going to see him for me! It's almost as good as me getting to go myself. Oh, you know what you should do?"

Orion's expression grew wary. "What?"

"You should hang out with Iason afterward and then tell me *everything*!" She turned her hopeful gaze to me once more. "That would be amazing!"

I tried not to let my giddiness show on my face. "We could arrange that." Her suggestion also made me wonder if she was more astute than I had expected. Did she suspect that there was something between me and her older brother? Was it her weird attempt at trying to set us up?

As she continued squealing with fangirl delight, Levi had to smother his grin behind his hand as he watched her antics. Mercifully, he didn't blow our cover.

While I didn't want Orion to leave, I forced the issue. "It's been such a long day for you both coming out here after school and work. You guys probably should head to the hotel to rest."

"I don't know how I'll ever sleep again!" Lyra exclaimed with a laugh. "Tonight was the most amazing night *of my life!*"

"I'll make sure tomorrow is even better." I figured it was worth taking a shot at influencing her bedtime. "You should sleep so you're ready to enjoy it to the fullest."

"It's like trying to sleep before Christmas!" Her girlish giggles were infectious.

"True, but everyone knows that the best part of sleeping on Christmas Eve is that it makes Christmas Day come faster," Levi pointed out. I could have hugged him for that.

"I'm sure when the adrenaline crashes, you'll pass out," Orion said.

She grinned. "Yeah, you're right."

"No matter what time you fall asleep, you'll still complain when I try to wake you up for breakfast." His voice had the weariness only an older brother could possess.

"You're just as bad as me!" Lyra protested, but her amusement was clear. "Maybe even worse!"

I had to cover my mouth with my hand to hide my grin at her words and the fact that Orion's cheeks flushed again when our gazes met. He slept like the dead, and waking him up took a herculean effort, so she wasn't wrong. I had no problem persisting in getting him to wake up for sexy times, though. As he shifted on the couch, I knew he was thinking of the same thing.

"He's right. We should go so that they can finish up and get back to their hotel, too," Orion suggested. "It's been a long day for everyone."

It was hard to not give him a look that promised his night was going to be longer still. "I'm glad you guys came out tonight. I'll see you tomorrow after the show."

"I can't wait!" Lyra exclaimed, clasping her hands together like she was praying. "There aren't enough words to thank you, Iason!"

"Have a good night." I couldn't stop my eyes from drifting over to her brother. "I'll see you later."

Orion got off the couch and ushered Lyra out of my dressing room. When he glanced over his shoulder for a last look at me, I blew him a kiss. His happy grin made my heart sing, even as I ached watching him walk away from me.

Once they left, Levi waited a few moments to let them get out of earshot before speaking. "Damn, Duke was right. You are like stupid in love with this guy."

He had become friends with Duke when we were at Sunnyside University together, so they kept in touch. Somehow, I wasn't surprised that Duke had told Levi how serious I was about Orion. I grinned at the undeniable accusation. "Truly madly deeply," I agreed, referencing a Savage Garden song I loved.

"Oh, you should sing that tomorrow," Levi suggested. "We haven't done that one in a while. It seems appropriate now."

The idea excited me, although I wasn't sure if Orion liked the song. Something told me he would, though. "Yeah, let's run it in rehearsal in the morning and see how it goes. We can swap it out for the Jeff Buckley one we did tonight."

Levi grinned at me with realization. "Which you did for him."

"Guilty as charged." The shocked awe on Orion's face as I sang it was what I had hoped for, and more.

Sal came over and knocked on the open door. "Hey, ready to go?"

Levi got off the couch and pulled him into a hug. "Are you that eager to be with me?"

The joking question earned him an eye roll from Sal. "Eager to get away from you, maybe." He grinned at their familiar banter.

As they continued their playful bickering, I smiled to myself as I left. I couldn't wait for the rest of my night once Orion came to my room. I looked forward to showing him exactly how much I loved him.

Chapter Twenty-Three

ORION

IT WAS agonizing waiting for my sister to fall asleep after the concert. But she eventually passed out, allowing me to sneak out.

He opened the door with a pleased expression, which sent butterflies fluttering through me. Lust burned within me at the sight of him wearing a white bathrobe with the hotel logo on it, his hair wet from a recent shower. I felt overdressed in my gray sweats, black T-shirt, and boots.

Once I stepped inside, I startled when the door closed behind me as the lock clicked into place. For some strange reason, I was suddenly shy in front of him as he led me to the center of the room.

He reached out to caress my cheek. The small touch sent a thrilling jolt through me. "I'm so happy you didn't talk yourself out of coming here."

"My sister would kill me if she ever found out."

"Are you sure about that? Because it seemed like she was trying to set us up next weekend by volunteering you to hang out alone with me." Iason looped his arms around my waist as he pulled me closer. "She was quite excited about it from where I was standing."

"No, she only meant it as friends. She's too in love with you to be fine with me dating you."

He didn't seem convinced. "She'll eventually find out. You can't keep living your life afraid of how a fifteen-year-old girl will react to you being in an adult relationship with a man."

Running my fingers through my hair, I sighed with frustration. "It's not that she'll have an issue with me being with a guy. It's that I'm with *you* specifically. She worships the ground you walk on and the air you breathe, and—"

"And someday, she'll understand that her teenage crush on me will never be anything more than that. I promise we'll laugh about this situation in ten years." He caught me by surprise at hearing him talking about our relationship long-term. "It's part of growing up. Her feelings have to be hurt so she can move past this."

"She won't be able to." My sister never half-assed an obsession—she whole-assed it with every fiber of her being. There was nothing she loved more on the face of this earth than Iason.

"She won't have a choice." His tone was gentler than his words. "She needs to come to terms and accept it, otherwise we're going to have some seriously awkward Thanksgivings, Christmases, and family dinners at your parents' house."

I laughed despite the seriousness of the situation. "I don't know if you're ready for Christmas with my family. Last year, Mom put up seven trees. *Seven.* All decorated with different themes."

"Please tell me Estelle has at least one tree that is decorated with nothing but twinkling lights and star ornaments. I'm going to be disappointed if she doesn't."

"Oh, she definitely does. You've never seen a more sparkly tree in your life. She has crystal stars she puts on spinners, so they catch the light, like diamonds glittering in the sky. It's pretty over-the-top, but so is Mom."

"It sounds magical." His tone was wistful. "I want to be a part of that with you without lying to your family."

The thought of Iason joining us for Christmas flooded my heart with warmth. "I want that, too, but Lyra..."

"We can worry about it later. All that matters right now is you and me." He leaned forward and brushed his lips against mine in a tentative offering, as if he was scared of driving me away by being too bold.

Filled with a need for more and eager to get off the awkward topic of my sister, I kissed him with the full force of my need for him. The unexpected taste of sweetness, cinnamon, and sugar surprised me. It was addictive when combined with the dark musk of whatever soap Iason had used in the shower.

When I parted for breath, my stupid mouth made a fool of me. "Snickerdoodle?"

His laughter was so genuine and bright that I couldn't help but grin. "Trying out a new nickname for me?"

"No, you taste like a snickerdoodle cookie."

"You can thank your mom for that." He gestured over to a pink box that was sitting on a side table by the windows. "She dropped them off at the hotel yesterday for me to take with me on the road. If you're good, maybe I'll let you have one later."

As much as I loved my mom's cookies, I was more interested in Iason at the moment. I delved deep for another taste, moaning as our tongues danced against each other and stirred my lust. I lost myself in him, my fingers entwining in his still-damp hair as I held on to stop myself from being swept away.

We paused long enough to get rid of my shirt and boots before Iason kissed me senseless again. I shivered as his fingers trailed down my back before he ran his hands over the swell of my ass to grope me. I needed more, which the large tent in my sweatpants couldn't hide.

He sank to his knees, trailing kisses along my body on the way down. My breath came in quick pants as he lowered my pants, causing my cock to spring free in front of his face. "No underwear? That's naughtier than I was expecting."

My cheeks flushed in embarrassment. "I forgot to bring them in with me to change into after my shower while waiting for Lyra to fall asleep."

He chuckled, sliding them down so I could kick them aside. I felt vulnerable being naked while he still wore a robe, but he didn't give me long to think about it. He started teasing me with lingering kisses on the tip of my dick while looking up at me with a lustful fire burning brightly in his mesmerizing blue eyes.

Part of me wanted to tell him to stop so we could move to the bed and continue, but I was powerless to say anything. I watched him take the head of my cock into his mouth, using his tongue to toy with it. He slid along my full length, taking in every inch until his nose brushed against my pubes. He then drew back at the same speed until my tip was resting on his plump lips. Once again, he tortured me with wet kisses that had the slightest hint of suction.

He repeated the process, then grabbed my ass to pull me closer. As his throat worked my length, I reached out to steady myself on his shoulder. My grip tightened when he slid two slicked fingers into me, teasing me open while he continued the erotic display of worshipping me in an unhurried manner. It made everything more intense than normal, leaving me torn between wanting something more while loving watching him taking me deep with such deliberate movements.

"Anise, *please*."

Pulling back slightly, he picked up the pace and started working my hardness with eagerness. It was a shock to my system after the gentle teasing. I trembled as he sucked my cock like it was the only thing giving him life. When he took me back into his throat again and worked me with a moan, I came hard with a gasp.

Iason swallowed before letting me fall from his mouth, one slow inch at a time, while also withdrawing his fingers. His full lips turned up into a cocky grin as he looked up at me.

Overcome by my feelings for him, I had him pinned to the floor before I realized what had happened. Despite having come, I still had a need for more burning inside me. I braced my hands on either side of his head as I hungrily kissed him. The taste of myself in his mouth mixed with the hint of cinnamon and sugar from the cookie earlier was unlike anything I had ever experienced before. I loved it.

It fanned the flames of my desire, causing me to reach between us to tug the belt undone. I pushed his robe open, revealing his glorious body. Surely, in all of antiquity, there wasn't a single statue as perfect as Iason and all of his chiseled muscles. Not to mention that none of them could compare to his huge cock, which strained from the need to be touched. There wasn't a fig leaf big enough to hide that from anyone.

I craved more, and I wouldn't be denied. Shifting further back to get a better angle, I started by kissing the mole on his collarbone that I found so beautiful for some inexplicable reason. From there, I covered his body with kisses and teasing touches.

Out of all the thousands of screaming fans tonight at the concert, by some miracle, he wanted me. Against all the odds, I was allowed to be with him. I was the only one blessed to see every inch of him exposed for my pleasure alone. It was surreal knowing I was responsible for his current aroused state. He sent fire through my veins with feverish desire for him. I didn't know what I had done to deserve such a gift, but I was forever grateful that he had chosen me to love.

While I wanted to return the blow job, I needed him inside me too much. I couldn't be bothered to relocate to the bed. Since he had slicked me earlier, I let his cock fill me as I slid down on it. There was no stopping after that as our bodies moved in search of more pleasure. It was a relief after spending so much of the concert aroused to be with Iason. His hands caressed me all over as his dick satisfied that intense ache within me, which had been building up from the moment I left him yesterday.

I didn't want to miss a single second of seeing him awash in bliss, but my eyes fluttered shut against my will. It was the best kind of pleasure to ride him hard, bracing myself on his impressive abs. It felt so good having him buried inside me, with each upward thrust of his hips driving me wild with lust. I hadn't known what real pleasure was until he showed me what I had been missing all of my life. I couldn't get enough of it now.

His hand wrapping around my cock and stroking it caused my eyes to snap open once more as I gasped from the sensation. My pace faltered from the intense sexual satisfaction in his gaze. His wet hair was mussed, making him even more attractive when combined with his arrogant confidence from knowing that he was making me lose my damn mind.

My body tensed as my climax started creeping up on me. It was all over when he commanded, "Let me hear your beautiful voice, Cherry."

I came hard, crying out, "Anise," as my cum splattered on his stomach. His hand worked my cock until it was completely spent.

It caused him to come, arching his back as he moaned my name. Only then did our bodies finally stop their frenetic pace.

Iason sat up and kissed me, making me gasp when he slipped out of me. He slid his tongue into my mouth, teasing me with more pleasure. It drove me to hug him when we parted for air. As I rested my head on his shoulder, he held me while we recovered from our intense climaxes. In that moment, everything was perfect in my world as I was with the one person who made me feel better than I knew was possible.

The responsible thing to do would be to go back downstairs before my sister woke up and discovered that I was missing. However, I was loath to give up the comfort of Iason's embrace. Not even Lyra bursting in on us would have been enough to make me move away from him. No, there was nowhere else I'd rather be than in his arms.

I kissed his neck with a happy sigh, lingering in the afterglow as long as I could. When he pressed his lips against my forehead in response, I smiled as we remained entwined, neither of us in a rush to separate quite yet.

Chapter Twenty-Four

IASON

"SHIT, THE SUN'S OUT," Orion groaned. He was sprawled on my chest, where he had collapsed earlier after another satisfying round of sex. "Anise, I seriously need to go."

I wasn't ready for our time to be over yet, so I hugged him closer. "Your sister's a teenager. She'll sleep until three in the afternoon if you let her. You can stay a little longer."

It pleased me when he stopped trying to move from his comfortable position on top of me. "It's only because I have to go, not because I want to."

"My point still stands." I grinned when my words caused him to huff. "The only place you're allowed to go right now is the shower. Otherwise, I'm not letting you up yet."

"And how am I supposed to explain my wet hair to my sister?"

His question made me grin. "There's this nifty little invention called a hair dryer. It'll take care of that problem for you." It amused me to feel the heat of his flushed cheek against my shoulder.

"Hey, it's early. You can't expect me to remember hair dryers exist when I never use them."

"Who doesn't use a hair dryer?" I asked, still chuckling. "Everyone uses them."

"I take showers at night before I go to bed, so there's no point in blow-drying my hair when it'll dry while I'm asleep."

My fingers traced lazy patterns over his back, sending a shiver through him. "How pragmatic of you."

"What I don't understand is how you wake up looking like this."

"Like what?" I asked, not understanding his meaning.

"A movie star who's ready for their close-up. It's not fair that you're this perfect and handsome all the time."

I laughed at the adorable reaction, ruffling his hair. "Am I supposed to be apologizing?"

"Not even Bernini could carve a sculpture as beautiful as you." His sigh was dreamy.

I wasn't familiar with the name. "I'm assuming that's a big compliment?"

"Yes, that was a huge compliment." He propped himself up to make eye contact with me. "He was a seventeenth-century sculptor who made some of the most beautiful statues in the known world. In one of his sculptures, despite being marble, the way Pluto's hand is holding Proserpina's thigh looks like actual flesh. It's remarkable."

Orion ran the backs of his fingers along my jawline, with a look of awe on his face as he continued. "But Bernini couldn't carve something as perfect as you." He cupped my cheek in his palm, brushing his thumb against my cheekbones in a tender caress. "You're more beautiful than anything that the Greeks, the Romans, Michelangelo, or even Canova could sculpt."

I wasn't familiar with art, but my ego purred under the praise all the same. Knowing that art history was Orion's biggest passion, it moved me to hear him talking about me in relation to that.

"You're beautiful enough that you could be a prized statue in a museum's collection, surrounded by signs that say 'Do not touch,' but somehow, I'm allowed to." He once again stroked my cheek with his thumb. "Against all odds, someone who looks like a flawless angel escaped from heaven to live on Earth fell in love with me, of all people. How is that possible?"

"That should tell you how incredible you are." I tilted my head to press a kiss against his palm. "It's proof of just how special you are, that you alone captured my heart. Don't you understand that you're more priceless to me than any work of art?"

Instead of answering, Orion kissed me. I wrapped my arms around him once more, enjoying indulging in his gentle affection. It didn't stir my desire as much as it comforted me. I could only hope that one day I could make him understand what he meant to me.

He looked at me in awe. "I'm so grateful that I get to live in this impossible dream for as long as possible."

"It's no dream, Cherry. This is all real."

His shy smile was endearing. "Somehow."

Unable to resist temptation, I reversed our positions to pin him on the bed under me. "Let me show you how real." I kissed him with more passion.

Orion groaned, even as he responded to me. "I'm supposed to be leaving. It's almost eight now."

"And checkout isn't until noon, so we've got plenty of time." I silenced his next protest with another kiss, turning his objection into a low moan of want.

When he reached up and pulled me closer instead of pushing me away, I knew I had my victory. I wasn't ready to give him up yet—or ever.

I WAS RIDING HIGH after my concert was over. Performing with Orion in the audience was a special pleasure. The way he looked up at me in awe and

me in a fierce hug. "Yes, because then you really will be part of our family!"

I hesitantly returned the hug. "You're not upset?"

She grinned as she stepped back. "I mean, I was for like a hot minute because you've always been my dream guy. But I'm not stupid. I'm literally half your age and illegal jailbait. Plus, I'm pretty sure you're gay, so that's three strikes for me."

"What makes you say that?"

She rolled her eyes in the dramatic way only teenagers could pull off. "Because you never use pronouns in your songs, duh. It's so obvious. If you were straight, all your lyrics would be about how much you love 'her,' but you always refer to the romantic interest as 'you' to keep it gender-neutral."

Her insight stunned me. "I'm impressed that you figured that out from my lyrics."

"They're what tipped me off about my brother." She shook her head. "It's so obvious now. I can't believe it took me so long to put it all together."

"Care to clue me in?"

She started laying out the facts in her case. "The first night you performed 'Wishes on Stars' was after you met Rion in the basement. I pretended the song was about me because I'm named after a star, but Orion is, too. Plus, he has gray 'stardust eyes,' and I don't. But it was obvious during family dinner that there was something going on between you two. You weren't exactly subtle."

I couldn't deny it. "And?"

"I'm fifteen, not stupid." Her grin turned wicked. "Luxurian Suites Hotels are a sponsor of your tour, which means you're staying at them. We also just so happened to be at the only Luxurian Suites Hotel near the venue. There's also the fact that Rion went missing last night and didn't come back until late this morning. I may be a teenager, but it wasn't hard to piece together he went to your room."

There was no denying it at that point. "Is it a problem?"

"Only if you aren't serious about him." Her expression turned concerned. "Nyla seriously broke his heart. I don't want you to do that to him, too. It would suck that I'd never be able to listen to your music again."

"I can promise you I'm very serious about your brother. All I want to do is love him with all my heart. This isn't a fling, Lyra. I'm moving back to Sunnyside to be together when my tour ends."

"Really?" Her excited squeal loosened the tightness in my chest. "That's amazing!"

She may have had everything figured out, but there was an important piece of the puzzle missing. "Have you talked to Orion about this?"

"No, I wanted to confirm with you before I embarrassed the hell out of him. I didn't want to be wrong and upset him."

"He's terrified that you won't approve of us."

She waved it away. "He always worries about the worst-case scenarios. But I can't be with you for all the obvious reasons, so having him be the person you love is the next best thing. I'll talk to him when we go back to the hotel tonight."

I was overwhelmed with relief. "Thank you. He's been worried about hurting you by following his heart."

She threw herself at me in another fierce hug. "I don't know how it happened, but I'm so glad you fell in love with him. Thanks for making him happy. It's all I've wanted for him after his breakup with Nyla."

"I promise you I'll do everything in my power to make him happy every day for the rest of his life."

She stepped back with a dreamy sigh. "He's *so* lucky." Her expression turned sheepish. "I guess this means I have to take down the posters of you in my room, though. It'll creep him out too much that his boyfriend is watching me sleep."

I laughed at that. "It might be a sacrifice you have to make."

"A worthy one." It was sweet how she wanted to do anything she could to support her brother. "Should we go put him out of his misery?"

"Yeah."

Before she opened the door, she turned to give me a mischievous grin. "I promise I'll pretend to fall asleep really early tonight." Just like her mom, Lyra was an incredible ally whose generous heart was full of love.

It filled me with gratitude. "You're the best."

"Yeah, I am." She preened at the praise before we left to go rejoin Orion, who was waiting with my band members.

Chapter Twenty-Five

ORION

I WAS in agony while waiting for Lyra to finish talking to Iason. His band members did a great job of trying to distract me, but I needed to know what she was up to. She revealed nothing after she came out to go to work at the merch table. All he had said was she'd talk to me about it later at the hotel. He then distracted me with his sexiness until I forgot about the problem.

But alone in the room with Lyra afterward, I had my chance to find out what the hell was going on. "Will you please tell me what you talked to Iason about earlier?"

She grinned at me when she dropped onto her bed with a bounce. "Why? Worried?"

"Incredibly." I frowned at her amusement. "Don't make me play Twenty Questions to figure this out. My anxiety can't handle it today."

A hint of remorse dampened her expression. "You have nothing to be worried about."

I gave her a look that told her how ridiculous I thought that claim was. "Then you should have no problem telling me."

She crossed her legs and gestured for me to sit on my bed across from her. I complied with a sigh as my heart hammered. She studied me with eyes that seemed to see straight through me before she spoke. "You like Iason, don't you?"

"Of course. I've always been a fan."

She crossed her arms with a huff. "That's not what I mean, and you know it."

I played dumb. "It's not?"

Her gaze never wavered. "You romantically *like him*-like him, don't you?"

My heart stopped as I realized she had figured out the truth I had been trying so hard to hide from her. I wanted to deny it, but I couldn't stop seeing the pain in Iason's eyes if I denied what I felt for him. It was time to stop running and face the consequences. My voice shook with fear. "I don't like him. I—"

She rolled her eyes. "Oh, bullshit! You totally do! It's so *obvious!*"

"If you'd let me finish, what I was going to say is I don't just like him. I love him, Lyra."

Whatever reaction I had been prepared for her to have, it wasn't her bouncing with joy. "I knew it!"

I blinked in shock. "Is that a good thing or a bad thing?"

"It's the *best* thing!" She looked at me with so much happiness that I finally could breathe. "I'm so excited for you both!"

"You are?" It was almost too good to be true. "You're not mad that I stole him from you?"

She snorted as if it was a ridiculous idea. "Sure, I was upset for a minute once I figured out what was going on during family dinner. I mean, tying a cherry stem knot to show off for him? *Really?*"

I blushed hard but said nothing.

"I'm not stupid, Rion. I'm an underage girl who has exactly *zero* sex appeal to a thirty-five-year-old gay man. I never stood a chance with him."

"I'm sorry." I still felt bad that I had unintentionally stolen her crush from her, although she was right about him never being attracted to her.

"If I can't have him, you being with him is the next best thing. You're *so* lucky." She gave a dreamy sigh. "And now he really will be a member of our family. I've gotta say, being his honorary younger sister is a pretty awesome consolation prize."

I could have cried from the overwhelming relief that she wasn't upset with me. Resting my head in my hands, I took a steadying breath. "I'm so glad you're not mad at me. I was so worried."

She got off her bed to sit next to me, throwing her arms around me in a bear hug. "You're the best brother in the universe. How could I be anything other than happy for you that you found someone as awesome as Iason to love you?"

I hugged her tightly. "Thank you, Lyra. I never wanted to upset you, but I couldn't stop myself from falling for him."

She laughed as she sat back. "Who could? He's *amazing.*"

"He really is." Now that I was calmer, I focused on the conversation instead of my panic. "Is this what you talked to him about?"

"Yeah. I didn't want to embarrass you if I had accidentally created a fantasy where he fell for you instead and was dead wrong about it." She grinned at me. "Thankfully, he told me how serious he was about you. I also warned him he's not allowed to break your heart because it would suck that I couldn't listen to his music anymore. Oh, and I promised I'd take down my posters of him. I figured it'd creep you out that he was watching me sleep."

That finally drew a laugh out of me. "It's definitely uncomfortable to think about you fantasizing about my boyfriend."

"Since he's off-limits for me, there's always Chance Prince. He's *gorgeous*, and his voice is amazing." He was the attractive and talented lead singer of the Devil's Chance band. "And as a bonus, he's bi in real life, so he'll be a good backup dream boyfriend.

Maybe once I turn eighteen, I'll ask Iason to introduce us."

I shook my head at how resilient my younger sister's relentless optimism was. "Thank you for at least waiting until you're an adult."

She laughed before she turned serious. "From the bottom of my heart, I'm so happy for you, Rion. Iason is the best, and he really loves you."

It was my turn to be sheepish. "Now, I feel like an asshole for assuming you'd never forgive me for dating him."

"In your defense, as fanatical as I am about him and as dramatic as I can be, it's a natural assumption to make. But I love you too much to be mad about it. All I've wanted is for you to be happy after Nyla broke your heart. I kept hoping that you two would get back together, but being with Iason is *so* much better."

I nodded in agreement. "It really is. Somehow, he loves the real me and *only* me." Because of how much he hated his father cheating on his mother, I knew I'd never have to worry about him doing that to me. "It still feels like an impossible dream."

Lyra theatrically stretched as she yawned. "Wow, would you look at the time? I should go to sleep."

I glanced at the clock on the nightstand separating our beds. "It's not even midnight yet."

"Well, the concert was too exciting, so this must be my adrenaline crashing." She gave me a fierce hug before crawling under the covers of her bed. "Love you. Good night!"

Her antics entertained me. "You're still wearing your regular clothes and not your pajamas."

"I'm too tired to change. It's fine," she assured me through another feigned yawn. She pretended to snore, making me laugh.

"What are you doing?"

"Snoring so loud I can't hear you sneaking out to go to Iason's room." She continued fake snoring until she realized I wasn't leaving. "I'm in such a deep sleep, I totally won't care that you're leaving to go be with him."

Her theatrics made me chuckle. I got up and placed a kiss on the top of her head. "Thank you for being the best sister in the world. Love you."

She cracked one eye open to glance up at me with a mischievous grin. "I'll love you more if you go to his room right now and let me sleep in peace."

"Well, since you insist, I guess I have to." I could hear her girlish giggles as I left. My heart was light and free now that I knew she supported my relationship with him.

Chapter Twenty-Six

IASON

IT WAS a surprise when Orion showed up to my room far earlier than I had expected. I greeted him with a warm smile as I stepped aside to let him in. "You're early."

"Lyra kicked me out. She said something about me needing to spend time with my boyfriend."

"She's the best." I hugged him, loving how he melted against me when he returned it. "I take it your talk with her went well?"

"It never occurred to me she'd be thrilled to be your honorary younger sister." He sighed, making me shiver. "I should have trusted her more and believed you when you said she'd be fine with us."

I stroked his hair in comfort. "The important thing is she's happy we're together. Don't waste time feeling bad about the past." I gave him a sweet kiss before leading him over to get into bed with me.

Leaning back against the propped-up pillows, I gestured for him to curl up at my side. "Come here."

He curled up next to me, draping his arm over me possessively as he rested his head on my shoulder. "This is nice, but don't you want to…?"

I pressed a kiss to his forehead. "We don't always have to. I'm sure you're sore after the workout I gave you yesterday."

"A bit, but in a good way." He rested his head on my shoulder with a soft sigh of contentment. "This is nice, too."

"It is. I've been looking forward to this all day." I wrapped an arm around him as I held him closer. "I'd love you to tell me about art."

"Seriously?" He laughed incredulously. "Nobody ever wants to listen to me talk about it."

"I want to hear all about it." To encourage him, I rubbed his upper arm. "Tell me about what time period you specialize in and why."

"My dissertation was about Jacques-Louis David, the artist who defined the Neoclassicism art movement that grew out of the French Revolution and continued through the Napoleonic era. Because of that, I work in the European art gallery at the Sunnyside University Museum of Art."

I wasn't familiar with anything he had mentioned. "Why him?"

"For one, he's an incredible artist who is unparalleled in portraiture. He also created the imagery that not only defined but perpetuated the beliefs of the French Revolution by essentially inventing the Neoclassicism art style. It's a cross of seventeenth-century Baroque chiaroscuro with Greek and Roman aesthetics in the 1780s."

"He invented his own art style? That's impressive."

Orion nodded. "His paintings told the story of the revolution, which bolstered the cause. But with the fall of the former Jacobins, they threw David into prison. He saved his life by painting portraits, which is incredible when you think about it."

"How did he do that?" It was hard for me to fathom.

"Because he reminded everyone he was the best at what he did. Napoleon recognized David's remarkable talent for defining eras through art, so he saved him. He used David to help legitimize him and the formation of his empire through the modified hallmarks of Neoclassicism iconography. For art and a single artist to have that kind of power to change history is astonishing, don't you think?"

I nodded in agreement. "It's unbelievable. I can see why you chose such a fascinating period."

"Because of the way David borrowed from the Greeks and Romans, I've also studied those periods of ancient art as well. And to understand what Neoclassicism grew out of, I've also extensively researched the Rococo period that came before it to see how it was a rejection of the frivolity of the art style of King Louis XV's court."

"That explains why you had so many books on different eras in your office."

Orion made a happy noise over me making that connection. "I'm not good at sticking with only one thing. The Renaissance, Baroque, Dutch Masters, and Post-Impressionist styles are also periods that I love. My bookshelves reflect that."

"I'd love to go to museums with you. I bet you give the best tours."

He shifted to look at me. "That wouldn't bore you?"

"Hearing you talking about your passion? Never." An idea came to me. "Maybe before I move back to Sunnyside, I could tempt you to come visit me in New York so we could visit the Metropolitan Museum of Art together."

Orion straddled himself over my lap as he gave me an intense kiss that told me how much he liked that idea. As it grew more heated, my intentions of not doing anything sexual faded fast. It seemed he felt the same way when he stripped off his sweater and threw it onto the floor.

It gave me an idea. "Take off all your clothes, and then get back on top of me."

I loved he was too turned on to argue. He got up and finished stripping down as I shrugged out of the robe I had on after my shower. I poured some lube onto my hand before he was on me again. He kissed me with so much passion I forgot how to breathe. I needed a moment to remember my intentions.

Reaching between us, I took his erection in hand with mine and started stroking them together with my lubed palm. His hips reacted by pumping into my grip as he kept kissing me senseless. The slick glide of our cocks against each other felt divine as he frotted against me with the cutest little whimpers of need.

He moved with more urgency as he got closer to climax. A soft moan escaped him. "Why is this so good?"

"Don't worry about why. Just enjoy it." I tightened my grip as I gave the tips a squeeze on my downward pump.

It didn't take much before he came with a shudder. My orgasm hit me hard as I shot my load onto my stomach to mix with his.

"That was incredible." He stared at me with awe.

I grinned at him. "Sometimes there's nothing better than a good frot."

He responded with another soul-searing kiss I savored. I couldn't wait for our museum date at the Met before I moved back to Sunnyside to be with Orion.

Chapter Twenty-Seven

ORION

IT HAD BEEN three days since I was with Iason in San Francisco. Three long days, with three even longer nights. Being with him had awakened a craving for his touch in a way I had never experienced before. Remembering our time together made me flush with a painful longing to have him filling the emptiness within me that ached when we were apart. I was going out of my mind with an uncontrollable lust only he knew how to satiate. However, he was performing in Portland, Oregon, for his adoring fans, while I suffered at home by myself.

Huffing in irritation as I readied myself for another miserable night alone in bed, I resented the desire crawling under my skin that begged for Iason. Like an addict, I was desperate for another euphoric high only he could give me. I tortured myself by reliving memories of his hands touching my body

like a burst of hot lightning. I thrust into my fist with desperation as he continued tantalizing me.

My toes curled in the sheets as all my muscles tensed in anticipation of my impending climax. Immersed in his voice intimately pleasuring me, it took a moment for the lyrics of "Midnight Magic" to filter through my haze.

Lost in lust and love,
I'll get down on my knees
And worship you all night long.

There's no greater pleasure than hearing
Your symphony of sighs,
Your chorus of cries,
As we make midnight music
Between the sheets tonight.

Hearing him singing and remembering how he had looked onstage when he performed the number at the concert, I neared my limit. When his voice soared to a big finish on the last notes of his seductive song like an aural orgasm, I felt it with my entire being. I came so hard I almost saw stars from the intensity of him penetrating me as intimately as possible. I couldn't move, breathe, or do anything other than lie there and *feel.*

As the next song played, I whispered Iason's name in a pleading tone that begged for respite from the overload. My body couldn't handle any more pleasure. With great effort, I reached out with my clean hand and paused the music. Satisfaction permeated every fiber of my existence as the echo of his voice resounded inside of me. It sent aftershock tremors through me. My reaction made me realize how lucky I was that I hadn't come in my pants during the concert. God help me at the LA one when I didn't have my sister's presence to pour cold water on me.

I wasn't sure how long I lay in bed, adrift in the afterglow, but I startled when my phone's ringtone filtered through my headphones. When I saw it was Iason, I hit the button to accept the call. Although I meant to sound casual, my hello sounded more like a moan.

"Did I wake you up?" Iason asked.

Looking down at the mess on my skin, the corner of my mouth turned upward. "In a manner of speaking."

"What does that mean?" Amusement radiated through his tone.

"I wasn't asleep."

It was easy to picture his grin. "Are you implying I'm responsible for your sexual awakening?"

I ran my index finger through the cum on my stomach. "Considering I'm covered in evidence, I would be lying if I denied it."

He hummed with interest, sending sparks of

desire skittering through me. "Are you saying what I think you are?"

"That it's your fault I'm covered in cum after giving myself the best orgasm I've ever had by myself?" I was too relaxed from my climax to be embarrassed by what I said.

"Fuck, why am I not there to lick you clean?" Iason moaned, making that insatiable want inside of me stir again. Because I was still wearing my headphones, it sounded like he was in bed with me. It was too much to handle after what I had just experienced. "Tell me what I did to get you all hot and bothered."

Leaning over and getting a tissue, I wiped myself clean. "No, it's too embarrassing."

"Oh, now you *have* to share what your fantasy was."

"I wasn't fantasizing about you." It was technically true. How was I supposed to admit that I felt freshly fucked by his dulcet voice alone?

He chuckled at my denial. "You said it was my fault, so clearly I did something for you."

The flush in my cheeks deepened to a full blush. "It'll go to your head."

There was rustling on Iason's end. "Please stroke my ego."

"Did you take your clothes off?" I sounded more scandalized than I intended.

He laughed at my reaction. "It was poor planning on my part to call you while I was wearing them.

Come on, how did I give you the best solo orgasm of your life?"

The note of desire in his voice sent shivers through me. "You'll think I'm weird."

"You should know by now I won't kink shame you for anything."

It was true, but it was still hard to admit what I had done. I stalled for time. "Wait, why did you call me?" We had texted every day since we parted, but it was the first time he had called me.

"Because I missed you."

His words filled me with a warm glow. "Really?"

"Why do you sound so shocked?"

I bit my lower lip before I answered. "Because I miss you, too. That's why…"

When I trailed off, he encouraged me to continue. "You can tell me, Cherry."

There wasn't a chance I was getting out of explaining myself, so I sucked it up and fessed up to the truth. "You know my ears are sensitive."

"I do," Iason said in an amused tone.

"It's not just to touch. I'm sensitive to sound in general."

I pictured his grin. "As evidenced by you shivering every time I murmur something in your ear."

"Because of that, I'm kind of an audiophile, so I have high-quality headphones." When I paused, he remained quiet so I could tell my story at my own pace. "The audio is crystal clear, making it sound like you're here."

"Are you telling me you listened to me singing while jerking off?" He sounded equal parts excited and aroused.

It was humiliating to admit. "Yes."

"Fuck, that's so damn hot. How many songs did it take before I made you come?"

"Two and a half." It embarrassed me how fast I had climaxed. "It was *intense*."

"Which song caused you to lose it?"

I told him the truth. "It won't surprise you that it was 'Midnight Magic.'"

Iason moaned at my response, making me aware of the sound of movement on his end of the call.

It gave me a sudden realization. "Wait, are you getting off on this?"

"You bet your sweet ass I am." He laughed without shame. "You heard 'Midnight Magic' and thought about us being together?"

"Not quite. That's why I said it was weird."

"Tell me more."

I shook my head. "No, it's too strange."

"Let me be the judge of that. Please tell me."

I didn't want to fess up to the truth, but I didn't know how to resist Iason, even when we were far apart. "It felt like your voice was caressing me. *Intimately*."

Rather than making fun of me, he encouraged me. "Keep going."

When he didn't laugh, it gave me the strength to continue. "It was like you were right here. Hearing you singing is a visceral experience for me. Your voice penetrated my body, then caressed and made love to my soul until I came harder than I ever have by myself."

"That's incredible." He gasped my name as he climaxed, filling me with an unbearable heat that burned in my veins. "Fuck, I would give anything to be there with you right now, Cherry."

I shuddered at the desire in his voice. "I feel the same way."

He sighed with longing. "Only a few more days and we'll be back together."

"Friday can't come soon enough." Our reunion would be worth the pain-in-the-ass commute to get down to LA to be with him again.

"I love you so much, Cherry. Sweet dreams."

I smiled at the affection I could hear in his voice. "Love you, Anise. Sleep well."

When we hung up, I sighed in the silence. I basked in being blissed-out from my incredible release and knowing that Iason really loved me.

Turning off my headphones and putting them on the nightstand, I forced myself to get ready for bed. I was eager for pleasant dreams about spending the night in Iason's arms again.

Chapter Twenty-Eight

IASON

DURING MY LUNCH BREAK, I video called my friends Kieran Aiello and Rook Warrick. They both were famous Hollywood action heroes, who had promised me they would wish Orion into my life. It seemed only fair to let them know how things had turned out with my new boyfriend.

I waved at them once we were all connected. "Hey, guys. How's it going?"

"I'd be better if I wasn't stuck in Canada shooting this movie," Kieran groused. "I hate being apart from Rory." That was his boyfriend he had met in Sweden while running away from a media scandal.

Rook was always the voice of reason. "At least someone hired you after what happened between us. And for an action film, no less."

"I told you it would be fine once everything blew over." Kieran waved away his complaints. "Ias, put us out of our mystery. Tell us if our wishes came true. Did you meet the love of your life at the show you performed at your friend's bar?"

"You both need to go into the matchmaking industry." I grinned as they both laughed. "You guys knocked it out of the park on this one."

"Did we get bonus points for a cosmic name?"

"Yes, I about fell over in surprise when he introduced himself as Orion Donati. Not only is he named after a constellation, his last name is also a comet named after a famous astronomer."

Rook shook his head in amazement. "Wow, it doesn't get much more cosmic than that."

"If you think that's wild, his mom's name is Estelle, and she's an astronomer turned astrophysicist."

Kieran's eyebrows arched up in surprise. "You've met his mom already?"

"I did better than that. I went to his parents' house for family dinner." The memory brought a smile to my face. "It felt like I was living in a movie. They were a perfect TV family. I didn't know it was possible for families to love each other that much. And somehow, I'm lucky enough to be part of that now. They adore me."

"Who wouldn't?" Kieran asked. "You're awesome."

"I'm glad it worked out for you. You deserve that kind of family to love you." Rook gave me an encouraging smile. "I'm guessing that means we can expect you to move to Sunnyside now?"

"As soon as my tour is over. I'm already looking at places."

"We can send you the contact info for Rune Tourneau's Realtor and PR people. They're both amazing and have helped us out a lot."

Rook nodded in agreement. "I can't recommend them enough."

"I sure hope Rune is getting a commission off all this," I joked.

"If he's not, he should." Kieran laughed at his joke. "So, tell us about the new love of your life."

"Orion is a sweetheart who works at the Sunnyside University Museum of Art as an assistant curator in the European art gallery."

"Damn, is being a sweetheart a requirement for attending Sunnyside University?" Kieran's boyfriend was a graduate student in their English department. "That's amazing, Ias."

"He specializes in an artist who was famous during the French Revolution, so I'd like to introduce him to Rune once I get settled out there. I think they'd enjoy talking with each other since that's the era he studies, too."

"Ambrosia is going to need a bigger table out in the garden for all of us to hang out." It was Kieran's favorite restaurant for a reason. We all loved it because the owners were wonderful people. The private grotto was invite-only and an amazing place to escape from the world and enjoy the best food on the planet.

"We'll have a nice housewarming party for you once you get out here," Rook offered. "Are you going to ask Orion to move in with you?"

"Absolutely. I don't want to spend one more minute apart from him than I have to." Before I could continue, there was a knock on my dressing room door. "Who is it?"

"It's Levi. Can we talk for a minute?"

"Yeah, just give me a second," I called out to him before returning my attention to my friends. "Sorry, duty calls. Thanks again for bringing such an amazing person into my life. I owe you guys big-time."

"You can repay us by being happy," Kieran said.

"I couldn't have said it better myself," Rook said. "We'll hang out once you're settled in Sunnyside again."

"Sounds good. Take care, guys." With a final wave, I ended the call. I got up to let Levi into my dressing room and shut the door behind him. "What's up?"

He made himself comfortable on my couch. There was an unusual hesitancy to him as he nervously rubbed his scruff. "I wanted to run something by you."

I sat next to him. "Sure."

"You're planning on moving to Sunnyside, right?"

"Yeah, as soon as I wrap up the tour. Why?"

He fidgeted as he built up the courage to ask me a question. "Would it weird you out if I moved back, too?"

It was a surprising question. "Not at all. But I thought you loved New York?"

"I do. Or at least, I did. But I don't know now." He shrugged with a frown. "I'm not really happy there, anymore. And when you leave, it'll suck even more. Plus, I was weirdly jealous that you were back in Sunnyside on your break. If we both move there, then we could still get together for a jam session whenever we wanted."

I felt bad that I hadn't realized he was so unhappy in the city. "It probably makes me a selfish asshole, but it would make me ridiculously happy if you came back to Sunnyside, too. You're one of the few good things about staying in Manhattan. If I didn't have to leave you behind, it would be amazing."

"It'll be like our good ol' days," he said with a grin. "It'd be worth the ribbing from Duke about me following you home. I'm pretty sure he low-key believes I'm in love with you."

I shook my head with a laugh. "Don't mind my guard dog. He means well."

"I'd be lying if I said I wasn't envious of what you have with Orion." He stretched his arm out over the back of the couch. "You're already so perfectly in sync even though you've known each other such a short time. He's an amazing guy, Ias. You're *so* lucky."

"I really am. But if *I* could find love, then you definitely will. You've never been closed off to the idea of it like I was." It was weird realizing if Kieran and Rook hadn't been teasing me about finding my soul mate, I never would have opened myself up to the possibility of meeting Orion. Thinking about what I would have missed out on was too sad. "Maybe moving back to Sunnyside is what you need to find your true love."

Levi looked at me in amazement. "Do you have any idea how much it's blowing my mind hearing *you* preaching about finding true love?"

"What can I say? Orion changed me for the better. It would be awesome if you moved back to Sunnyside with me, Levi. I think we'll both be a lot happier there."

"Then that decides it." He leaned over and gave me a hug. "Thanks, man."

"You know I'd do anything for you, including self-ishly begging you to follow me across the country." I grinned at him when he laughed. "Any other requests?"

He shook his head as he got off the couch. "No, but we need to head back to rehearsals. Poor Sal is in a mood today. He probably needs to get laid."

Sal was great, but he was tightly wound. Levi most likely wasn't wrong. I stood up and suggested, "We should convince him to come out with us, too. He's too stressed-out for Manhattan. He needs to learn how to relax Sunnyside-style."

"Good luck with convincing him." Levi snickered at the thought of Sal overreacting to the suggestion. "If you can persuade him, you are a far better negotiator than I am."

"I'll give it my best shot."

Levi slung his arm over my neck. "Let's go tell the band the great news. If we get lucky, they'll all say fuck it and come out to California with us. Wouldn't that be awesome?"

"It definitely would. And hey, dreaming big has worked out for me so far, so let's aim high."

We laughed as we rejoined rehearsals with our friends.

Chapter Twenty-Nine

ORION

AS I WAITED for the LA concert to begin, two women in their early twenties sitting near me caught my attention. The one with auburn hair exclaimed, "Can you believe we're here? And so close to the stage!"

"I know!" The brunette squealed in excitement, reminding me of my sister. "I'm in a dream I never want to wake up from."

"If it was a dream, he would be naked, and we would be alone together without you here." Her comment caused them both to laugh. "I guess I'll settle for hoping he notices I exist."

"God, could you imagine if he looked at us and smiled?" The brunette gave a dreamy sigh. "I might actually die."

As they continued joking back and forth with outrageous talk about their reactions to Iason, it was an interesting reminder about his fame. I kept forgetting that he was Iason Leyland, the famous musician. He had become my Anise, who loved me and only me. I was the luckiest man in the world.

After Mirror Mirror finished opening the show, I checked my phone during intermission. It surprised me when I saw a text waiting for me.

Iason: *I have a surprise for you.*

His promise intrigued me. I texted him back, although I wasn't sure if he'd see it before performing.

Orion: *What kind of surprise?*

Iason: *One I can guarantee you're going to love.*

Orion: *And when do I receive this mysterious surprise?*

Iason: *As soon as I walk on stage.*

I furrowed my eyebrows as I tried to guess what he was planning. Normally, I hated surprises because they made me anxious. However, I was curious despite my normal aversion to them.

Orion: *Is that the only hint I get?*

When he replied with only a winking kiss emoji, I

rolled my eyes with a grin. I couldn't figure out what he had planned. My intrigue made me even antsier for the show to begin.

After the longest thirty minutes of my life, the lights dimmed. I burned with curiosity about the surprise, but I hoped it wasn't something that was going to embarrass me in front of over fifteen thousand people.

Iason walked onto the stage to thunderous applause. He wore tight jeans, a white T-shirt with the *Winged Victory of Samothrace* dripping multicolored paint from its wings, and a metallic black suit jacket. The sight of the beautiful statue on his shirt made my heart skip a beat. How had he known it was one of my favorite statues from antiquity?

It was surreal realizing that he was wearing it for me. Although it was such a simple thing, it was a sweet gesture that touched me. Most of the people in my life got so bored whenever I talked about art, but Iason genuinely seemed to enjoy learning about my life's passion. It made me feel loved in a way I had never experienced before.

My mind refocused when he picked up his blue acoustic guitar from the upright stand to slip the strap over his shoulder. "Is everyone as happy to be here as I am?"

The audience shrieked so loud that they could probably be heard in space. He grinned at the reaction, strumming the strings to check the sound.

"Glad to hear it. We're going to have a great time tonight."

More cheers rang out as he began playing his latest single, "In My Arms." Everyone quieted down as he sang the upbeat number, his fingers nimbly moving over the frets. It was a beautiful sight that made me grateful for my first-row center seat he had reserved for me.

When he reached the chorus, his eyes met mine.

You belong
In my arms.
Let me love you
And hold you tight.

Whispering promises
For all our tomorrows,
I'll give you an eternity of love,
If you stay in my arms tonight.

There were over fifteen thousand people in the amphitheater, but they all disappeared when he held my gaze. It was like he was singing a private concert just for me. The venue may have been large, but it was stunningly intimate. His words made me ache for him to embrace me again. A thrill raced through me from knowing it would only be a little longer before I would enjoy the pleasure of being in his arms again.

As I watched him working the fretboard with

practiced ease, I admired his long, slender fingers. It filled me with the strange urge to suck them into my mouth and worship them under his heated gaze. I longed to have him play my body the same way as his guitar. It sent tendrils of hot want curling through me as he transitioned to the next song. Hearing him singing in person exacerbated that desire. While he sounded amazing on recordings, it couldn't compare to hearing a live performance.

Without having to worry about my sister seeing my reactions, I was free to enjoy the experience to the fullest. My eyes fluttered shut for a moment as I let his voice wrap around me. It was like a palpable caress on my skin. I shivered from the intensity of his honeyed tone seducing me with every note. It was more intense than hearing him through my headphones the other night.

I was powerless to resist the visceral effect he had on me. My body responded to the teasing rise and fall of his voice that somehow filled the entire space of the large arena, while also penetrating the innermost parts of my soul. And it felt so very good.

His next key change into a higher register made me shudder as my back arched off the chair. I had to bite my lower lip to hold in the whimper that almost escaped. Having his voice making passionate love to every part of me was the single most incredible experience of my life.

My pants were uncomfortably tight, causing me to

shift in my seat. I was self-conscious that I was so aroused already. Part of me feared I would make an embarrassing mess of my underwear before he finished the concert. It was a valid concern when I hadn't even made it three full songs when I had experimented with getting myself off while listening to him through my headphones.

When he locked eyes with me again, my heart stuttered in my chest as an electric shock of lust shot through my body. My indignation flared at the self-satisfied smirk he couldn't hide. He knew exactly what he was doing to me and enjoyed every second of being able to arouse me without a single touch.

Just when I thought I couldn't endure any more aural teasing, he took a break to drink water. "Are we having fun yet?"

The crowd roared and applauded in response, making Iason smile so beautifully it stole my breath away. It was amazing watching him in his element as he made small talk and joked with the band while strumming random chords.

He introduced everyone to the audience. I was a little surprised at the number of shouts that Levi received from the women in the audience. That thought was soon forgotten as Iason then launched into the next part of his set. It got me all hot and bothered again as his voice reduced me to trembling arousal.

When I was in actual danger of losing my battle

against my desire, he took another break. It was almost as if he sensed I needed a moment to recover my equilibrium before it was too late. My muscles were tight with tension from being edged to the precipices of pleasure and stopped just short. It was as much a relief as it was frustrating.

It was the best kind of hell to be toyed with by Iason's performance. I experienced the concert as a full-body sensation, with all of my senses attuned to his overwhelming presence. As many live shows as I had been to in my life, I had never had such a visceral reaction to anyone before Iason. But everything about him pushed me higher and higher in my spiral of lust. It would get out of control if I didn't have a reprieve soon. I had been hard for so long that it verged on painful. However, getting relief would have to wait until afterward—provided I didn't explode before it was over.

I lost all track of time as I enjoyed seeing Iason doing what he did best. After another one of his breaks, he announced, "This next set of songs are ones that have been inspiring me lately. I hope you enjoy them as much as I do."

My jaw dropped when he played the opening chords of Rufus Wainwright's "The Art Teacher." I had never mentioned to him how much I loved that song because of the Metropolitan Museum of Art reference. It didn't matter how many thousands of people were in that theatre when he was performing just for me. I loved every second.

When it ended, they played the opening bars to Jeff Buckley's "Grace." My whole body flushed with heat. I remembered Iason telling me in the car that first night about how much he liked to tear into it and let go. I didn't know if I could handle it, but he launched into it, anyway.

The gentle lilting rise and fall of his voice teased my senses with the promise of what was next. It thrilled me when he did the wordless runs. He started off sweet and easy before reaching into the highest parts of his register. There was a brief instrumental interlude before he aggressively began the last verse. The intensity of it tantalized me. But when he tossed his head back and gave it his all on the long vocalization section, I almost came. Each note was bigger than the last. As he held the final sustained howl for as long as he could, my entire body trembled as I felt it down to the essence of my being.

It was a small mercy that the song ended almost immediately after. I was so close to climaxing that I didn't know how I was going to make it through the rest of the concert. The huge note echoed through me, like a shotgun shell ricocheting through my soul. I tried to think of anything that might kill my arousal, but nothing worked.

I was so caught up in not giving in to my urge to come that I missed what Iason said after it was over. It took a supreme effort to focus on him as he once again started plucking random fragments of melodies on his guitar while addressing the audience. "I've always loved the magic of music." Iason's sky-blue eyes looked straight into my soul. "The right song can be a magic spell capable of seducing you and making you fall in love. It can touch you in the most intimate of ways, all the way to the hidden parts of your heart. It's magic at its finest."

My chest felt so tight I almost couldn't breathe. It didn't let up when he looked away to gaze out over the crowd. Despite expecting what happened next, I thought my heart would stop when he announced, "For tonight's final song, let's make some 'Midnight Magic' together right now."

The resulting shrieking was damn near deafening as he played the opening bars of the song that had pushed me over the edge of pleasure when listening to it in the privacy of my bedroom. It was one thing to hear it through headphones. Watching in person as his fingers caressed his guitar like a lover while staring at his beautiful face was too much to handle on top of his electric performance of "Grace." It got harder to control myself when he licked his lips, making me remember what that gorgeous mouth could do to me.

When he tilted his head back to vocalize the sexu-ally satisfied–sounding moans, I clamped my hand over my mouth to suppress the lusty sound that almost broke free. I didn't know whether to plead for more or

He picked up his guitar with a grin. "Well, look at that. You pulled a rabbit out of the hat. Neat trick, guys."

The crowd tittered with laughter as everyone took their seats once more.

Iason continued his one-sided conversation. "I guess fate is its own kind of magic, isn't it? That incredible moment when all the cosmic forces align to bring you the person who gives your life meaning and makes you realize that forever will never be enough."

Once again, he strummed random chords on his guitar. "For my last number tonight, I want to share a brand-new song with everyone about that kind of love. It's called 'Museum of My Heart.' Enjoy."

Taking a deep breath, Iason played a beautiful melody as he started to sing. I recognized it as what he had been practicing in the hotel when I had returned from work.

A constellation brought to life,
I've studied every inch of you,
Admired you from every angle,
But every time I see you,
I fall in love with you all over again,
My beautiful dream come true.

I'll never say a last goodbye
Because I'll never let you go.
Forever isn't long enough,

So let's walk together
Through the halls of time.

More beautiful than any painting,
More lovely than any sculpture,
You're a priceless masterpiece
That belongs in a museum of art,
But I selfishly keep you
In the museum of my heart.

I fell in love with shy eyes,
With cherry kisses,
And your soul made of stars.
There's no greater pleasure in this world
Than being yours.

More beautiful than any painting,
More lovely than any sculpture,
You're a priceless masterpiece
That belongs in a museum of art,
But I selfishly keep you
In the museum of my heart.

When the song ended, the audience was on their feet with cheers and applause again. My body automatically stood up to join them, but all I saw was Iason smiling down at me with an open look of love. It made me forget what air was as tears welled up in my eyes.

With a few more parting words, he left the stage after taking a final bow and waving at the crowd.

The clapping continued until people realized he wasn't coming back out again. I collapsed into my seat once more. My mind swam with too many thoughts competing with my haywire hormones. Holding my head in my hands, I took several steadying breaths to calm my overly sensitive body. I was sore from the tightness of my muscles as Iason's voice fucked me from the inside. He had kept me right on that edge of raw sexual need before sending me careening over the cliff.

My thoughts bounced around too much to be anything close to coherent. I was distantly aware of the noisy chatter as people filtered out of the theatre. But all I could hear was the reverb of his melodious voice moving inside of me like sensuous smoke as his words echoed in my soul.

Someone touching my shoulder pulled me from my distraction. The unexpected sensation startled me. My head snapped up to see Iason's tour manager, Dylan, standing in front of me with a knowing smile. "You doing alright over there?"

"Yeah, sorry." I cleared my throat as I tried to remember how to be a normal person. "How's your night?"

"Not as good as yours will be." Her flirty wink made me blush at the implication.

The reminder of what would happen tonight

made my cock twitch in the sticky confines of my pants. I stayed a few steps behind Dylan to readjust myself as subtly as possible. If she noticed, she at least had the decency not to say anything about it.

Guiding me to the dressing room, she gestured for me to go in. "Ias will be in as soon as—"

She didn't get to finish her sentence as he walked past her without a word and kicked the door shut behind him. When the lock clicked into place, we heard Dylan's laughter as she left.

Before I talked myself out of it, I aggressively pulled Iason closer by his belt loops and crashed my mouth against his. The moan I had fought so hard to hold in during the concert finally escaped as I backed him against the door. It was a desperate and demanding kiss, our mutual desire devouring us. There was no finesse as our lips and tongues searched for what we both were going out of our minds for.

When we parted for breath, I saw another drop of sweat roll down his neck. Without thought, I leaned forward and did what I had fantasized about during the concert by licking it away. Whereas normally it was gross, somehow the salty taste ramped up my desire even more. My tongue continued trailing up his neck until my mouth was by his ear.

"Need you," I gasped in a voice I barely recognized. I thrust my renewed hardness against his answering one. "Holy fuck, I need you so bad, Iason."

He reversed our positions to pin me against the

wall, pressing his body against mine. It wrung a strangled whimper from me as I gave myself over to his dominating kiss. When he undid the button of my jeans, I realized that he was going to discover *exactly* how much I enjoyed the concert. It humiliated and excited me in a confusing way.

When he reached his hand into my underwear, his eyebrows arched up in surprise at the mess in my pants. A look of immense satisfaction darkened his eyes. His voice was an arousing, feral growl. "When?"

My reaction had embarrassed me until I saw how turned on he was from it. "You almost had me with 'Grace,' but it was the big note of 'Midnight Magic' that got me."

"Fuck, that's so sexy." He captured my lips in a fierce kiss with a growl that made me shudder. "Do you have any idea how hot it is that I can make you orgasm without touching you?"

He didn't wait for me to answer before he kissed me hard. I wanted to tell him what his encore song meant to me, but I couldn't while he worked my cock. The only thing I resisted was my urge to come again.

My mouth babbled without my permission. "I need you inside me. Please, Iason, I *need* you." My shameless wantonness would have humiliated me if I wasn't so damned turned on.

"And I need you just as much." He yanked down my pants, exposing my flushed erection.

He dropped to his knees and didn't hesitate to

take my cock all the way to the back of his throat. I slapped my hand over my mouth to muffle my sharp cry at having that wet warmth on me after so much aural teasing during the concert. My other hand embedded in his sweat-dampened hair.

Seeing him on his knees with my erection in his mouth after the show was downright surreal. Those lips that had formed such beautiful sounds onstage were now stretched around me and sucking me for everything I was worth. The man that so many people were going to go home tonight and fantasize about was pleasuring me and me alone.

When he hummed "Museum of My Heart" around my length, I smothered a shout from the intensity of my climax. I loved the way he greedily drank me down.

My legs gave out on me as I sank to the floor. I trembled from the overwhelming feelings crashing into me. While it had been amazing, I still suffered from a hollow ache to feel him inside me. It took a moment for me to gather my wherewithal to raise up onto my knees to return the favor.

He stopped me from proceeding. When I looked up at him questioningly, he caressed my cheek with his clean hand. "While I can't wait to have your mouth on me, wait until after I've had a shower."

"I don't care how, but I need you inside me." I swore as I attempted to remove his pants. Although I had come, I still needed more.

Grinning at my reaction, he stopped me once more. "I've been marinating under those hot stage lights for almost two hours. Trust me, you will thank me for showering before you go down on me."

I sat back with a heavy sigh. He was right, but my craving for more refused to abate.

Holding his hand out to me, he pulled me up to stand. I barely got my pants up before he tugged me closer. He pressed his hardness against me with a look of dark hunger that sent a primal thrill through me. His voice lowered to the sensual part of his register. "There is one thing we could do."

My need for him pushed me beyond my normal reservations. "Anything."

Iason led me over to the vanity mirror, where he stripped off my sweater. He then shrugged out of his jacket and pulled off his T-shirt, throwing them both aside to embrace me from behind. I inhaled at our bare skin coming into contact. His body was so hot— in both the gorgeous sense and the literal temperature. He hadn't been kidding about the broiling effect of the stage lights.

Pressing his lips next to my ear, he held my gaze in the mirror. "You weren't the only one affected during the concert. I couldn't stop thinking about you pleasuring yourself to my music. I kept wondering if I had made you come in your pants tonight without touching you. Thank god my guitar hid the fact I was hard for most of the show."

"Shit, you're killing me." I groaned and pressed my ass against his arousal.

He didn't relent. "I'm going to bend you over this vanity and fuck you hard while we watch in the mirror."

Although our gazes were only meeting in the reflection, his dark gaze sent molten lava surging through me at the sexiness of his words and how close his voice was to my ears. My only answer was a strangled whimper escaping past my lips.

"I take it that's a yes?" Iason asked with a smug grin.

My arousal made me unusually bold. "*Please.*"

That was all the permission he needed. He pulled my pants and briefs down, exposing me in front of the mirror.

Seeing myself naked and aroused in a mirror was a strange experience. The thought didn't last long as he peeled off his tight jeans with some amount of effort. His hard length pressed against the crack of my ass made the ache to have him inside me intensify.

He reached around me on the counter and got a bottle of lube out of one of the vanity drawers.

The foresight impressed me. "You planned for this?"

"Provided you were willing." He slid a slicked finger into me. I widened my stance a little to make it easier for him. "I haven't been able to stop thinking about it since the first night you came to my dressing room in San Francisco. This time, there's nothing stopping us."

"Don't you have to leave here by a certain time?" I pushed against his fingers when he added another one to spread me open.

"This place could burn to the ground around us for all I care. I won't stop until we've both come." His growl made my ass clench in anticipation. "Nothing will stop me from being with you, Cherry."

He worked a third finger into me, putting just enough pressure on that spot inside of me to make me weak in the knees. I had to brace my hands against the counter edge to steady myself.

"That's it." He withdrew his fingers and shifted my hips into a better position before sliding his hard length into me.

It was great and not enough at the same time. I pressed back to take him deeper. Getting the hint, he pushed all the way in until he was balls-deep in me. He gave me a moment to adjust as he wiped his hand off on a nearby towel, but after that, it was a flurry of motion.

There was nothing gentle about our coupling. As he had promised, he fucked me hard, straight from the start. After the prolonged and intense arousal I experienced during the concert, it was exactly what I wanted. I was so turned on by the rough, almost animalistic way he was thrusting into me. It drove me to rest my forearms on the countertop as he continued pounding into me with all of his pent-up need.

"Look at us," he ordered, tightening his grip on my hips as he mercilessly pleasured me.

Unable to disobey, I looked up at the mirror and watched. It was downright surreal seeing a sex god behind me, possessively fucking me as I shamelessly moaned. I thought it would embarrass me, but it was sexy watching us lost in lust. It was further confirmation that *I* was the one that he chose to be with.

"There's nothing more beautiful to me than the sight of you moaning my name while I'm inside you." His words made me tremble with a rush of arousal. "I want you to remember this anytime you doubt why we belong together. You're *mine*."

"Yours," I gasped, the single word thrilling me.

"All of you." He reached around to grope my cock, teasing it back to full hardness.

Dropping my head onto my forearms, I whimpered. "Ias, it's too much."

"I told you I wasn't stopping until both of us come." His hand worked me as relentlessly as his hips.

"I already have," I protested. "Twice! Oh, *god*!"

Iason made a smug noise as I scrambled for a hold when he shifted angles. He thrust into me so hard that things were falling off the countertop, but nothing stopped him. I held on as I muffled my cries against my arm.

"No, let me hear you."

"But everyone—" I interrupted myself with a loud gasp when he rubbed his thumb over the head of my cock, spreading the precum that had leaked again. I didn't know how I had anything left in me after the two orgasms he had already given me.

His voice was firm and commanding, sending a thrill through me. "Let me hear you, Cherry."

The merciless pleasure overwhelmed me past the point of reason. I whimpered Iason's name as I looked up at him in the mirror. My heart would give out at the rate we were going.

Running his other hand up my spine until he entangled his fingers in my hair, he used the grip to pull me up against him. It allowed him to bring his lips to my ear once more. His smirk was the only warning I got before he breathily sang the chorus of "Midnight Magic" for me and me alone.

It was more than I could handle. I came so hard that my vision swam, crying out Iason's name at the height of my pleasure. It triggered his orgasm as he growled my name and filled me with his cum.

I collapsed against the vanity counter, completely spent from the experience. It was a struggle to remain upright when my legs had turned into jelly.

Iason withdrew from me, then took the time to wipe me off before he pulled up both of our jeans. He then dropped onto the couch and pulled me into his lap. I melted against him, incapable of thinking about anything other than the blissed-out haze dulling all of my other senses.

As much as I wanted to tell him how much I enjoyed his T-shirt surprise and loved his new song, I was too adrift in the afterglow. I was content to stay in his warm embrace until Dylan told us it was time to leave. It was enough to let myself be loved by Iason. Words could wait until later.

Chapter Thirty

IASON

"I DIDN'T GET a chance to thank you for yesterday," Orion said as we sat in the chairs by the window and waited for room service to deliver our breakfast.

I grinned at the reminder of how he had passed out in an oversexed coma as soon as we returned to the hotel after the concert the night before. My ego was incredibly gratified I had pleasured him to that degree, although it meant I had to take care of myself in the shower while he blissfully slept. "You don't have to thank me for anything."

"Maybe not, but I wanted you to know how much everything meant to me yesterday." His shy smile was endearing. "Your *Winged Victory* T-shirt, the covers you sang for me, the song you wrote about me, what happened backstage, all of it was incredible."

"I'm glad you enjoyed your surprises." Orion coming in the middle of the concert without being touched was still one of the greatest highlights of my life.

The faintest flush of color graced his cheeks. "I'm serious. What you did for me yesterday was unbelievable."

"It was my pleasure." I had to resist the urge to tug him onto my lap.

"I've never been able to enjoy art with anyone before." It wasn't right that he couldn't share that part of himself with others. "Knowing you cared enough to find a T-shirt with one of my favorite sculptures on it is mind-blowing to me."

I grinned at him. "So, how much will it shock you to find out I've started doing art research because of you?"

His happiness at the news made it more difficult to resist my need to embrace him. "What did you do?"

"After your comments last week about the different sculptures, my curiosity got the better of me. I wanted to see what you were ranking me against, so I started digging online."

His shock was precious. "Seriously?"

"You made me curious talking about how Bernini made marble look like actual flesh," I said. "You were right. It looks lifelike on a level I can't comprehend."

His disbelief morphed into excitement. "Pictures are one thing, but in person, it's even more impressive."

"I'll add the Borghese Gallery to the list of

museums we should go to someday." The suggestion earned me an adorable smile. "When I was looking up Bernini, I found out he sculpted a bed for a beautiful Hellenistic statue. I went down that rabbit hole next, since you said ancient Greek sculptures were something you had researched."

"The *Sleeping Hermaphroditus* is stunning," Orion agreed with a nod. "It's so impressive that his mattress looks like it's always been a part of the sculpture."

It wasn't surprising he knew what I was referencing. I continued telling him about my findings. "I've obviously seen the *Venus de Milo* before through pop culture, but the *Winged Victory of Samothrace* is one of the most beautiful things I've ever seen. And I was even more surprised it's sometimes called the *Nike of Samothrace*. I had no idea the athletic company took their name from that goddess."

"It's one of my personal favorites." His admission thrilled me. "You can almost see her taking flight. The way the fabric flows and the wing details are exquisite."

"I can only imagine how much more impressive it is in person."

He smiled at memories. "The first time I visited the Louvre, I stood on the Daru staircase looking at her for at least an hour. I studied her from every angle possible."

"Since I can't go see it right now, I did the next best thing and found a T-shirt," I said with a laugh.

"It's a poor substitute, but I hoped it would be a fun surprise for you."

"I loved it." He smiled at me with so much adoration, it took my breath away. "I didn't know they made shirts with her on them, so I was definitely surprised. I can't believe you researched all of that. Thank you."

"Touring leaves me with a lot of downtime, so I doubt that will be my last deep dive into art history." I couldn't resist teasing him a little. "Plus, it's the only way I can look at naked men in public that won't have Dylan all over my ass."

"If you want to look into something interesting, Hadrian's—*oh*." He had a startled expression.

"What's wrong?"

Blinking several times as he came back to the present, he shook his head. "No, nothing's wrong. I just realized something, sorry."

"What?"

Instead of answering, he asked a question. "Do you know anything about the Roman Emperor Hadrian?"

It sounded vaguely familiar, but I struggled to remember why I knew that name. After racking my brain, I guessed, "Wasn't he famous for building a wall or something?"

"Yeah, he built a famous wall in England, back when it was known as Britannia. Do you know anything else about him?"

I shook my head. "Nope, that was my one lucky guess."

"Hadrian fell in love with a Greek youth named Antinous, and they became lovers," he said. "Although the emperor had a wife, he was devoted to his beloved Antinous, whom he loved above all others."

The information genuinely surprised me. "That definitely wasn't in any history book I read in school."

Orion's smile turned sad as he continued. "Hadrian took Antinous with him on all of his travels. Once, the emperor famously killed a lion to save Antinous's life. However, one day when they were traveling on the River Nile, Antinous mysteriously died. Nobody knows if it was an accident or murder, but there are several theories."

It wasn't the turn I had expected the story to take. "Which theory do you believe?"

"I don't buy into human sacrifice. It's also too suspicious to be an accidental drowning."

That left one option. "You think he was murdered?"

He frowned with sadness. "Antinous didn't have any political influence over Hadrian, so someone killing him to get him out of the way never made sense to me. Having said that, I could believe somebody was jealous enough of Hadrian's affections for Antinous to murder him, maybe hoping to take his place."

"That's awful."

His expression turned sympathetic. "Hadrian was beyond devastated by the loss of Antinous and publicly wept for him, but it still wasn't enough. He not only built a city where Antinous died called Antinopolis, but he deified his lover as a god and started a religious cult for people to worship him throughout the Roman Empire."

The story stunned me. "Wait, are you seriously telling me there was a Roman emperor who started a religion dedicated to his dead boyfriend, and this is the first I'm hearing about it?"

He nodded. "It's true. Hadrian had many temples built and thousands of statues of Antinous commissioned in his likeness to house in them for worship, as well as for his personal estate in Tivoli. Unfortunately, a lot of them were destroyed by the Christians for the obvious reasons. Although surprisingly, quite a few of them ended up in the Vatican Museums, which is where I first learned about Antinous."

The last piece of information was baffling. "Wait, why would the Vatican Museums display statues of a Roman emperor's *boyfriend?*" It was almost beyond comprehension. "Shouldn't they have been leading the crusade to destroy them because they think homosexuality is the greatest of sins?"

"I don't actually know the answer to that." He shrugged as he continued. "On my first visit, I saw a stunning statue of Antinous as Bacchus. It was one of the most beautiful sculptures I had ever seen, but I wasn't familiar with it. I checked the plaque next to it, which referred to Antinous as 'Beloved by the Emperor Hadrian.' That wasn't an epitaph I expected to see in the Vatican Museums, of all places."

"Yeah, that sure sounds like coded language for a lover."

He nodded in agreement. "I noticed another statue of him in the same room looking over at a bust of Hadrian, with a plaque calling him Hadrian's young 'favorite' in quotes. I got curious and made a mental note to research it later when I had time."

"Wow, I can't believe the Catholic church actually did that." It was unbelievable, given their stance on homosexuality, that they would showcase sculptures celebrating gay love.

He took his phone out of his pocket and pulled up an image before passing it over to me. "That's the Antinous as Bacchus statue I saw first."

The sculpture was a gorgeous god of a man. Zooming in on the face, I saw he truly was a divine kind of handsome. "Damn, no wonder Hadrian turned him into a deity. If someone existed today who looked like that, there isn't a man or woman alive who could resist him."

He chuckled at my comment. "It wasn't only that one room, though. There were more statues of Antinous in Egyptian iconography from a reconstruction of an area at Hadrian's Villa."

I passed Orion's phone back to him. "Now I know why you didn't add him to the list of sculptures I was prettier than."

"Technically I did, since I said any Roman statues." He put his phone away.

"True. What a story, though."

"After I returned to the hotel and researched it, I couldn't believe that as interested in ancient Rome as I was, I had never heard that story before," Orion said. "Afterward, I noticed Antinous statues in other museums. Rufus Wainwright even wrote an opera about their romance."

Everything surrounding the tale fascinated me. "What was your realization earlier about all this?"

"I always thought that their love story was beautifully tragic," he said, although it didn't answer my question. "The scale of it is astounding. Hadrian loved Antinous enough to turn him into a god for others to worship. Not to mention he commissioned thousands of beautiful statues, built a city, and temples in his honor, so some part of him still exists all these centuries later. I'm in awe of that level of devotion."

"And this was a sudden realization to you?"

He shook his head. "No, it just never occurred to me until then that it was weird for me as a straight guy to think one of the most romantic love stories of history was between two men, one of whom I thought was the most beautiful works of art ever created."

I bit my lower lip to hold in a chuckle at how cute it was that he was oblivious to that side of himself. "In your defense, Antinous was seriously hot. It's no wonder even an emperor worshipped him."

"Huh, I thought I just appreciated his aesthetic."

I had to laugh. "That's the most academic way of saying you found him sexy I've ever heard."

Looking away, he paused for a moment before continuing. "But I also realized you writing a song about me is the same thing."

Unable to resist the urge any longer, I reached out and took hold of his hand to guide him to sit in my lap. "It may not be a statue, but I like knowing even centuries from now, people will hear my song and understand how much I love you."

His voice trembled as he whispered my name in awe.

"Always and forever," I murmured, meaning it with all of my heart.

He cupped my face in his hands as he leaned closer and gave me the sweetest kiss, making me fall for him all over again. I really was the luckiest man in the world to love someone as remarkable as Orion.

Epilogue

ORION

ONE MONTH LATER

HAPPINESS RADIATED from deep within my soul as we sat in front of Jacques-Louis David's portrait of Antoine-Laurent Lavoisier and Marie-Anne Lavoisier. It was one of my favorite paintings by him, although it was a portrait that most people only spared a quick glance at before moving on to look at his more famous work, *The Death of Socrates*.

The story of the Lavoisier family was fascinating and full of heartbreak and triumph. Iason listened to me as I talked for almost an hour about their lives during the tumultuous French Revolution. I would have been self-conscious about talking for so long, but he was paying rapt attention and asking questions that showed he was engaged and interested.

When I finished, he gazed at me in awe. He

looked amazing in his black-rimmed glasses he used as a disguise. I adored his navy T-shirt that had a drawing of a bust of Michelangelo's *David* with the swirls of Vincent van Gogh's *Starry Night* escaping from his head. It was paired with a badass leather jacket and tight jeans that made it hard to keep my hands to myself. "That was an incredible story, Cherry."

"You weren't bored?" My family wouldn't have been able to sit through the entire thing like Iason had.

"Not for a single second." He gave me a reassuring smile. "You said the stories drew you to art history. Now, I see why."

His praise made me happy. "It adds a lot of meaning to what would otherwise just be a painting of two dead people." I looked up at the portrait. "Marie-Anne is so remarkable. She was so strong to make it through the revolution without bending to the pressure of it. Plus, her contributions to the scientific community are invaluable, although she doesn't get enough credit. And you have to admire Antoine for sticking to his principles, even though it cost him his life in the guillotine."

"They were an amazing couple." Iason gave me a warm smile that heated me up inside. "Thank you for inviting me into your world. It's been incredible to learn so much from you today as we toured the galleries."

"I'm glad you've had a good time." It meant a lot to me that he cared about spending time with me in a museum. It was something I had never been able to do with any of my previous partners, let alone in one of the greatest museums in the world. "I can't thank you enough for bringing me here today. This has been a dream come true."

"What do you say next time we go to Paris to visit the Louvre Museum? Or maybe Italy to see some of their amazing ruins and museums?"

Every time I thought I couldn't love Iason more, he said something that made me fall for him all over again. "You'd really want to do that?"

"As long as you agree to be my docent." He winked at me, making me laugh. "Although, it's hard as hell controlling myself while you're being so sexy talking about art."

I snorted at the ridiculous idea. "How is that sexy?"

"Do you have any clue how incredibly attractive it is that you have centuries of knowledge in your mind that you can recall without any effort?" He looked at me with genuine admiration that left me flustered. "It makes me wish I could show you how much I appreciate you, but I'm not allowed to touch a masterpiece in the museum."

The perfect punchline overrode my normal shyness. "Well, somebody needs to nail the artwork on the wall."

Iason burst into laughter before he leaned over to give me a kiss. It was twice as amazing because we were out in public and he loved me enough to risk the show of affection where anyone could take a picture of us. "I'll have to see what I can do about that once we get back to my place."

"I'm looking forward to it." The mere thought of what he would do to me once we were alone made me shift on the bench as the first tendrils of arousal worked through me. I rested my head on his shoulder as we continued admiring the portrait of the amazing Lavoisier couple. "And to answer your previous question, if you're willing to let me drag you around all the museums, I would love to go to France and Italy with you."

He kissed my temple. "It's a date, then."

I snuggled against him with a contented murmur. Life didn't get any better than spending it with someone who loved me for all that I was. It still amazed me that person was Iason Leyland, but I was so grateful that he had chosen me. Our love had been written in the stars, and we were only at the beginning of our happily ever after. It made me excited for every day we spent together.

What special surprise does Iason have planned for

Orion on their Italian vacation? **Claim your copy of Undying Love to find out today**.

The series continues with Levi and Noctis! The two neighbors enjoy singing shower duets together, but they've never met in person before. Will sparks fly when they meet at an open mic night? **Read Make Music Together to find out what happens next**.

Want to see where the Sunnyside universe begins? **Check out Bet on Love to start the adventure**.

Thank You

Thank you for reading **Play By Heart**. Reviews are crucial for helping other readers discover new books to enjoy. If you want to share your love for Iason and Orion, please leave a review. I'd really appreciate it!

Recommending my work to others is also a huge help. Don't hesitate to give this book a shout-out in your favorite book rec group to spread the word.

Next in Series

AVAILABLE NOW

It all started with a song. Two neighbors singing duets in the shower finally meet at an open mic night. Sparks fly, but will it lead to true love?

If you love neighbors to lovers, insta love, musician, first time, opposites attract, gay romances that make you laugh and swoon, **read Make Music Together today by using the QR code below**!

Acknowledgments

I hope you enjoyed Iason and Orion's romance! This is a book that took me seventeen years to publish, so it means so much to me to finally share their story with you.

Connecting with my readers in my Facebook group is one of the best parts of being an author. If you'd like to become a Sunnysider, we'd love to have you!

A special thank you goes out to my amazing team of beta readers of Amy Mitchell, Niki Cosgrove, Lindsay Porter, Tammy Jones, Lisa Klein, Kylie Anderson, Cilla May, Dylan Pope, Jennifer Sharon, and Missy Kretschmer! I feel so truly blessed to be friends with such amazing people.

I'm very grateful to Shelia Kilgore, Beth Barton, Tammy Jones, Gabriela, and my other Ko-fi supporters who helped make it possible for me to become a full-time author. Their support means everything to me. If you want to see book covers and full chapters months or even years before they get published, please join my Ko-fi.

I also want to thank all of you who recommend

my books in Facebook rec threads. It means so much to me that you enjoy my work enough to share them with other readers to help them discover their new favorite books. I'm also filled with endless gratitude to Katie from Gay Romance Reviews and all of their ARC readers for their kind and helpful reviews.

I'm blessed to work with my dream team of Pam, Sandra, and Cate. It makes writing books even more of a joy when I know they help polish it to perfection.

I can't wait to meet again in **Make Music Together**!

About the Author

WWW.ARIELLAZOELLE.COM

Ariella Zoelle adores steamy, funny, swoony romances where couples are allowed to just be happy. She writes low angst stories full of heat, humor, and heart. But sometimes she's in the mood for something with a bit more angst and drama. If you are too, check out her A.F. Zoelle books.

Get a bonus chapter by using the QR code below!